FROM THE AUTHO...

...COMES A CHILLING NOVEL OF
SUDDEN DISASTER
TSUNAMI

The bridge under Kirstie's feet began to shudder; flakes of grey paint and orange rust fluttered down from the upper deck. The roar of the wave had been relatively quiet after the first sound blast, but grew louder again as the tsunami ran south along the waterfront.

Docks snapped away from their pilings; one of the freighters tilted and capsized. A long segment of the freeway toppled into the wave. Moments later the Ferry Building disintegrated, and the wave rolled over it.

Below her, Kirstie saw the water steepen as it neared the shore of the island. Then a breath later, it struck and exploded. She spun and lunged away, too slowly. Water crashed over her with enough force to fling her hard against a car. Fist-sized chunks of rock clattered down around her....

Tsunami

a novel by
Crawford Kilian

SEAL BOOKS
McClelland and Stewart-Bantam Limited
Toronto

For Alice

*This low-priced Seal Book
has been completely reset in a type face
designed for easy reading, and was printed
from new plates. It contains the complete
text of the original hard-cover edition.*
NOT ONE WORD HAS BEEN OMITTED.

TSUNAMI

*A Seal Book / published by arrangement with
Douglas & McIntyre, Ltd.*

PRINTING HISTORY

Douglas & McIntyre edition published March 1983

*Hardcover publication of this book was assisted, in part, by a
grant from the B.C. Cultural Fund.*

Seal edition / August 1984

ISBN 0-7704-1857-0

*Seal Books are published by McClelland and Stewart-Bantam
Limited. Its trademark, consisting of the words "Seal Books" and
the portrayal of a seal, is the property of McClelland and Stewart-
Bantam Limited, 60 St. Clair Avenue East, Suite 601, Toronto,
Ontario M4T 1N5 Canada. This trademark has been duly registered
in the Trademarks Office of Canada. The trademark, consisting of
the words "Bantam" and the portrayal of a rooster, is the property
of and is used with the consent of Bantam Books, Inc. 666 Fifth
Avenue, New York, New York 10103. This trademark has been
duly registered in the Trademarks Office of Canada and elsewhere.*

PRINTED IN THE UNITED STATES OF AMERICA

H   0 9 8 7 6 5 4 3 2 1

1

"Three hundred and three metres," Don Kennard said into the microphone. "I'm about two metres above the bottom. Visibility is fair."

"*Copy.*" The radio operator's voice came fuzzily through the loud-speaker of the submersible's radio.

"I'll retrieve the first core here, and then follow the current across Butler Canyon before the next core."

"*Very good.*"

Don shifted on the narrow couch, grateful that a tall man had designed it. Lying flat on his belly, he was still fairly comfortable; after a few more hours he would be stiff and clumsy. The cabin of the submersible, though designed to hold two men, was barely wider than a double bed. Its curving ceiling was only a metre above the couches. The bulkheads, painted black to reduce reflection on the portholes, were beaded with moisture: humidity inside the cabin was close to one hundred per cent, and the temperature was a cold 12° Celsius.

As usual, Don was dressed for the dive in jeans and a black wool turtle-neck sweater, with a watch cap pulled down over his thick brown hair. He was rawboned, not very heavy for his height, but with powerful shoulders and arms. His face was long and a little heavy-jawed; like all the men in his family, he had a slightly protruding lower lip. He was clean-shaven and, like most people these days, sunburned, except for a pale stripe around the eyes. His complexion, reddened and coarsened, made him look older than his actual age of thirty-six.

Don looked through one of the portholes at the grey sediment illuminated by the submersible's floodlights and gripped the handle of the external manipulator.

The mechanical arm reached out and down, and poised for a moment above the mud. The submersible tilted a little; it was too buoyant to be really stable, which had earned it the ironic name of *Plummet*. Instability, though, had its advantages: as he drove the core tube into the mud, Don lunged forward on his couch. *Plummet* tipped, forcing in the tube a little deeper. A cloud of fine particles puffed up, mixing with the yellowish mist of dead phytoplankton in the water. The marine biologists were really interested in only the top millimetre of sediment, but a long core would give them a better data base.

He pulled the core tube free and manoeuvred it into the lazy-susan rack mounted outside the forward porthole, just below the wet compass.

"First core secured. Moving on. Can you give me a bearing?"

"Bearing one-six-seven at one knot."

"One-six-seven. Copy."

He looked sourly at the useless wet compass. Three weeks ago, the earth's magnetic field had abruptly disappeared after fading for several months. Its loss made navigation underwater a difficult job.

That, of course, was the least of the problems. Since the previous summer, solar flares had been erupting with unusual violence and frequency on the surface of the sun.

Each flare had bombarded the earth's ozone layer, forming nitrogen oxides that quickly broke up the triple-oxygen molecules of the ozone layer. Loss of the magnetic field had accelerated the process. With the ozone reduced by at least fifty per cent, ultraviolet radiation was penetrating the atmosphere.

The sun's normal output of uv, sharply increased by the uv in the flares, was reaching the surface of the earth. It burned into the cells of plants and animals; crops were withering, and livestock was going blind. Humans could scarcely venture outside in daylight without eye protection, and whites needed sunblock cream on exposed skin, or they would start to burn in less than a minute.

The effects on the upper layers of the sea were, perhaps, even more threatening: phytoplankton, the microscopic marine plants that formed the basis of the oceans' food web, were dying off under the uv onslaught. The core Don had just taken would help to determine the rate at which different species of plankton were affected.

The flares had also smashed the ionosphere, blacking out long-range radio, and had burned out most communications satellites. Electromagnetic pulses, like those associated with high-altitude nuclear explosions, induced voltage surges in power networks; whole continents blacked out. Electronic devices behaved with an eerie unreliability, sometimes working beautifully and sometimes burning out. The earth's electric field became highly charged, and caused violent thunderstorms. The ozone had trapped some of the heat reflected from the earth's surface; that heat now escaped into space, so the stratosphere cooled and weather patterns changed.

That, of course, was outside his scientific domain. His wife Kirstie knew far more than he about the impact of the flares on the weather. But she and her fellow climatologists at Berkeley were going crazy trying to make sense out of events. For example, *Ultramarine*, the research vessel that was *Plummet*'s mother ship, was being battered in the latest of a series of storms which should have stayed in the Gulf of Alaska. Instead, a branch of the circumpolar jet stream had moved far south, dragging the storms onto the California coast. The winter had been one of heavy rainfall on the coast and snowfall in the Sierras. Flooding and mudslides had thrown whole cities into chaos. Don, a physical oceanographer, preferred the peace and quiet of the continental shelf to the endless harassments of life on the surface.

Those harassments, he reflected, weren't limited just to the weather. On the surface he had to contend with people who did not interest him, whose problems and desires did not stir his sympathy. Solitude suited him; even Kirstie, involved in her own career, left him comfortably alone. In ten years of marriage they had spent much of their time apart: he on diving expeditions, she on research projects, in five countries on three continents. Their last six months in Berkeley was one of the longest times they had lived in one place, and together; Don was even getting to know some of his colleagues at the Pacific Institute of Oceanography. But people and organizations were too transient to care about. —Or too dangerous to care about, he admitted to himself. Once you invested your feelings in them, they tried to take you over, to tyrannize you. His grandfather Geordie had done it to Don's father, and then to Don and his brother Steve. His father had escaped only by dying of a heart attack; the grandsons had escaped into science and distance. For Steve, what was important was seismology in the Antarctic; for Don, it was cruising like this, alone through the cold darkness three hundred metres down.

The floodlights abruptly shone on foggy emptiness.

"I'm over Butler Canyon," he said. "The current in the canyon may push me a little west of south until I get across."

"Copy."

Don knew the canyon fairly well. The continental shelf off California was a network of such canyons; many of them were drowned rivers, relics of the last ice age when sea level had been much lower. This canyon was small, less than a kilometre wide and about fifty long. After ten thousand years of sedimentation, mud and silt lay almost a kilometre thick above its bedrock, so that it was only one to two hundred metres below the average level of the continental shelf.

Somewhere out in the middle of the canyon, *Plummet* rose suddenly, nose up; the yellow mist of dead plankton thickened and swirled. Then the submersible shook and began to drop.

"What the hell was *that?*" he shouted.

"What was what?" the operator asked. *"—Hey, Don, are you descending?"*

"I sure seem to be. Just got a real jolt, up and down again. I'm down to three-twenty metres."

"Are all your systems functioning?"

"Yes."

Earthquake? Sandfall? Whatever it had been, *Plummet's* descent had stopped now. Visibility was nearly zero. The mist swirled in the lights, thickening and darkening from yellow to brown. *Plummet* was still vibrating and yawing.

"I'm going back up to three hundred metres. I can't see a thing. If visibility doesn't improve, I'll come all the way up. What's it like at the surface?"

"Getting worse. The wind's out of the west at forty knots. We have a hell of a sea running."

"Any weather reports?"

"You're about as far as our radios can reach right now. We're two hundred kilometres off San Francisco and can't raise anything."

He started the motor, feeling relieved when its three horsepower kicked in, and reached for the switch that would force compressed air into the ballast tanks.

Without warning, *Plummet* turned over and nosed down.

Don fell full-length against the low, curved ceiling and slid headfirst into the black-painted forward bulkhead. Something—*Plummet* or something outside—was rumbling softly. Impossibly, the hull clanged as if struck.

Very slowly, too slowly, the submersible righted itself, and Don fell back onto the couch. What the hell could keep *Plummet* upside down for that long? Its centre of gravity was too low—

It turned over again. He could feel it start to roll and was braced for it: this time only his feet hit the ceiling, and he kept his grip on the wheel. Loose equipment bounced and clattered around him. Gauges twitched. The interior lights burned serenely on.

"Wait a minute," Don muttered. The rumble grew louder, so loud he couldn't hear himself talk. What must have been a fist-sized stone clanged against the hull.

Plummet swayed and righted itself, but began to spin rapidly on its vertical axis. The portholes showed a grey-brown murk. The million-candlepower external floodlights were either torn away or unable to penetrate the mud.

The spin slowed. The rumble was changing, rising in pitch to a rattling hiss. *Plummet* yawed and pitched. Don groped for the emergency weight-release, but his sight was blurred; his lids felt sticky when he blinked. He wiped his eyes, and his fingers came away smeared with blood. The top of his head hurt; he must have gashed his scalp on one of the gauges.

Before he could reach again for the weight-release, *Plummet*'s starboard side scraped violently against what must be the canyon wall. The submersible spun completely around and struck the wall again, stopping dead with an impact that flung Don hard into the thin cushion of the couch.

Plummet was lying nose-up at a steep angle. He must have struck a slope on the canyon wall, and now something was holding the craft down. The depth gauge read 450 metres. Stones rattled and banged against the superstructure; the strange, surflike roar went on. Don caught his breath.

A turbidity current.

It had to be. A quake must have dislodged unstable sediments farther up the canyon. In a frictionless mix with water, millions of tonnes of mud and sand and rock had started to move. Like an avalanche, the current had fed on what it scoured from the canyon floor, increasing in force and speed. He was the first person ever to witness one, but their effects were well known: they could snap undersea cables like threads and carried enormous masses of sediment far out onto the ocean floor. If he hadn't struck the canyon wall, the current might have swept him onto the abyssal plain, into depths far greater than *Plummet* could endure.

"Lucky," he muttered. He would be buried alive instead of being crushed. Rocks were beginning to pile up the superstructure and along the sides of the craft; he could see a couple through one of the portholes.

Yanking the weight-release did nothing. Either the switch was broken, or the eighty-kilogram steel plate had released without any effect at all. *Plummet* no longer shook as violently under the barrage of stones: they were piling up fast.

Don pressed his fingers against his ears, trying to muffle the noise. He was angry at himself for being frightened, for letting fear slow his thoughts. Blood trickled stickily over his hands from the cut on his scalp. He shuddered, closed his eyes, and opened them again. Maybe he could push the sub away from the canyon wall before the rocks built up and buried him for good.

He grasped the manipulator control and pushed the arm forward. It responded, grating against stone, and *Plummet* shifted a little. If the ballast tanks were still intact, and the emergency weight came free, *Plummet* might manage to ascend out of the current.

Cautiously, Don pressed the switch that fed compressed air into the ballast tanks. He was trembling uncontrollably, frightened and excited at once. Taking a deep breath, he pushed the manipulator arm hard against the wall and heard rock scrape against the nose. He pulled the arm back and pushed again. The stern lifted slightly, and rocks thumped down the length of the superstructure.

Don pulled back again, and threw himself forward as he pushed the arm against the wall.

He felt the unmistakable shudder of the emergency weight coming off. *Plummet* heaved towards the horizontal, banged its nose against the sloping canyon wall, and spun out into the current.

He watched the depth gauge: 410 metres. 408. He was rising slowly through the current. The brown swirl was as dense as ever, with only momentary thinning. *Plummet*'s rotation slowed.

At 320 metres, the water cleared a little. At 300 metres, the submersible began to ascend more steeply. The water was a chalky-coloured mist; the rumble of the current was still loud, but now came distinctly from below. At 280 metres, *Plummet* shuddered through the turbulence of the shear zone between the current and calmer water.

Don was still shivering, enough to make it hard to unscrew the cap on his canteen. Wetting a cloth, he wiped blood from his face and hands. His watch cap was stained red. The hair above his left temple was sticky and matted, but he seemed to have stopped bleeding. He rested his forehead on his crossed arms. He could think only in disjointed images: walking along a Vancouver street as a little boy, holding his father's hand; struggling to the surface after falling into the deep end of a swimming pool; Kirstie's blue eyes reflecting the Mediterranean sky. He felt sad, somehow, and unaccountably lonely.

Twenty minutes later, *Plummet* neared the surface. The storm was raising big waves, but fifteen metres below them the sea was calm. Don turned on the VHF and raised *Ultramarine* at once. Owen Ussery, the ship's chief scientist, answered.

"*You're okay?*"

"A little banged up, but yes, I'm okay."

"*You gave us one hell of a scare, Don. We clocked you at twenty-three knots before we lost you. Do you realize you must have been caught in a turbidity current?*"

"Yes! It sure gave me a ride. I was almost too excited to be scared. There must have been an earthquake offshore."

"*No, it was a tsunami, Don. We finally raised San Francisco a few minutes ago. Apparently there was a hell of an earthquake or eruption or both, down in the Antarctic yesterday. Hilo issued a tsunami warning last night, but it's taken hours to get the word out. The waves got here before the message did.*"

"He was right! By God, he was right," Don whispered.

"*Say again?*" asked Owen.

"My brother Steve is down there, at a research station on the Ross Ice Shelf. He's been predicting a big quake in the Antarctic."

"*Well.*" Owen paused. "*I hope he's all right. Listen, Don, We've got a fix on you and we'll be picking you up in about two hours—maybe less if this damn storm lets up. We're going straight home.*"

"What for?"

"*From what we heard on the radio, San Francisco's been hit by several tsunamis. Really hit.*"

Suddenly, Don felt trapped. Kirstie, he remembered, wasn't in Berkeley today: she was at a climatology conference—in San Francisco.

2

The morning session of the conference ended at last. Kirstie Kennard was eager to get out, away from San Francisco University and back to the relative sanity of Berkeley. For the past three-and-a-half hours, she had listened to grown men and women, with advanced degrees, debate whether losing fifty per cent of the ozone layer in six months should be described as "temporary" or "transient" or "short-term."

Kirstie had kept very quiet except to deal with technical issues. The report which the conference was about to issue was more political than scientific, intended to calm the public yet alarm the government. Kirstie suspected the effects would be just the opposite.

She paused in the lobby of the auditorium to smear a little sunblock cream across her face, pull on her raincoat and gloves, and adjust her sunglasses. Even with the rain pelting down like this, enough uv got through the overcast to start a nasty burn in five or six minutes.

This afternoon's meeting, she thought as she pushed out the door, would be depressing but funnier: helping

Sam Steinberg plan strategy to fight the nonrenewal of his contract. More politics. He was in physics, she just a visiting professor of climatology. But she'd been shoved into helping him. The rest of his colleagues didn't want to go near Sam, but Kirstie, with just a few more months left in her appointment at Berkeley, could risk contamination.

The poor bugger didn't stand a chance, of course, not in the present political climate. Sam was a throwback to the 1960s, from his long hair to his romantic leftism. The fact that he was an absolutely brilliant scientist only demonstrated to others than no one was safe from what was called a "shakeout."

Except for security officers in ponchos, crash helmets and goggles, the campus was almost deserted under the cold February rain. It reminded her of real Vancouver weather, while Vancouver itself was enjoying its sunniest winter in years. The rain made her homesick—not for Scotland, but for Vancouver, Don's home town. Apart from a couple of brief jobs and one unhappy family reunion, they hadn't been there in seven or eight years. In retrospect, though, it seemed like a lost paradise where no one ever heard of shakeouts, and climatologists didn't worry about the political aspect of their work. Perhaps she might even persuade Don to move back there for a year or so. Good God, his grandfather Geordie must be nearly a hundred years old by now; he couldn't be such a dragon any more. Even if he were, he couldn't last much longer. And Don's mother Elizabeth was a dear woman who deserved better treatment from all her men.

Poor Don, she thought. He really had his knickers in a twist about his family. The Kennards had been in British Columbia since the gold rush of 1858; one of Don's great-great-grandfathers had founded a logging dynasty that was still powerful politically and economically. David Kennard, Don's father, might have become provincial premier if he hadn't died of a heart attack. Don and his brother

Steve had been in high school then; they'd gone to university, graduate school and careers in science, abandoning the family business and what was left of the family.

She half-envied Don; her own parents had died when she was young, and she'd grown up like a gypsy among various distant cousins. It would have been marvellous having bloody great battles with parents, instead of the absent-minded affection of cousins. Yet she'd grown accustomed to the pleasures of independence. Don had married her on the understanding—even stronger on her side than on his—that they would have no children, set no suburban roots. They had lived and worked all over the world, enjoying each other without hindering each other. Sometimes Don's quietness and stubbornness drove her mad, but she knew they were only aspects of the strength she had relied on from the start. And he still had a talent for surprising and delighting her.

She reached the parking garage, which looked bleak with its surrounding flowerbeds full of dead plants, and ran up three flights of stairs without even breathing hard. Jogging in the Berkeley hills had its hazards—she had to run at night, of course, to avoid the uv, and some of the neighbours' dogs were really vicious—but at least she'd stayed in shape. Not many people realized she was all of thirty-four.

Before getting into the old orange Volvo station wagon, Kirstie checked the new lock on the gas cap. No one had tampered with it. A week before, with three days to go before her next gas coupon could be used, she'd found the tank siphoned dry.

Gas rationing had at least reduced traffic problems; she was on the freeway, bound for the Oakland Bay Bridge, within minutes. The rain and uv had kept most hitchhikers off the streets as well. Sometimes they threw rocks or bottles at cars that didn't stop for them; often, they robbed the drivers who did.

She saw she'd missed the top of the noon news, but switched the radio on anyway. The announcer's voice was so excited that she glanced at the dial, thinking it had been turned to one of the rock stations. It hadn't.

"—*warning was delayed by poor radio conditions and disruptions in ocean cable systems that may have been caused by the tsunamis themselves. The tidal waves are expected to reach the San Francisco area by twelve-thirty this afternoon and they may go on for several hours. Persons living in low-lying areas along the coast are advised to be ready to move to higher ground if necessary. The waves are not, repeat not, expected to affect communities inside San Francisco Bay. Back with more tidal-wave stories after these—*"

Kirstie spun the dial: country & western, rock, rock, a rabid right-wing commentator. Static buzzed behind everything.

Her first thought was about Don: but he should be safely at sea, where tsunamis were unnoticeable. Then she decided to keep going, to cross the Bay Bridge and get home to Berkeley. She glanced at the dashboard clock: twelve minutes after noon. She would be on the bridge in five minutes or less, across it in ten more. The announcer had said the waves wouldn't cause problems within the bay, but she had heard too many stories from Don and his colleagues about what could happen when a seiche got going in an enclosed body of water. As long as she was across the bay and well away from the water—

The traffic thickened and slowed as she reached the bridge. Six lanes of trucks and cars and motorcycles were moving at walking speed. Jockeying from lane to lane, she managed to move relatively quickly. But as she neared Yerba Buena Island, where the western half of the bridge ended, the traffic came to a complete halt.

"Oh, for God's sake," Kirstie muttered. People were leaving their cars—not to continue on foot, but to walk to the north side of the bridge and cluster along the railing.

They were looking for the tsunami, waiting for it; some even had cameras slung around their necks.

Trapped, Kirstie got out of the Volvo and walked across two lanes to the railing. Just to her right was the steep, rocky slope of Yerba Buena Island; to the north was the straight edge of Treasure Island, a navy base built on a precise rectangle of fill in the middle of the bay.

It was 12:23. The city looked normal enough, half-hidden in veils of rain and mist. A stiff breeze blew from the west. The surface of the bay was a dull grey, flecked with wind-driven whitecaps. Not far to the west, a big fishing boat was moving north between the footings of the bridge. Farther away, tugs hooted along the San Francisco waterfront, and a couple of freighters were pulling away from their berths. Lights flashed and winked on the streets of the city: the white of car headlights, the red and blue of police cars. The distant wail of sirens was almost lost in the normal deep rumble of the city.

Kirstie looked down again and saw that the fishing boat was moving surprisingly quickly; then she realized that it had turned around and was pointed south. The current was pulling it stern-first. And the footings of the bridge were exposed; two metres or more of crusted barnacles and weeds showed above the choppy grey water. She looked directly below her and saw bare rock and mud where water had been moments ago.

The normal white-noise rumble of the city changed pitch, deepened; from the west came a series of low, hard concussions. The bridge began to tremble in response to each of them. Beyond the city's northern skyline, a pale mist rose against the darker overcast.

That's the wave, Kirstie thought wonderingly. The spray from the wave, and it's rising as high as the hills.

Then the wave itself came into the bay.

Nothing so large should have moved so swiftly. It looked to Kirstie like a snow-streaked black moraine, a long, steep ridge that must have been well over fifty metres high, spanning the Golden Gate. It grew taller, steeper, gliding under the roadbed of the bridge, exploding in twin geysers against the towers. It was just beginning to break as it struck the Marin shore and blew apart into an enormous burst of whiteness.

"Thousand one; thousand two—" Kirstie whispered to herself, counting seconds as she watched the shock wave moving towards her at the speed of sound, a sharply defined curve on the surface of the bay.

When the sound blast struck the bridge, Kirstie clapped her hands to her ears and screamed with pain. She dropped to her knees, seeking the shelter of the railing; dimly she noticed other people staggering under the impact of the noise. Part of her was terrified, but another part kept her watching through the open grid of the railing, observing, estimating, even predicting.

The wave rebounded through the spray, away from the Marin hillsides, smashing again at the towers of the Golden Gate Bridge. The southern end of the wave bounced off the San Francisco shoreline and pulsed out into the channel. The tsunami peaked in the centre of the Golden Gate, just east of the bridge, reaching a height near its original maximum of fifty metres. The wave had lost its sharp definition and was now a shapeless mass wrapped in mist. As it spread north and south and east it looked more like fog than solid water.

Kirstie could see nothing of Marin; Sausalito and Tiburon, and Angel Island, were lost in billowing clouds of spray. But along the San Francisco waterfront the tsunami was moving with what seemed, from a distance, to be an eerie slowness. Its true speed was probably over a hundred kilometres per hour, for it overtook a police car that was hurtling south along the Embarcadero.

The bridge under Kirstie's feet began to shudder; flakes of grey paint and orange rust fluttered down from the upper deck. The roar of the wave had been relatively quiet after the first sound blast, but grew louder again as the tsunami ran south along the waterfront.

Docks snapped away from their pilings; one of the freighters tilted and capsized. The other ship was swept over the docks and struck broadside against the concrete pillars of the Embarcadero Freeway.

A long segment of the freeway toppled into the wave. Moments later the Ferry Building disintegrated, and the wave rolled over it. From some other building, fire spurted in a burst of orange, vivid against the grey and white of the wave. Through the thickening mist, Kirstie could glimpse tentacles of the wave reaching up the hillside streets.

In the bay itself the tsunami was a chaotic mass of foam, five to ten metres high except where it rose higher on crossing shallow water. It ran south under the western end of the Bay Bridge, engulfing the fishing boat Kirstie had seen a few moments before. The bridge swayed and groaned under the blows to its footings.

Below her, Kirstie saw the water steepen as it neared the shore of the island. Then, a breath later, it struck and exploded. She spun and lunged away, too slowly. Water crashed over her with enough force to fling her hard against a car. Fist-sized chunks of rock clattered down around her, bouncing off the cars and trucks.

Gasping, she staggered away from the car. The water was ankle-deep, mixed with stones and mud hydraulically blasted from the side of Treasure Island. People were wading through it, or crawling, or lying motionless.

Wiping mud from her face, Kirstie marveled that her sunglasses were still in place. She made herself walk back to the railing. Below, several metres above the normal level of the bay, brownish-grey water boiled past under the bridge. The spray was clearing over much the bay, and she could see the Golden Gate Bridge. As she watched, the roadway broke from the north tower and dropped into the water. The north tower of the bridge was tilting. The tilt increased and then the tower fell into the water. Gouts of spray shot up and sank back.

"The bugger is going to seiche," she muttered. "It's going to seiche."

Kirstie waded to a woman lying face down nearby and helped her get to her hands and knees. Blood-streaked mud covered her face; the woman moaned and coughed. Kirstie tried to talk to her, but the roar of the wave, pouring back down the hillside and running under the bridge, obliterated all other sounds. The woman stood up and staggered to a yellow Rabbit. Ignoring Kirstie, she got in and started the engine.

People were moving all over the bridge: helping each other, driving away, walking slowly towards the tunnel to Oakland or back towards San Francisco. One man directed traffic around abandoned cars; three others were pushing those cars to the sides of the pavement. A few more cars arrived from the city and roared through without stopping, their drivers and passengers looking terrified.

Wondering if she were in shock, Kirstie started the Volvo and drove. The station wagon bumped over the gravel and rocks left by the wave. The windshield was cracked, and the hood and fenders were scratched and dented. Off to her left she saw seething white water where Treasure Island had been. What she could see of Berkeley seemed all right, but to the southeast a huge column of smoke was rising into the rain. Fires burned at the Army Terminal, a sprawl of docks and warehouses on the Oakland waterfront; an odd, greenish-yellow cloud was spreading from the Terminal across Oakland towards the hills to the east.

She got off the bridge onto the East Bay Freeway. The mud flats that ran beside the freeway were deep under water, and as she approached Berkeley she had to drive through flooded stretches. Just as she reached her exit and turned off, she glanced in her rearview mirror and saw what looked like a tidal bore sweeping up the freeway and mud flats from the south. It was the seiche, a tsunami trapped within the bay. The long hump of grey foam and black water extended across the bay and well inland.

Slamming the car into first, Kirstie accelerated up Ashby. A roar grew behind her; the seiche was coming fast. Glancing back, she saw it engulf three, four, six cars, one of which was flung spinning into the air.

San Pablo Avenue: once across it, she knew, Ashby began to rise a little. The wave, now only a metre high, hissed into the intersection and paused.

A few blocks farther on, Kirstie realized that she was clutching the steering wheel so hard that her hands hurt and that she was still in first gear. She made herself slump back in her seat. Up ahead, the Berkeley hills looked comfortingly close and high, but she did not want to go home to an empty house. Turning left, she drove into a neighbourhood of small apartments and stucco houses, west of the Sacramento Avenue BART station. On a street lined with dead palm trees, she parked in front of an old Hollywood bungalow. The rain was getting heavier. She locked the car and ran to the door of the bungalow.

Sam Steinberg opened the door as she came up onto the little porch. He was a small, lean man in his forties, with a wrinkled, deeply tanned face above a bristly black beard.

"You look like hell," he said. "Come in."

The living room was small but snug, with bookshelves lining the walls. The furniture was nondescript: a couch, a couple of easy chairs, a small desk, all utilitarian. Sam Steinberg was a bachelor with little evident interest in physical comfort or in esthetics.

"Do you know Einar?" Sam asked. A blond giant rose from one of the easy chairs and gently took her hand.

"Einar Bjarnason," he said. "How do you do?"

"I'm Kirstie Kennard," she said faintly. "You're Sam's graduate student?"

"The one and only," Sam grunted. He tossed Kirstie's raincoat over a pressback chair while she kicked off her sodden boots. "All the others have found safer advisers. Einar's too crazy to be scared."

"No, I am not too crazy." Einar's white teeth flashed in his sunburned face. "When I finish with you, I go back to Iceland. We do not have shakeouts."

"A primitive people, the Icelanders." Sam sat her down on the couch. "What's up? I thought we were supposed to meet up in my office."

"Don't you know about the tsunami? I was on the Bay Bridge when it came in. And then there was a seiche. The whole bloody bay is just sloshing about with huge waves, like water in a bathtub. M-my God, you mean you didn't know?"

"We've been sitting around all morning doing physics," Sam said. "Is that why the lights are off? We thought it was just another damn thunderstorm."

"Sam, have you anything to drink in this house?"

She drank two beers as she told them what had happened in the last hour and a half. When she was through, Sam asked:

"Where's your husband?"

"At sea, in *Ultramarine*. He'll be fine. They won't even have noticed the tsunami out there."

"Good. Hope he doesn't worry about you."

"I suppose he might, if he knows what's happened. With radio communication being so unreliable, they may all be as blissfully innocent as you two."

"We are neither blissful nor innocent, after what we worked on this morning and what you told us now," Sam grunted. "Come and help fix lunch before you're completely bombed."

Sam refused to talk shop or even to discuss the disaster while they ate. He launched into a diatribe on the sad political level of current American movies. Einar argued with him, manifestly unworried about annoying his adviser.

"Have you seen this bloody thing called *Gunship*?" Sam demanded. "It was on cable all last month again. It's turning into a damn cult movie, like *The Texas Chainsaw Massacre*."

"It is only a cowboy movie with helicopters," Einar said.

"It's a pornography of violence. What *Gunship* says is that this country hasn't learned a goddamn thing. Don't examine your motives, put your trust in guns and more guns, and kill everybody you can because maybe they'll kill you. And the guy who made it is a millionaire because he peddles that crap."

"Anyway," the Icelander said, "it is not on cable now. Nothing is on cable any more."

"It's an ill solar wind that doesn't blow someone some good," Sam said. "Okay, enough—looks like we'd better get out and see what we can do to help. The authorities are probably a little overstrained."

They walked out into wind and spattering rain, and headed west. Sirens screamed everywhere. The wind smelled of smoke. A surprising number of people were on the street, or standing on their porches watching the smoke rise in the west. Kirstie realized they were mostly black; in her own all-white neighbourhood, up in the Berkeley hills, people went out only after dark these days.

Ambulances seemed to be concentrating a few blocks away, around an elementary school at San Pablo and Francisco. The seiche wave had come across San Pablo, right to the edge of the blacktopped schoolyard; across the street, people were carrying casualties out of the flooded buildings, wading through the mud left behind by the wave, and putting them down gently on the blacktop.

Teenaged blacks were stringing ropes across basketball courts and hanging tarpaulins and plastic sheets from them, improvising shelter for the injured.

Kirstie paused as they were about to enter the school building. The air reeked of smoke and excrement. She touched Sam's arm; his dark eyes looked into hers, and she saw something gentle, powerful and sad in them.

"I'm sorry—I'm scared," she mumbled.

"Of what?"

Two orderlies carried out a screaming, blood-splashed man with a sodden red bandage where his right forearm had been.

"Of—that."

"Come on, Kirstie. You're needed."

Without quite willing herself, she walked up the steps and through the door into a dark hallway echoing with screams.

3

Rain drummed on the bedroom skylights. Robert Anthony Allison woke up and, as always, rolled right out of bed. Shauna, as always, slept on. He went to the bathroom and flushed the toilet, knowing nothing would wake his wife.

How many men, he wondered as he shrugged into his favourite silk robe, how many men had fantasies about sleeping with Shauna Dawn McGuire? Five million? Twenty? He'd done his best to encourage those fantasies: three movies in two years, each a blend of violence, romance and sex that nobody else could bring off. Shauna was a big part of the blend—some of his competitors said he'd still be directing drive-in horror movies without her—but who else could live with a sex goddess and still keep the objectivity a director needed to exploit her properly? Not her last two husbands.

He padded back into the bedroom, studying Shauna's face. The fantasies couldn't include her merely human traits: her catatonic style of sleeping, her allergies, her humourless and self-absorbed lovemaking. As a husband he might resent those traits; as a director, his personal feelings never interfered with artistic concerns.

A narrow flight of stairs led directly from their bedroom suite to the kitchen. Allison plugged in the coffee maker and watched the rain slash down. He looked west and north, down the hill to the willows along Escondido Creek, up the far slope to the ridge almost a mile away. It was all his own land. He knew every one of those scattered oaks, right up to the ridge where the land fell away almost vertically into the next valley. He knew the course of the creek, from the pool a mile upstream (on the eastern boundary of his land) to the canyon three miles southwest (just outside his land) where the creek met the Carmel River. At the age of thirty-two, he was landed gentry, just like the rich pricks up and down the Carmel Valley. But unlike them, he had earned his land, over ten square miles of it; the pricks had inherited it from grandfathers who'd paid next to nothing for it.

Allison picked irritably at the peeling skin on his nose. Sunburn: he had pale and vulnerable skin, and the ultraviolet seemed to get past even broad-brimmed hats, but he was not about to run around like a clown, his nose painted white with sunblock ointment. At least the heavy overcast today would block some of the uv. He envied Shauna; she just turned a deeper and deeper brown.

Breakfast was two cups of coffee, black, strong and unsweetened. Then fifty push-ups and fifty sit-ups on the cold tile floor of the kitchen before he went back upstairs to his dressing room.

Allison had thought carefully about the clothes for today's interview: khaki trousers and safari shirt, dark-green ascot, glossy Wellingtons. A light-brown leather jacket with a broad sheepskin collar. He studied the effect in the mirror of his nineteenth-century wardrobe: out-doorsy, macho, semimilitary. His close-cropped black beard and gold-rimmed glasses might make him look a little too bohemian, even left-wing; the beard might have to go soon. His hair was getting shorter with every styling—not yet a soldier's white sidewall haircut, but close enough. The hole in his left ear lobe had closed up nicely. He put on a flat-brimmed Stetson, almost like a drill sergeant's.

Not a bad effect, he decided. It helped to be over six feet, with big shoulders and no belly. Even the sunburned nose helped a little, made him look less . . . studied. Sometimes your production values could be too good.

"Who are we today—Ernest Hemingway or Smoky the Bear?"

Shauna stood in the doorway to the bedroom, wrapped in an old terry-cloth bathrobe. Allison framed her between his hands, the great director visualizing a shot.

"Kid, you got funk. Real funk. The robe is a genuine *objet trouvé*, but I think I see pink plastic curlers in your hair, plus fuzzy pink slippers on your tootsies. Then in the background we see in deep focus the five-piece dinette set, genuine Formica and wood-grain vinyl trim, a K-Mart special this week only, plus a seventeen-inch TV set playing afternoon soaps."

"Wow. What are you popping?"

"Caffeine, real Colombian brown. But I don't drink it, I just snort it."

Shauna leaned against the doorframe and stretched in a big yawn. Not bad; remember that. It would look better in a black lace nightie, real Rita Hayworth, or even nothing at all. She doesn't know the killer is lurking in the closet with the butcher knife, but the audience does.

"Where you going?"

"Fort Ord. Lunch with our old buddy General Miles. Two or three drinks, burger and fries, then I ask to borrow the Sixteenth Airmobile Cavalry for a couple of months."

"Gee, thanks for not inviting me."

"Kid, you don't get invited—you get deployed. You're my *force de frappe*. I don't waste you in these little skirmishes." He put his arms around her.

"God, you say the sweetest things to me, I mean, really, God."

They lurched companionably downstairs to the kitchen, arms around each other. Shauna poured herself a cup of coffee, took the mandatory sip-before-first-smoke-of-the-day, and lighted a Marlboro. She slid into a chair at the kitchen table, next to the window.

"Know what I miss? I really miss the hills being green." She waved her cigarette at the hillside across the creek: it was a dull beige, with here and there a green bush or weed.

"Wait'll next year, kid."

"Do you think it'll be okay again by next year?"

"Kid . . . No. It won't be okay. It'll be worse. A whole lot worse."

"Hey, Bob Tony. It's such a beautiful morning, don't spoil it."

He looked around the high-ceilinged kitchen, at the gleaming copper pots, the used-brick fireplace, the microwave, the doorway to the sauna and hot tubs.

"Okay, it's a bad setting for a prophet of doom," he said. "But I'm getting an intuition. Like this next project could be the last for a long time, because already there's no cable and soon there won't be any more movie theatres."

"Okay," she shrugged. "This is the way the world ends. So what?"

"The oracle is working on it. —Listen, I'm late, I'm due for lunch in half an hour. What are you doing today?"

"Thought I'd go into Carmel, do some shopping."

"Mmmh. Okay. I'll be back around three or four. Talk to Lupe about dinner before you go." He kissed her with husbandly absent-mindedness and left.

The house was part of a compound on the crest of a

narrow ridge. On the north stood a barn and stables; on the east, a garage, sheds and two-story guest house; on the south, a big greenhouse and the low, flat-roofed servants' quarters. The area within the compound was partly garden and partly swimming pool.

Allison sprinted through the dead garden, past the swimming pool, and into the garage. Hipolito Vasquez, the gardener and handyman, was changing the spark plugs in the Chevy van. Next to the van were Allison's red Mercedes 450 SL convertible and Shauna's silver Jaguar XJ sedan.

"Buenos días, Don Roberto."

"Buenos días, Hipolito. Y como están los ojos, hombre?"

Hipolito grinned under his salt-and-pepper mustache. "Mucho mejor, gracias a Dios." He had made the mistake, a few days ago, of working outside without sunglasses. The UV had given him a mild dose of snow blindness. A lot of people got it these days, but usually only once: two or three days of agony were enough to teach caution to anyone.

Allison got into the Mercedes; Hipolito opened the garage door, and the convertible backed out into the rain. Allison let it glide down the long, curving blacktop drive to the gravel road along the creek.

He didn't like the road because it gave others access to his land. Farther up the creek was a ranch run by some weird religious sect called the Brotherhood, and farther still a handful of cabins that had been taken over recently by four or five families. Both groups left Allison and each other alone, but it was still an annoyance to see their jeeps and vans going past.

The creek was high, running fast and brown. Allison worried about it. The willows and oaks along the stream seemed to be handling the UV pretty well so far, but most of the local grasses were dying off. Erosion was getting serious, and in places the creek had undercut healthy trees and toppled them into the water.

The valley narrowed as he drove southwest, until the road wound through a steep-sided canyon just a few feet above the creek. As he came round a corner, Allison swore and stamped on the brake. Walking in the middle of the road was a tall figure in a hooded green poncho.

Without even glancing over his shoulder, the man moved to the side of the road. Allison roared past him in a spray of mud and gravel, then stopped and backed up.

"Need a ride?"

The man was young, with a blistered red face beneath sunglasses. He smiled shyly and nodded.

"Where you headed?" Allison asked.

"Monterey, sir."

"Jesus, that's still eight or nine more miles. Come on, get in. I'm going right into Monterey."

"Bless you, sir. It's very generous of you."

One of the Brotherhood. Allison cursed the guilty charity that had made him stop, while the young man got in and dripped on the leather seat.

The canyon twisted around a long, steep spur of rock and ended abruptly; the road dropped through a stand of oaks and met the Carmel Valley highway. From the valley, it was hard to see any clear break at all in the hills; Escondido was indeed a hidden creek.

Allison drove fast, with his usual brusque aggressiveness. Not many other cars were on the road; the fields and orchards of the Carmel Valley looked bleak; the only livestock in sight were six or seven cows in a meadow, bunched around a stack of hay. Each wore clear plastic goggles—too common a sight to be funny any more. Cattle without them went blind in a day, and the pain in their eyes drove them crazy. A blinded bull had killed a rancher up the valley a couple of months ago.

"How are your livestock doing?" Allison asked, though

he knew they must be alive—his passenger smelled strongly of cowshit.

"They're mostly well, praise God."

"Hell of a time to be ranching, though."

"It's the time of Tribulation, sir. We bear what the Lord sends us. Are you saved, sir?"

"Afraid not."

"I'll pray for you. And I'll ask Mr. Lamb to pray for you too. Once you're saved, these troubles don't burden you."

"Who's Mr. Lamb?"

"He's our leader. A very holy man. He's drawn us together here to care for one another and endure the Tribulation."

Allison was tempted to wonder whether a truly holy man would hole up on Escondido Creek when the world outside was falling apart; but he had wasted too much of his youth arguing with cranks and cultists in the film business to bother arguing. He said nothing, and the young man fell silent also. The Mercedes hissed through the rain.

Carmel, with its kitschy doll-house roofs among the pines, had all the charm of an out-of-season amusement park. A hand-lettered sign had been stuck into the gravel shoulder of the road: NO WORK KEEP GOING. The hospitality of Old California, Allison reflected, didn't extend to unemployed drifters.

North of the town, Highway 1 was really deserted, and he drove fast until he reached Monterey. With the tourist trade dead, the city was sustaining its revenues by nailing speeders; Allison kept carefully within the limit.

"Where can I drop you?" he asked.

"Anywhere along here will be fine, sir." Allison pulled over to the curb. Three men, loafing in the entrance to a bar, stared opaquely at the car. Out-of-town drifters could be chased away, but not the local boys.

The young man put out a big, calloused hand. "Thank

you, sir. May God bless and keep you."

"And you," Allison replied solemnly. The kid was a zombie, all right, but a likeable one. Put a machete in his hand and he'd make a great psychopathic killer, stalking the unbelievers. Too bad you couldn't make a nickel from a religious-nut movie any more, not with half the audience just as cracked as this kid but not so polite.

Allison accelerated again as he passed the shabby store-fronts of Seaside. The few businesses still open had heavy wire screens over their windows, and signs on their doors: Guard Dog on Duty, Max. Two Customers in Store at a Time, Clerk Is Armed. Tough times. The only laugh any-one had had in ages had been President Wood's inaugural boast that the recession would be over in sixty days. That had been three weeks ago; nothing had changed yet, except that people had stopped saying "recession" and started saying "depression," just like the Reagan years.

Highway 1 curved northeast around Monterey Bay. The view was spectacular, even in the rain: to the west the long dark arm of the peninsula, to the north the open grey waters of the bay, to the northeast the long dunes that marched along the coast. Out in the bay he saw a tanker coming in to its offshore moorage, three or four miles due west of the refinery at Moss Landing. A mon-ster, one of the half-million-tonners that had come out of moth balls recently. With almost no oil coming out of the Middle East anymore, the North Slope of Alaska had become crucially important; tankers were running up and down the coast nonstop, but even so the supply was never enough. To overcome the bottleneck, they were even refining some of the oil in Valdez and sending it down as gasoline and diesel fuel. Allison toyed with the idea of a tanker-hijack story; half a million tons of gasoline would be worth a hell of a lot these days, when it cost six dollars a gallon with a ration card, and fifteen on the black market. Well, save it for later—

He was at Fort Ord. To his right were the boxy little prefabs of married-personnel housing; to his left, the firing ranges, closed off from the sea by steep dunes. Despite the rain, many of the ranges were in use. Most of the trainees were blacks; the whites stood out because of the antisunburn ointment on their faces. They all looked wet and miserable. The irregular popping of rifle fire made him think again about buying some guns; it was getting easy to imagine Shauna being pulled from her car and raped, himself being beaten up by some mob. Paranoia—the stock response of the middle class in hard times.

The three black guards at the main gate looked a little paranoid too: brisk, alert, suspicious. Even in the rain, their sunglasses looked more sinister than silly. They checked his driver's licence, car registration and credit cards, made a phone call, and only then allowed him through.

A disquieting thought occurred to Allison: how the hell could he shoot exterior scenes in a war movie, when white actors would sunburn in minutes and risk snow blindness in an hour? Make-up—he'd have to get his make-up people working on it. Most of the filmmakers he knew were convinced everything would be back to normal by spring; Allison's intuition told him nothing would be back to normal for a long time. And he trusted his intuition. Three times now, he had guessed—*known*—what kind of movie would be popular in two years, and each time he'd been right. The last one, *Gunship*, had been such a screaming success that he'd let himself be pressured into another war movie even though it hadn't felt right.

The hell with it. *The Longrangers* had a good script, a small cast and a modest budget. It would still turn a profit and stir up the critics. Then he could sit back and choose the next project without so much hassle—

Doublethinking. The world is coming to an end tomorrow, but next week will be fair and warmer.

He parked outside the Officers' Club, a rambling two-story building with the mandatory stucco walls and red-tile roof, and walked slowly across the lot to the front doors. Discipline. You don't lose your cool, you don't run, least of all when you'll get wet anyway.

A young second lieutenant, freckled and sunburned, was waiting for him. He escorted Allison to a small dining room on the second floor, overlooking a stand of eucalyptus and a woebegone flowerbed. General Ernest Miles was already there, looking out the rain-streaked windows. His eyes were brilliantly blue, his square face deeply tanned. Allison found himself standing straighter.

"Hello, General. Hope I haven't kept you waiting."

"No, just got here myself. I'm drinking Perrier, but help yourself to whatever you like." Miles waved a thick hand towards the bar in the corner.

They settled companionably in easy chairs by the windows, reminiscing about the filming of *Gunship* two years before. Miles had been the commanding officer at Fort Polk, Louisiana, where they'd done the location shooting, and he had helped a lot. Allison privately suspected that Miles's transfer to Ord was largely due to the success of *Gunship*, which among other things had been a terrific recruiting film.

Waiters brought lunch; Allison and Miles moved to the table across the room.

"Good salad," Allison remarked.

"Hothouse lettuce. Can you believe it? Here we are in the middle of some of the finest farm country in the world, but they have to grow lettuce under glass." Miles regarded his plate with a kind of perplexed regret. "God knows where this will all end up. Ozone, flares, uv, weird weather—" He shook his head. "You wouldn't believe what we're contending with."

Uh-oh, thought Allison. "Well, you seem to be coping pretty damn well, General. The troops here look sharp."

"It's communications that's killing us, Bob. Every time one of those solar flares goes off, we get an instant power surge that blows hell out of microchip circuits. Knocks out computers, telecommunications, missile electronics, the works. Knocks out all our satellites as well. Washington is putting in fibre-optic cables as fast as possible, and they'll help some, but it'll be—oh, a couple of years before we're back to an adequate communications capability. The Russians could invade Germany tonight and we wouldn't know about it until next Tuesday."

"At least the Reds have the same problems, right?"

The general's grin returned. "Worse. We hear rumours that a couple of their missiles have blown up in their silos due to electronic malfunction."

"They didn't—?"

"Not nuclear explosions, no. But they showed that the Reds can't trust their hardware. We can't either."

"Should I even be hearing this?"

"It's common knowledge, Bob. These damn flares have the upper atmosphere all churned up. Launch a missile, you can't tell if it'll come close enough to its target to take it out.

"Are you telling me World War Three's been postponed because of the weather?"

Both men laughed and turned their attention to lunch. But within a minute or two Miles was brooding again about his troubles.

"The kids in basic training are taking it hard. At least the whites and Chicanos. They're mostly farm boys, small-town boys, they worry when they see what the uv is doing to the land. Then Mama writes a letter about how all the horses went blind and had to be shot—boy, you got a kid with a problem.

"What about the blacks?"

"Thank the good lord for those boys. They can take a dose of uv that would fry an egg, and they're city kids—

they don't know what colour grass is supposed to be. Except maybe the kind they smoke. We'd be out of business without 'em. You know, they're actually getting a kick out of all this."

"A kick?"

"Sure. The rest of us can't go outside without gloves and all that crud on our faces, except at night. The black boys think it's funnier'n hell. Well, I guess it is. We got the world's first indoor army."

Allison saw the chance to make his move. He raised his glass of Perrier: "Here's hoping the ozone will be back by June, or I'll have to shoot *The Longrangers* in a studio."

"Ah! Tell me about it."

Allison launched into his spiel, knowing Miles would be interested and sympathetic; the general had commanded long-range reconnaissance and patrol outfits in Vietnam. The pitch was going well, and Miles was nodding enthusiastically, when a stocky, red-faced captain burst in.

"Sir—sorry to disturb you, but we've got an urgent message from the Presidio in San Francisco. Uh, some kind of tidal waves are coming up the coast. They say San Diego and L.A. got clobbered, and Vandenberg—" He stopped himself, looking suspiciously at Allison.

"Spit it out, captain."

"Vandenberg Air Force Base reports heavy casualties and extensive damage. They expect the waves to reach the Monterey area about twelve-twenty. That's ah, twelve minutes from now, sir."

The general looked more annoyed than alarmed. "Okay. I don't think this will amount to much, but evacuate the firing ranges at once, and the dependents' quarters within half a mile of Highway One. Get everyone moved east of North-South Road. Notify the hospital, fire services and MPs. And get me a chopper out in front of this place by twelve-fifteen."

"Yes, sir!" The captain vanished, leaving the door ajar;

the hum from the main dining room, downstairs, seemed to change pitch.

Miles rose from the table. "Well, Bob, looks like we'll have to get together another time real soon. Sorry about this. I don't think we'll have any real trouble, but no sense taking chances. Boy—if Vandenberg got flooded, they must be some big waves."

The general was already halfway to the door. "Remember me to that lovely wife of yours."

—Oh Christ, thought Allison, she's in Carmel.

Allison followed Miles out and raced to his car. Just as he was unlocking it, the fort's PA system thundered into life: loud-speakers bawled unintelligibly, the noise blurring into echoes. Sirens moaned. Allison backed out of the parking slot and roared onto the street.

The main exits would be jammed with trainees from the rifle ranges pouring across Highway 1. He'd do better taking North-South Road and coming out at the southwest corner of the fort.

Once past the dependents' housing, Allison met little traffic, and soon reached Highway 218. He used a roundabout route to get back onto Highway 1 on the south side of Monterey; Carmel was only four or five miles farther on. He drove fast, splashing through flooded stretches of the road.

Belatedly, Allison turned on the car radio and tried to get KMPX, but it was off the air. He tried 640, the emergency frequency, but heard only a high-pitched whine. He switched off, swearing.

Sirens were screaming as he neared the junction with Highway 1: ambulances and police cars blocked off the streets leading down to the water. Even without radio, word had travelled fast in Monterey. Cars were almost bumper-to-bumper, heading for the high ground on the road to Carmel.

—Why was the engine running so loudly? He downshifted into second; the noise was louder. It wasn't the car. The whirring, rasping roar was coming from the north, from the waterfront.

The roar ended suddenly with a single sharp boom; the Mercedes shuddered as the pavement thumped beneath it. What sounded like machine-gun fire followed almost at once. Crossing Pacific, Allison got a clear look down to the waterfront.

It was gone. A black-and-white wall of water stood where the beach and wharves had been. The crest of the wave was level with the roof of a four-story building, which exploded when the water struck it.

A long tentacle from the wave shot up Pacific, a white mass twenty feet high and moving fast. It overtook a yellow Datsun station wagon, flipped it over, and engulfed it. The front of the tentacle was armoured in debris—boats, trees, fragmented walls, chunks of concrete, a long black shaft that must have been a piling from one of the piers.

The wave slowed long before it could reach the intersection, but Allison didn't pause. He spun the Mercedes around a stalled Volkswagen and accelerated. Others had the same idea and blocked him, until he turned on his headlights and leaned on the horn. Like sheep before a barking dog, the other cars drew aside and let him by.

Away from town, the broad highway to Carmel was crowded with cars moving slowly and steadily in both directions. Allison wondered whether Carmel had somehow escaped, until he glimpsed a sobbing woman sitting in the back of a northbound pickup truck. They'd got it, all right. He watched the oncoming cars, looking for Shauna's Jaguar.

He came over the ridge and looked south. West of the highway, almost nothing was left of Carmel. Trees, houses, the tea shops and boutiques on Ocean Avenue—they were all just wreckage now. Men and women ran or walked up the road, many without protection against the driving rain; many didn't even have sunglasses, and their eyes were vague and unfocussed with shock. One bearded man, barefoot and wearing only a T-shirt and jeans, slapped the hood of the Mercedes as he shambled past.

"Hey man, too bad, show's over. You missed all the fun. Missed all the goddamn fun!" The man went on up the line of cars, shouting and laughing.

The wave had almost reached the highway before receding. No one was trying to keep traffic out of the ruined village; most of the drivers pulled off the road and abandoned their cars, running downhill through the wreckage to look for family or friends. Allison shook his head and muttered, "Morons." It was obvious that anyone caught in the western, downhill part of Carmel was dead. All the little doll-house cottages, the stores and restaurants, were smashed flat and scattered up the hillside like driftwood. Muddy water ran in streams through the debris. Carmel Bay was a mass of heaving water that looked like boiling milk.

Uphill from the highway, the high school and the houses around it looked almost obscenely normal. Kids and teachers were crowded against the chain-link fence on the edge of a playing field, gaping down the hill. One of them had vaulted the fence and was standing on the hillside above the road, a portable videotape camera held to his face. Allison admired the kid's presence of mind.

He was still about a mile from the Carmel Valley turnoff when the second wave came in. Allison saw it first as a geyser erupting around the rocks of Carmel Point—a geyser that rose higher and higher, then vanished as the crest of the wave rolled over the point and onto the wreckage-strewn beach.

Hidden behind its own spray, the wave rolled over the ruins like a fog bank. When it struck the wall of debris left by the first wave, it shot straight up, higher than the few trees still left standing; then it curved and fell roaring onto the steep slope below the road.

Allison turned into the empty northbound lanes and jammed the accelerator to the floor. Rain and spray mixed in a dense grey cloud too thick for the windshield wipers; he guided himself by the line of red taillights to his right. Just a few hundred yards now, and he'd be on the road up the valley.

The taillights, glowing blurrily, suddenly drifted closer. A little orange car materialized in front of the Mercedes, skidding slowly sideways—

He felt the wave hit: a foot deep, still powerful, thick with debris. It swept across his side of the highway with a grinding noise. Cars were all over the road now, crunching together and spinning apart. The Mercedes drifted left, almost to the concrete barrier at the side of the road, before its tires came back into solid contact with the pavement. Allison had automatically put the car in neutral; now he gently tested the brakes. They felt mushy, but they worked. The car stopped. He pressed a button to retract the top, another to lower the windows. Rain drenched the leather seats. He put his hat on and looked around.

The wave was retreating from the highway in a sheet of chocolate-brown water, leaving an uneven layer of branches, lumber, rocks and mud on the asphalt. Wedged against the right front wheel of his car was the body of a German shepherd, its teeth bared and its fur caked with mud.

A young woman in jeans got out of a stalled Audi nearby and ran screaming across the road towards the hillside below the school. She stepped on the corpse of a small child and ran on without stopping.

Allison stood up on his seat. A few cars were turning around, skidding in the mud, and heading back north. To the south, a van lay on its side. Water sounds assaulted him: the hiss of rain, the roar of the ebbing wave as it ran in torrents back through the smashed village. Not far from the road, someone was screaming for help.

He slid down behind the wheel and put the car in first. The tires spun, flinging mud and pebbles against the underside, and then found traction. Slowly, slipping through mud and bumping over rocks and shattered lumber, Allison drove south to the turnoff. —Don't let me hit any nails, he prayed. God, please, no nails, no glass.

Other cars followed him, weaving around those deserted by their drivers. In his rearview mirror, Allison saw three or four men leave their cars and stumble downhill into the ruins.

They wouldn't get far; neither would he, if he were fool enough to follow them. Better to get home, change, and come back with Hipolito. If Shauna was in Carmel she was almost certainly dead anyway. Tears stung his eyes.

Rain soaked into his Stetson, and the brim began to sag. The sheepskin collar of his jacket smelled of wet wool. He drove slowly, avoiding the bodies scattered among the wreckage; weeping, he turned onto Carmel Valley Road, into country that had seemed forlorn this morning but now looked like an untouched paradise.

A silver Jaguar came around a corner, headed west. Allison saw it from half a mile away, braked, and pulled off the road. He flashed his headlights, then leaned on the horn. Shauna cut smoothly across the road and halted just in front of the Mercedes. He saw her face in the spattered semicircle of clear windshield and giggled at her surprised expression. The giggles took a long time to stop.

Deliberately, savouring the moment, he got out and splashed over to her. She rolled her window down.

"What in God's name are you doing, Bob? And what have you done to the car?"

Allison glanced back and noticed absently that the sides and front of the Mercedes were scratched and gouged. He turned to her, reaching out to touch her cheek, her perfect dark hair.

"Kid, y'know—you're cute enough to be in the movies. Anybody ever tell you that?"

"Are you ripped? Driving the Mercedes with the god-damn top down, and it looks like you were in an accident, and all you—"

"Turn around. We've got to get home."

"Hey, I'm getting all wet. —Oh shit, *was* there an accident? Are you okay?"

"Turn around, kid. I'll follow you home. Tell you about it there."

She nodded slowly, looking scared, and rolled her window up. The Jaguar boomed in reverse, off the shoulder and onto the rainswept pavement.

Allison followed close behind her, without bothering to put the top back up. His sodden clothes made him shiver. But he felt very clear-headed. Just an hour or two ago he'd been dithering, planning a movie one moment and worrying about social collapse the next. The time for doublethink was past; middle-class paranoia was a futile self-indulgence now.

He made his plans swiftly and easily. Every step fell into place, like the preproduction phase of making a film. By the time the two cars turned up into Escondido Canyon, most of the details of the plan were set, most of the contingencies were allowed for. One question remained, and it hung in his mind all the way back to the ranch: How do I get Sarah up here?

4

Plummet pitched and swung wildly as it was hoisted up and onto *Ultramarine*'s deck. They were hove-to in the lee of the Farallon Islands, thirty kilometres west of San Francisco, but the sea here was calm only in comparison to the storm-driven waves nearby.

Don crawled to the rear of *Plummet*'s cabin. Grunting, he straightened up and opened the hatch. Rain sluiced down on him as he climbed out.

A couple of crewmen helped him down from the superstructure; he was stiff and clumsy, and a little dizzy.

"How do you feel?" one of the crewmen asked.

"Okay." He turned to look at the sub. "Poor *Plummet*."

Ignoring the rain, Don walked around the submersible. He had seen at once, when the hatch opened, that the sail—a metal skirt around the hatch—had been torn away. *Plummet*'s bright yellow paint was pitted and chipped, in many places right down to the steel. Rocks had gouged and dented the hull; the protective screens around the propellers were clogged with gravel. The manipulator arm was mangled.

"I hope Owen won't be too sore when he sees this."

"He already has." The crewman pointed to the bridge, where two pale faces showed through rain-blurred windows. Don waved; the men waved back.

He left the deck and went down a corridor to his tiny cabin; on the way he met Shirley Yamamura, the ship's doctor. She cleaned the gash on his scalp and put a bandage over it.

"A real turbidity current, huh? You're lucky," she remarked.

"Pretty sloppy kind of luck. Ow."

"Poor baby. No, really—too bad it didn't happen when the networks were still operating. You'd've been the biggest thing since Cousteau."

"Maybe I'm lucky at that. What's happened to San Francisco?"

"They've had at least three big tsunamis, maybe four or five. I'm afraid I'm going to be awfully busy when we get back." Her lined face was set. "See you later."

Don got out of his wet, bloodstained clothes and pulled on dry jeans and a red flannel shirt. Then he went up to the bridge.

Except for the rattle of rain on the windows, the bridge was quiet and dim. Bill Murphy, the skipper, stood beside Owen Ussery, the ship's chief scientist. Bill was a short, compact man with a soupstrainer mustache and curly black hair that stuck out around a Giants baseball cap. The cap, together with his wrinkled plaid shirt and brown corduroys, made him look more like a suburban father than a master mariner. Owen was tall and thin, with a long sallow face and short white hair. He wore a baggy grey cardigan and shapeless blue slacks tucked into gumboots.

"Glad to see ya," Bill said, punching Don's arm. "How's your head feel?"

"Like a hangover. Good to see you guys. Uh—sorry about the sub, Owen."

"That's the least of our problems. We'll just take it out of your pay." Owen nodded towards the window. "Look."

Just above the wave-chopped eastern horizon, a dark cloud merged into the overcast.

"Is that the city?"

Owen blew his nose. "Yes, that's the city. We've been trying to raise the Institute, but there's no reply."

"What we're picking up from CBers and hams is really bad," said Bill. "So I'm staying put until the waves are all finished."

Owen pursed his lips. "We've been discussing our options," he said dryly. "I feel we should get home as soon as possible. Sitting out here is not doing anyone any good."

"Sorry, Owen." Bill Murphy's dark eyes met the chief scientist's. "We stay put until the waves stop."

Don eased himself into a chair. He ached, and felt a little seasick. "That could be a long wait, Bill."

"How come?"

Don seemed to ignore the question. "Owen—was this really from a quake in the Antarctic? Any details?"

"Not much. There was a quake, eight or a little better on the Richter scale, somewhere in West Antarctica. Mount Erebus is erupting too, but that's all we heard."

"Look, I don't know enough to be sure, but these waves could go on for days or weeks."

"How so?" Owen walked with practised ease across the swaying floor and took the chair next to Don's. Bill glanced at his steersman and then joined them.

"I told you my brother's in the Antarctic. He's got a theory that a quake down there could start a surge of the ice sheet. That would dump a lot of ice into the ocean, all at once. And if the surge is periodic, we'll get more tsunamis."

"We can stay out for two weeks more if we have to," said Bill.

"Not much point," said Don. "If the waves are caused by an ice surge, and the surge is periodic, the next series of waves could come at any time. We might as well go in now."

"Not in this storm," Bill said. "Wait until morning. It'll blow itself out by then. And if it hasn't, at least we'll be able to see where we're going."

"Fair enough," said Owen. "Don, let's get you down to the wardroom and feed you something. You must be starving."

The thought of food made Don feel queasy, but he got to his feet and went out with Owen. He listened only absently to Owen's talk about the tsunamis and the turbidity current and the need for more biological samples.

The wardroom was hot and smelled of pea soup. Don walked unsteadily to a table and sat down, leaning on his elbows with his hands on his face. It occurred to him that his brother might be dead, far away on the ice. He began to shudder.

Owen handed him a plastic tumbler with two fingers of brandy in it. Don took a small sip and felt a little steadier. He saw that the wardroom was crowded with scientists and technicians, all of them too busy to greet him with more than a nod or wave. Charts had been taped onto bulkheads, showing the California coast in detail. A loudspeaker was linked to the radio shack. The men and women in the wardroom were very quiet as they scrawled lines across the charts based on reports that came over the loud-speaker. A rough picture was emerging.

Tsunamis had travelled up the Gulf of California, between Baja and the Mexican mainland, and had swept over the low-lying Imperial Valley. El Centro and several other farming towns were under water. San Diego and La Jolla had been flooded, but the coast around San Clemente had escaped. Long Beach and Wilmington were in ruins. The waves had bypassed Los Angeles's western beaches and densely populated shoreline, but from Topanga to Malibu the coast highway and hundreds of houses had disappeared.

The small towns and cities from Santa Barbara to Big Sur were silent. So were Carmel and Monterey. The 500 000-tonne tanker *Sitka Carrier*, preparing to offload a cargo of diesel fuel and gasoline at Moss Landing, had gone down in Monterey Bay. Santa Cruz, and the north end of Monterey Bay, had been flooded up to three kilometres inland.

Details were clearest about the Bay Area. The waves had destroyed the Golden Gate Bridge and virtually all of the San Francisco waterfront. Seiches in the bay were scouring out the landfill on which thousands of houses had been built. Fires were spreading across San Francisco, Oakland and Tiburon. The huge tank farm in Richmond, storing millions of tonnes of oil and gasoline, had been flooded. Many of the tanks had been breached and were on fire; the northeast corner of the bay was covered with a burning slick. The wind from the west was confining most of it to the Richmond shoreline, but the outgoing tide was drawing the slick towards San Francisco and the Marin shoreline.

A chlorine spill in Oakland looked really bad. Two policemen in Piedmont had reported seeing a greenish haze spreading across the freeway towards the hills on the east. That meant that scores of thousands of people in the path of the chlorine cloud were almost certainly dead.

North of California, the waves had done relatively little damage on the steep, thinly populated coast. A ham operator relayed a report from Oregon that several fishing ports had been seriously hit. No news had come from Washington, British Columbia or Alaska.

"Pretty goddamned depressing," said Owen. "It'll be even worse when we get in and people start looking for their families."

"Yes." Don knew that Owen was divorced; his wife and two daughters lived in Chicago now.

"Kirstie should be okay."

"God, Owen, I hope so. She was supposed to be in the city today, at a conference of climatologists. She could be fine or she could be dead."

"She'll be fine. I'm certain of it. But I'm worried as hell about all the people at PIO, right on the waterfront."

"I'll bet they got out in time," said Don. "They're plugged right into the Hilo tsunami alert system, so they'd have known as soon as anyone. They would have moved fast."

Owen nodded.

"Even if the Institute is wrecked," Don went on, "we'll be back in business right away. There'll be a hell of a lot to do."

"I know. But we may be way down the priorities list. Think about the economic impact of all this, coming on top of a depression. The government will be scraping around for money just to pay its own people, let alone us. The insurance companies will be wrecked, the banks will start failing—can you imagine how many mortgaged houses must have been smashed into kindling today?"

"And all the computers have been haywire for months," Don added. "Still, they'll have to do something. They can't just let everything fall apart."

Ultramarine hove to a few kilometres northwest of the Golden Gate and waited for sunrise. Don slept for a few hours and woke gritty-eyed and sluggish. His head hurt. The air smelled sour and strange.

The lights were on in the wardroom, but he found no one there. Don got a cup of coffee and took it with him to the bridge.

Bill Murphy was there, red-eyed and hoarse from staying up all night. Owen, by contrast, was freshly showered and shaved, and seemed relaxed and casual. On deck below, most of the rest of the crew and scientists were lined up along the port rail, looking at the Marin coast.

"My God," said Don.

The sea was strewn with wreckage: lumber, trees, an almost-intact shingle roof, a capsized fishing boat, tangled masses of yellow nylon rope, carcasses of cows and sheep, a man's naked body caught in the branches of a floating oak. Here and there, the flotsam was thick enough to form islets. Oil slicks gleamed in long streaks across the choppy grey water. Despite the westerly wind, the air was sour and heavy.

The Marin shore, five kilometres to the west, showed the scars of the tsunamis. All the lower slopes had been scoured clean of life; bedrock gleamed wetly. Above the scars, houses stood undamaged along tree-lined roads.

"They haven't had a big wave since midnight," Bill rasped, "and the seiches in the bay have died down. But the slick is all over the northeast corner, and across to Marin, and up into San Pablo Bay. Lot of fires in the city."

"Anything from PIO?" Don asked.

"Uh-uh."

The ship picked its way inshore, steering around islands of debris; a lookout in the bow used the ship's phone to guide Bill through clear water.

Don went outside as *Ultramarine* entered the Golden Gate. Grey sky hung low over the sea. The two peninsulas faded into mist not far to the north and south; over San Francisco, smoke coiled up into the overcast. It was fairly quiet, except for the drone and thump of the engines, the susurration of water against the hull, and the distant white noise of the city.

Just to the right of the ship's course, the south tower of the Golden Gate Bridge rose above the incoming tide. The roadway it supported ran out from the steep bluffs of the Presidio, between the twin orange pillars, and ended in ragged steel and concrete. Support cables trailed into the water. Steel had twisted, concrete had shattered, but somehow the structure held together.

A line of surf showed where the north tower lay beneath the surface. On the gouged bedrock of the Marin Headlands, the northern end of the roadway lay twisted and shattered.

Straight ahead, Alcatraz stood out clearly against the smoke cloud of the burning slick; the hills behind Berkeley were just visible through the tattered edges of the cloud.

Don turned to look at the San Francisco shoreline again. The old bastion on Fort Point was gone; on the muddy slopes of the Presidio, soldiers and civilians wandered without obvious purpose. Beyond the trees and red-tile roofs of the Presidio itself, more smoke rose in streaks of black and grey, white and yellow. Don saw a helicopter rise from somewhere inside the army base and vanish into the smoke.

The surface of the water was a matted mass of uprooted trees, capsized sailboats, oil drums, furniture, tires and corpses. Despite the lookout, *Ultramarine* kept striking debris. The smell in the air thickened into a smoggy stink.

Now they were within the bay, and keeping well offshore. Although he had the harbour to himself, Bill Murphy kept *Ultramarine* moving dead slow. The ship crept south along the ruined docks; apart from the broken concrete pillars of the Embarcadero Freeway, Don could see little of the city through the thickening haze of smoke. Beyond where the Ferry Building had been, the smoke was a solid black wall, blotting out everything on the far side of the bay. Coughing, Don went back up to the bridge.

"Looks really bad," Bill said. "I don't think we'll find much left of PIO." He picked up a microphone.

"This is Bill." His voice echoed from loud-speakers all

over the ship. "*I want everyone below decks. Everyone. Secure all portholes and ventilation.*" He put the mike back on its hook and tugged his baseball cap lower over his eyes. He crossed himself.

Darkness fell over the ship. Smoke swirled in grey cones in front of the spotlights, and the foghorn blatted every few seconds. Bill watched the radar and sonar screens; their green lights were reflected in his eyes.

One of the Bay Bridge's huge concrete footings loomed through black haze; the roadway above was only a darker smudge. Don went to the starboard windows.

The footing was pitted and scarred for almost ten metres above the surface of the water. Deep cracks ran through the concrete; fragments of wood and plastic had been forced into them, and hung like moss.

"That high—this far inside the bay—" Don shook his head. "There won't be a thing left of the Institute."

PIO's buildings had stood on China Basin Road, near Pier 48. Dozens of pilings still jutted from the water, but the Institute's converted warehouses were gone. Where they had been, oily water reflected the orange glare of the burning city.

"Well, well," Bill muttered. Owen stared out the windows, expressionless.

A low, dark peninsula stood beyond the ship's bow: the naval shipyards at Hunter's Point.

"Maybe the navy will take us in," Owen said quietly.

While flotsam thumped against the hull, the ship crept south. It was still several hundred metres from the north side of the shipyards when everyone on the bridge could see that the docks were wrecked here as well. The seiches had swept back and forth across the low peninsula of Hunter's Point, turning the machine shops and dry docks into rubble.

Bill and Owen spoke together for a few minutes, quietly and gravely. Then Bill ordered the anchors dropped. He picked up the mike.

"*We're going to anchor here and assess the situation, people. If it's at all possible, we'll ferry you ashore in the Zodiacs. I know you all want to get to your families as soon as possible, but I'd like some people to stay aboard for a day or two.*"

"Company's coming," said Don.

A small motorboat was approaching across India Basin; behind it was a high wall of rubble where Innes Avenue had been, and beyond that the long hill with the housing projects that were the heart of the Hunter's Point ghetto. As the boat drew nearer, the people on the bridge could see that it carried four young men. All were black and all carried rifles.

5

The old woman lay on the wet blacktop of the school's playing field. Her skirt and sweater were muddy and sodden. Kirstie lifted the old woman's head, and held a styrofoam cup of water to her lips.

"I'm not thirsty, thank you," the old woman whispered.

"All right, then. We'll have you inside soon. The doctors will take a look at you, and then off you'll go to a nice warm bed."

"What's your name, dear? Are you from England?"

"My name's Kirstie Kennard, and I'm from Aberdeen, in Scotland. And what's your name?"

"My name is Susan Smith. I live at ten-twenty-five Francisco Street. Where am I?"

"Just a couple of blocks from home, Mrs. Smith. At the school up the street."

Kirstie glanced across the crowded field, over the crude shelters made of plastic sheets or slabs of plywood. The school was on the east side of San Pablo Avenue, and the disaster zone started across the street. From there to the bay, a distance of nearly two kilometres, almost every building had been damaged or destroyed. The old woman had been pulled from the ruins of her home and carried on the shoulders of two nameless men, men who had waded knee-deep through oily mud to bring her here.

"I'm cold. I don't feel well." Her breath rasped in her throat. She found Kirstie's hand and squeezed it. For a long time she lay still; at last Kirstie put a hand gently on the woman's narrow chest, feeling for a heartbeat. Beneath the skin she felt only the sharp ends of broken ribs. The old woman had died.

Rain pattered again on the plastic sheeting just above her head. The air stank of smoke and wet ashes and excrement. All around her, people lay or sat on the blacktop. Most of them were hurt; many were dying. Susan Smith had been the fourth person to die in Kirstie's company in the last two hours. The schoolyard buzzed and hummed with voices: screams, shouts, weeping, laughter.

Standing up, Kirstie signalled to two black women standing in the school's main doorway. They came over, lifted Susan Smith's body onto a stretcher, and carried it around the building to the growing pile of corpses.

Kirstie went into the school for a drink of water. The halls and classrooms were filled with more people, mostly children, awaiting emergency surgery. Some cried out and wailed, but most were strangely quiet, even those who lay by themselves along the side of the main corridor. Above them, on the walls, were construction-paper murals of tulips and raindrops; in the middle of the floor was a thick trail of mud and blood.

Someone was screaming in the cafeteria, now being used as an operating room. A young medical student in jeans and a blood-spattered apron came out of the cafeteria and looked around. He saw Kirstie and waved her over.

"Doing anything important?"

"Not really."

"Okay, you can go to this address." He ripped a paper tulip from the wall and scrawled on it. "It's a medical-supplies warehouse. Grab all the sulfa drugs and dressings you can carry. Somebody brought in some backpacks, okay, I think they're behind the reception desk up in the school office. Fill 'em up."

"How do I get into the warehouse?"

"Uh, you may have to break in, okay, but we need the stuff. You'll find the dressings in big boxes near the rear door. The drugs are in a locked room between the warehouse and the front office. The key to the room should be in the top right desk drawer in Ken Berkowitz's office, okay, with a red Dymo tape on it."

The young man turned and pushed through the swinging doors back into the cafeteria. Fluorescent lights, powered by a portable generator, glared over a dining table where four men held down a writhing, shrieking girl while a fifth man bandaged her arm.

"Oh, and morphine, okay?" added the young man over his shoulder.

"O-kay," Kirstie murmured, feeling both relief and guilt at escaping from the schoolyard. She found the backpacks, by a cupboard containing a flashlight; if she had to go into a darkened building, the light would be useful. Going outside, she looked around for Sam and Einar, and spotted them by their yellow ponchos.

"I need you two," she said. They followed her out of the schoolyard and down Francisco Street.

"Where are we going?" Sam asked. She told him; he whistled.

Walking across San Pablo and down to University was easy enough; the waves had been less than knee-deep when they reached San Pablo, and had left only a scatter of rubble. But the farther west they walked down University, the harder it became. Most buildings had collapsed into piles of masonry and splintered wood. Cars were tumbled and scattered, their interiors packed with mud, across streets and sidewalks and parking lots. The Southern Pacific Railway station, an old tile-and-stucco landmark, had vanished; where the building had stood, a derailed train lay toppled on its side.

The streets were swamps; in some places, the asphalt had been torn off and the underlying gravel scoured out, leaving waist-deep gullies. Fires burned in the ruins. A hotel, big and massive enough to have survived the waves, was now only a smoking shell.

Kirstie and Sam and Einar were not the only ones floundering through the rubble. Dozens of people were picking over the remnants of jewellery and grocery stores, or wandering aimlessly. One old man, in a long overcoat and mud-caked trousers, carried a new waffle iron in a string bag as he high-stepped through the mud.

"No cops," Sam said as they paused beside an overturned Chevy pickup. "Where the hell are the cops?"

"Some are taking people to the hospitals," Kirstie answered. "I think a lot of them with families just took off for home. I don't blame them. We had some firemen working across San Pablo, but they all left in a mad rush—something about a chlorine spill in Oakland."

Sam touched her arm. "Are you serious?"

"Well, of course."

"How big would a chlorine spill have to be, to draw firemen away from this?"

"Pretty big."

Through a gap in the smoke overhead, a helicopter chattered south at low altitude. "Bloody television," Kirstie muttered. "They were circling around the school like vultures this afternoon, but would they land and help? Now they must be looking for something even worse."

"Is that where we go?" asked Einar, pointing to a two-story cement-block building half a block away.

"I think so."

The front entrance was buried behind drifts of twisted metal and shattered wood, including a part of a sailboat's hull. Carefully, they worked their way through the adjoining parking lot to a side entrance. It was a glass door and had been smashed open.

"Looks like someone got here before us," said Sam quietly. He rubbed his beard. "A building full of drugs. Mmmh." He looked at Kirstie. "I think you maybe ought to stay put until we check out the inside."

"Don't be so bloody chivalrous, Sam." Kirstie got the flashlight out of her backpack and stepped through the aluminum doorframe. Water was ankle-deep inside. The entry led up two steps to a corridor; she squelched up and found it lined with offices, most of them unlocked.

Sam and Einar followed her in. The three of them moved slowly; their only illumination was from the flashlight, throwing a restless yellow ellipse on floors and walls. After looking into the first office, Kirstie turned to Sam and whispered in his ear:

"Someone's been in here, all right. Maybe they're still here."

The office had been ransacked: desk drawers ripped out, house plants knocked over, filing cabinets dented. Kirstie swung the flash around, and changed her mind: not ransacked, just vandalized by someone feeling very frustrated. Maybe the key to the drug room would still be in Ken Berkowitz's desk.

That office was two doors up the hall. It hadn't been touched. The desk looked as if its owner had just stepped out a moment before; papers were strewn over the desk, and a brown-paper lunch bag sat beside colour photos of two small girls and their attractive mother.

The key with the red Dymo tape was easy to find. Kirstie took it and went out into the hall, where Sam and Einar were waiting. She patted Sam's arm and went on down the hall to the locked door of the drug room.

Someone had obviously tried to break into it, using a hammer: the grey paint on the steel door was chipped away in little circles and crescents. Silently, Kirstie unlocked the door. Warm, stale air puffed out.

It didn't take long to find the sulfa; the morphine, though, seemed to be in a padlocked cupboard.

"What now?" Kirstie hissed.

"Wait," said Einar. He took the padlock in one big hand, and tugged at it. Then, gripping it with both hands, he put one foot up on the steel door of the cupboard and pulled.

Something snapped metallically. Einar grunted and pulled again, twisting. The hasp came away from the door, and he pitched backward across the room.

"Jesus Christ," said Sam. "Did you know you could do that?"

"I think maybe I can do it. No harm to try."

They were talking normally now, relieved and surprised, as they took box after box of morphine and methadone ampoules out of the cupboard.

"My God," Sam chuckled. "If we'd done this two days ago, Einar and I could've retired to Rio. Son, you're wasted in astrophysics. You should've been a burglar."

"Fuckin' A," said an unfamiliar voice. Then, unnecessarily: "All right, everybody freeze."

Kirstie saw Einar spin round, and heard a thump. The intruder cried out. Another thump followed, and then a second voice yelled out incoherently.

She swung her flashlight to the doorway. Lying in the hall was a young man with blood on his lips. Just beyond him was Einar's broad back. The Icelander turned, holding another young man in a half nelson.

"Oh jeez, oh shit, man, my arm—hey, easy, we're not doin' anythin', honest, shit my arm. Please."

Kirstie walked quickly to the doorway, keeping the light on the young man's face. "Shut up!" Her voice sounded shrill in her own ears, but he obeyed. "Sam, you'd better search him."

"He's got a knife."

"What about his friend?"

"A gun," said Einar. "He dropped it. I kicked it into the room."

"Good, got it," Sam said. "What the hell did you do to him?"

"I threw the padlock."

Kirstie stepped closer to Einar's prisoner. "I take it you two were looking for drugs."

"Uh, well, yeah. So?"

She fought down an urge to kick him. "Sam, give me the gun." She studied it for a moment: a snub-nosed revolver, finished in dull blue. It sat in her hand, heavy and ugly. She turned the flashlight back on the young man, who looked terrified.

"Now listen to me. You and your friend are going to help us get this stuff to where it's needed. If you try anything, I'll shoot you. Do you believe me?"

"Yeah, yeah, Christ."

"All right, then. Sam, get the other one up."

They filled their backpacks and then emptied the plastic bags in the wastebaskets to use as sacks. Leaving the room, Kirstie locked it. The five of them went to the storeroom at the rear of the building, and found big boxes of gauze and bandages. When everyone was carrying as much as possible, they went back out the side door.

The grey afternoon was dimming into dusk. The two would-be looters looked small and almost pathetic, skinny men with long wet hair and sodden denim jackets.

"Right," said Kirstie. "Let's get back to the school."

"Hey, lady," said the unhurt one, "you gonna walk up the street with a gun on us?"

"Yes."

"Thass ki'nappeen," the other one mumbled. Fresh

blood oozed from his split lips.

"And if I shoot you, it'll be murder. Get going."

With their arms full, Sam and Einar and their prisoners made slow progress. The streets were deserted now. The fires were spreading, and a sullen orange glow shimmered over everything. The noise of burning was loud. Smoke was thin at times, then thick, as gusts of wind blew in from the bay.

Kirstie looked over her shoulder and saw an enormous cloud, black laced with orange, blotting out the western sky. Its base blazed hot yellow, and it seemed to extend far to the northwest. What could be burning like that, out on the water? A ship?

She was stepping on a fallen telephone pole when a growing rumble from behind made her pause. Before she could turn, the pole heaved beneathed her feet and toppled her backward into black, stinking water. It washed over her, carrying slimy lumps of debris.

Gasping, Kirstie fought her way back onto her feet. The water was receding already, but the four men were clambering onto cars. She waded towards them.

"Come on, come on!" she shouted. "It's not much of a wave, then, is it? Let's go."

Sheepishly, the men slid down into the water. A storefront crashed noisily into the street, exposing a show room crowded with refrigerators and ranges. One of the looters staggered and cried out.

"Jeez, I just stepped on a dead body!"

"Go on!" Kirstie shouted.

It was full dark by the time they reached the school. With lights glowing in its windows, it looked warm and welcoming in the black-and-orange night. An ambulance parked nearby flashed red and blue, and the plastic shelters in the schoolyard reflected the colours.

"About time," grunted the medical student when they met him in the hallway. "I thought you weren't coming back. Thanks." He looked curiously at the gun. "What's that for?"

"Persuasion."

"Huh."

"Doc—can you do so'thin' for my 'outh?" asked the injured looter.

The medical student looked dispassionately at him. "Wait your turn."

Kirstie handed the pistol to Sam, who delicately unloaded it before stuffing it in a pocket of his windbreaker.

"Look," said the medical student, "you're soaking wet and you look bushed, but can I ask you and your friends for one more favour?"

"Sure," Kirstie nodded.

"We got over fifty people too hurt to be moved, even if we had someplace to move 'em to, okay? And we got maybe a hundred other injured and three hundred with nowhere to go, most of 'em relatives of the casualties. We got to start feeding these people."

"You want us to scavenge food for five hundred people?" Kirstie said, slowly and incredulously.

"Grab everyone you can find to lend a hand. Try the Co-op supermarket or wherever, okay?"

Kirstie sagged against a wall. "Oh God."

A few minutes later, she and Sam and Einar and fourteen other people were walking through the darkened streets. Candles burned in a few houses, but most looked deserted. From one pitch-black house, though, music blared; shadowy figures stood on the front porch, smoking dope and giggling. In a dark back yard, a dog howled.

Above the housetops to the west, fire pulsed under orange-and-black clouds of smoke. Fine soot stung their eyes and tasted bitter.

Kirstie, Sam and Einar led the others up several blocks to the Co-op. It was a big building, part of a chain of consumer-owned supermarkets in the Bay Area. They were surprised to see its beige facade was glaringly illuminated by floodlights from a big white van parked near the entrance. Across the sides of the van was written: KSRA ACTION NEWS—All the News for Sacramento!

A reporter stood on the sidewalk, with a cameraman and sound girl behind him, and a cluster of uniformed National Guardsmen between him and the entrance to the market. The reporter was interviewing their commanding officer, a young lieutenant who looked self-conscious. Standing around the van were dozens of civilians, most of them shouting angrily.

"I realize it seems unfair," the lieutenant was saying to the reporter, "but our mission here is to protect property. It's other people's job to look after persons in distress. I'm sorry if that disappoints some of these individuals, but that's our job."

Kirstie shouldered past a guardsman and tapped the lieutenant on the arm, ignoring the news crew.

"Lieutenant, I must insist that you allow us into the market." He gaped at her, startled as much by her Scottish-schoolmistress accent as by her boldness. "I have to feed five hundred homeless and injured people."

The young officer's girlish mouth set hard. "I have my orders, ma'am, and those orders are to prevent looting. The Office of Emergency Services will be in action here as soon as possible, and that means your people will be looked after. Now would you please move on."

"I will not move on."

He turned and walked stiffly away; Kirstie would have followed him, but the reporter turned his attention to her. He was a boyish, curly-haired man in baggy jeans, a leather coat and rimless glasses.

"You say you're trying to feed five hundred people? Where are they? What kind of shape are they in?"

She hesitated, imagining the effect of TV cameras and

inane questions on the people in the schoolyard. They'd gone through enough without having to entertain viewers sitting comfortably in undamaged homes far away.

"Many of them are badly hurt, even dying," she said at last.

The reporter put down his microphone, and his cameraman stopped taping. "My name's Jason Schwartz, KSRA News. Could we see these people? Maybe interview some of them?"

"I don't think that would do much good, Mr. Schwartz. —No, wait a moment. If you'll help us, you can interview anyone you like."

"How?"

"Take us somewhere, where there's food. A market, a warehouse—I don't care. And help us bring the food back in your truck."

"Are you asking us to help you loot some unprotected store?" grinned the cameraman.

"No, to help us feed some unprotected people."

"Why not?" asked the sound girl. The reporter nodded slowly.

"I can see the humanitarian angle," he said. "Sure. We can only take three or four of you, though."

"That's fine." She told the volunteers to go back and help get the cafeteria ready; then she and Sam and Einar climbed into the back of the van. The cameraman got in behind the wheel and doused the floodlights on the roof; the guardsmen were left to protect the Co-op in almost total darkness.

"Never seen anything like this," Jason Schwartz said over his shoulder, one arm resting comfortably on the sound girl's shoulder. "We got tape you wouldn't believe. We came on down Interstate Eighty into Richmond, and boy, you should've seen those tank farms burning!"

"It was really, you know, far out," said the sound girl. "Like almost a religious experience, you know?"

"Shut up, Michelle. Listen, if we get a chance before the chopper pickup we'll run some of that tape for you guys. Just un-fuckin'-believable. These big, big, orange flashes, you know, and the stuff pouring like lava down into the bay, sort of like the last days of Pompeii, you know? Wow, and we got really, really close; there wasn't any police or firefighters there. I seriously think we got a chance for an award."

They had turned south onto Sacramento and were driving past block after block of two- and three-story apartment buildings. Candles glowed dimly in many of the windows. The only stores they saw were small convenience markets and corner groceries; most had been looted, except for a few guarded by armed civilians.

Then they were in Oakland; the apartment buildings here were older, taller and grimier, interspersed with used-car lots and funeral homes and Polynesian restaurants. To the south, fires reflected pink and orange off the low overcast, silhouetting the high-rise towers of downtown Oakland. A few fires burned just ahead, but no sirens wailed and no one moved in the streets. All the apartment windows were black.

"Christ!" The cameraman jammed on the brakes, too late, and the truck bounced over two bodies in the middle of the street.

"Fred, Fred, stop!" yelled the reporter. "That's hit-and-run, for Christ's sake!"

"Shit, Jason, they were already dead. Look, oh God, the whole fucking street is full of 'em."

He slowed to a stop. In the truck's high beams, the street and sidewalk ahead were littered with bodies. They lay in heaps and singly; their clothes looked strangely tattered and discoloured, and their skins were mottled. A black woman had fallen from the door of the taxi she'd been driving. Her face was puffy and looked scarred. Two dachshunds lay stiffly beside a boy of nine or ten. The air was sharp with the smell of chlorine.

"Like Jonestown," Jason whispered. "Jesus. Fred, get your camera."

"My eyes sting. I think we should get outa here."

"The hell with your eyes. C'mon."

Kirstie and Sam and Einar talked quietly while the others got their gear together.

"This is the chlorine spill," Sam murmured. "God knows if it'll get thick again. A shift in the wind and we could all be dead."

"Oh God," said Kirstie. "That's why their skin is like that, and their clothes are in shreds. It was raining. Some of the chlorine must have formed hydrochloric acid."

"It could start eating the hell out of our tires," Sam murmured. "We'd better get out of here while we can still move."

"There's a supermarket on the corner," Kirstie said. "If we're quick and lucky, maybe we can get what we need."

She turned and started walking quickly towards the supermarket. Behind her she heard Sam and Einar following, and Jason's voice as he improvised a report. Fred's floodlights threw her shadow ahead of her.

The supermarket's entrance was piled with dead people, men, women, children, lying among spilled shopping carts and scattered groceries. Their faces were puffy, mottled and contorted in the light of her flash. The doors to the market were open, but barricaded by corpses.

Kirstie stopped. The men caught up with her.

"I can't go in there," she said. "I'm sorry—it's—I'd have to—"

"We will go around," said Einar. "In the back."

There were all coughing: pockets of chlorine trapped between buildings were embittering the air. At the rear of the supermarket, an alley led to a loading dock. Two men in blue coveralls were curled up on the dock; their eyes glinted in the beam of the flashlight.

"Ho-ho," Einar said.

Backed up to the loading dock was a big truck; on its aluminum sides were the words NORCAL WHOLESALERS—THE BEST FOR LESS! Einar ran up some cement steps to the dock, stepping lightly over the dead men, and shone his light into the rear of the truck. "Ho-*ho*," he said again.

"What is it?" Sam called in an urgent whisper.

"This truck is almost full. Mostly canned food."

Kirstie wanted to howl in triumph; instead she gasped and wiped her watering eyes.

"Can you drive it?" she wheezed. The alleyway lit up as a burning apartment building collapsed suddenly in a whirl of sparks. Einar leaped down, ran to the cab, and pulled out the body of the driver.

"Yes. Let us go."

"Let us go then," Sam echoed hoarsely, "when the city is spread out like a patient chloroformed upon a table." He and Kirstie climbed into the cab.

"That is not an accurate quote," Einar said, starting the engine.

"Shut up and drive."

The headlights glared. Einar swung the truck up the alley, turned left, and left again onto Sacramento. Jason was standing before the market's plate-glass windows, illuminated by Fred's lights. Einar honked the horn and braked beside them.

"We have got some food now," he called down to them. Fred had already started taping the truck; he followed Jason around to Kirstie's side of the cab and grinned excitedly at her.

"Far out," he coughed. "Listen, give us a fifteen-second clip and then we'll follow you back to your people."

"Well—" Fred's light was an added injury to her streaming eyes. Jason asked her a few questions, and she coughed her answers. "Now we've got to go. The school is at Francisco and San Pablo in Berkeley. Thanks."

"Thank *you*. See you there."

The truck raced north on Sacramento, but had to detour west, just inside Berkeley, to avoid a fire in the middle of the street: an office building had exploded nearby, scattering burning fragments across several parked cars which had then caught fire. Sam fiddled with the truck's radio, picking up bits of news bulletins through heavy static.

"*The President has declared the states of California, Oregon and Washington disaster areas, and vowed tonight to visit personally the worst-hit areas such as San Diego and San Francisco ...*" "*... says there is no cause for panic and the National Guard is on duty in the stricken areas. General Ernest Miles, commander of Fort Ord, has declared martial law in the Salinas-Monterey area. No word as yet on whether Sixth Army Headquarters at the Presidio of San Francisco plans a similar declaration for the Bay Area ...*" "*... reports of looting in the Los Angeles area are exaggerated, the city's mayor says. The power is still out in most of the Southland as far east as Palm Springs, and hospitals using backup generators are reported running short of fuel.*"

"Jesus, what a day," Sam said. "I feel like I accomplished something. I stole a bunch of drugs, kidnapped a couple guys, and hijacked a truck. And got on TV. Maybe we ought to make a career out of this, Kirstie."

She laughed, and then couldn't stop. Bent over, she gasped and howled. Sam started laughing too; even Einar chuckled.

They got back onto Sacramento and rolled north into thickening smoke. Einar slowed at Sacramento and University, and they looked west towards the Co-op. It was on fire. A few people moved back and forth before the flames, but they didn't seem to be guardsmen. Farther west, the fires had coalesced into an orange blur.

They turned at the south side of the BART station, and were stopped by a pair of Berkeley policemen, one white, one black.

"Where you people headed?" the black one asked.

"The school at Francisco and San Pablo," Kirstie answered. "We have a lot of people to feed."

The policemen, who looked exhausted, smiled faintly.

"Well, we ain't supposed to let anyone go west of here unless they're on official business. But I guess that means you—sure haven't seen many officials."

"Neither have we, except for the National Guard over on University."

The policemen shook their heads. "Those turkeys," the black one said. "I understand they actually opened fire on folks. Shit. The folks had more armament than the soldiers did."

"Dear God. When?"

"About an hour ago."

The TV van caught up with them. "They're with us," Kirstie said.

"Okay. Good luck."

"You too."

They drove slowly west, then jogged south to Francisco. Einar parked where the ambulance had been. The two black women who had been on stretcher duty that afternoon came out of the school building.

"My gosh, it's you!" one of them exclaimed. "Where you been so long, honey?"

"Out shopping."

"And look at what you got. Hate to think what the bill must have been. What's this TV truck?"

"They gave us a ride down into Oakland." Kirstie and the men got out. "They want to tape some interviews."

"Gonna talk to some angry people, then. There was a gunfight, a real battle, over at the Co-op."

"We heard."

"They brought back twenty-two bodies, and sixteen wounded."

The news crew began taping while people unloaded the

truck. Kirstie leaned against the door of the cab as people jostled around her: black faces, brown faces, white faces. Hands reached out for hers.

"Thank you, ma'am," someone said. "You done real good."

She smiled unsurely, pleased and embarrassed. She thought about the corpses in the silent streets of Oakland and Susan Smith dying long ago in the rain. She wished Don were with her. She wished they were in Vancouver. She wished she could stop shaking.

6

The little boat zigzagged through masses of shattered lumber until it was alongside *Ultramarine*. The four black men tied up the boat at the foot of the boarding ladder and trotted briskly up to the deck.

Bill Murphy met them with handshakes. They looked around the ship with interest.

"You came through the Golden Gate!" their leader exclaimed. He was a tall, young man wearing a rust-coloured leather jacket and a broad-brimmed black hat. His name was Mitchell Eldon. "Boy, that's dangerous. Any damage?"

"No." Bill looked proud of his answer.

"Well. Uh, we are here to see what you can supply, like in terms of food, clothes, blankets, medical stuff, like that."

Bill's smile faded. He looked impassively at Mitchell, then at Owen. "I'm not sure we've got anything. That's more the kind of stuff you get from the Red Cross or Civil Defence."

"Forget *them*. They give us nothing yet. Everything is

mightily fucked up over there. Nobody doin' nothing."

"Look, uh, Mitchell—I'm willing to help any way I can. But we need the supplies we carry. And I can't just, you know, hand 'em over to the first guy who asks."

"Captain Murphy." Mitchell's voice was gentle. His eyes were masked behind dark glasses. "You see those buildings up there on the hill? That's the housing project. We got no lights, no water, no food except for what's left in a couple little supermarkets. We can't get into the rest of the city 'cause of the fires and floods. We got two-three thousand folks up there with no homes now. Lots of 'em hurt. Lots of 'em slept out in the rain last night."

Mitchell's rifle, a .22, swung to point at Bill's chest. "I am not goin' back and tell Mrs. Debney I come back empty-handed."

Bill stared disgustedly at the muzzle of the rifle. "And I am not going to be dictated to on the deck of my own ship."

"Could I suggest something?" Don said. Mitchell and his friends glanced away from Bill, and the .22 wavered. "Let a couple of us go back with you to talk things over with Mrs. uh—"

"Mrs. Debney?"

"Mrs. Debney. Chances are we can help you better if we know exactly what you need, and you know what we can offer you."

"Sure, uh-huh. And while you're talking, your ship sails off somewheres."

"Where to?" Don asked, waving to the north and east. Mitchell smiled wryly and nodded.

"Okay." Everyone was relieved at the compromise. "You and the captain can come with us."

"No, me," said Owen. "I'm responsible for our supplies."

"Right, fine. Let's go."

Six men in the little boat nearly overloaded it. Mitchell

settled himself in the stern and whipped the outboard motor into life. The boat moved slowly west across India Basin.

The seiches had transformed it, churning up an archipelago of sandbars and wreckage where only mud flats had been a day ago. As they neared the shore, Don saw almost a dozen small craft—sailboats and motorboats—anchored in the shallows or moored to the irregular dike of rubble, three to five metres high, left by the seiches.

"They was floatin' all over," one of the young men said. "We went out and brought 'em in las' night and this mornin'."

"Weren't you worried about the seiches—the waves?" Owen asked. "It must have been pretty rugged, at least last night."

"Aw well, you know, it was kind of fun." The young man half smiled at the boats and looked up through his sunglasses at the overcast. "It really was fun. Makes a change, you know?"

Owen glanced surreptitiously at Don, who said nothing.

Now they could see that men and women were working all over the dike: chain saws whined and snarled, cutting paths through the debris, and work gangs passed salvaged lumber up the hill.

"No lack of firewood," Don said to Mitchell.

"No indeedy." He brought the boat in alongside an improvised dock, made of six logs lashed and stapled together. "C'mon, you guys are gonna burn bad, we don't get you indoors."

The six men walked rapidly up the path that had been cut through the dike from the dock to what was left of Innes Avenue. The dike had buried the east side of the street, and half filled the storefronts and empty lots on the west side. As they came through to the street, Owen stopped short and gripped Don's arm.

"My God, my God," he muttered. "It's all starting to

sink in on me."

The stink of smoke and rotten mud hung in the air. Fires smoldered in the dike. The anonymous housing projects up the hill looked intact, but Don and Owen could see a solid wall of smoke rising up in the Bayview district.

Along the half-buried street, young men and women stood guard outside the stores; they held rifles or pistols and looked self-conscious. Work parties were carrying goods out of the stores and up the hill: bedding, tools, bolts of fabric and food. No children were in sight. No policemen or firemen. No obvious officials. The people clearing the stores and working on the dike gave and took orders, laughed and complained, in an atmosphere of bustle and excitement.

"Why so many guns?" Owen asked. Mitchell shrugged.

"Just makin' sure everything goes where it's s'posed to. We got some mean mothers in the neighbourhood, you know?"

Don and Owen, with their escort behind them, started up a long flight of concrete stairs. It was slow going up the hill: dozens of people were moving up and down the stairs. All were black; some gave Don and Owen curious glances.

"Here come supper!" a teenager yelped as he passed them.

"Get away with you!" Mitchell laughed. Hilarity rippled up and down the stairs. Don grinned; Owen did not.

Tents and lean-tos crowded together on the playgrounds and dead lawns of the housing project, and plastic sheets and tarpaulins were strung everywhere. But not many people were in sight.

"Where is everybody?" Don asked Mitchell as they walked down a muddy lane between tents and camper trucks.

"Kids are in the gym at the school. Old folks are lookin'

after the babies. Sick and hurt folks, they're in the apartments. Everybody else is workin' indoors or down the hill."

"You people really landed on your feet," Owen said. Mitchell grinned, not very pleasantly.

"Well, you know, this new president, he talks about 'dynamic self-reliance.'" He mimicked an educated white accent: "'We don't want black people to grow up in a welfare-oriented culture, we want them to be proud and self-supporting.' What that means is, they got tired of paying to help folks. So we been lookin' after ourselves, just like the man says."

"What can you tell us about Mrs. Debney?" Don asked.

Mitchell chuckled. "You call her *ma'am*."

They reached the community centre, a low, rambling stucco building. Inside, the noise and smell were overpowering: bawling children, blaring cassette players, dozens of high-pitched conversations, the ammoniac stink of wet diapers. The rooms and offices were dim, lit only by daylight falling through the windows. Mattresses and sleeping bags carpeted the floors, and children bounced happily over sleeping babies.

Mitchell led them to a big kitchen at the rear of the building. More than a dozen women were working there. Kettles of soup simmered on two big gas ranges; the soup's aroma mingled with that of baking bread. Dirty dishes clattered in sinks, and everyone seemed to be working hard and having a good time.

A tall woman was kneading bread dough on a countertop. She might have been thirty, or fifty: robust, broadshouldered and handsome. Under her apron she wore jeans and a white jersey that set off the darkness of her skin.

"Mrs. Debney? These gentlemen, they're from the ship."

"How do you do?" Mrs. Debney kept kneading as Don

and Owen introduced themselves.

"We understand you need food and medical supplies," Owen said, raising his voice over the commotion.

"We're down to twenty pounds of flour, Mr. Ussery." Her voice was deep and powerful. "I sent some of my boys off to find more, but they haven't come back yet. Yes, and medical supplies. We got lots of people hurt, lots of burns, broken bones."

"What about the government—the Red Cross, the National Guard? Civil Defence? The Navy?" Owen gestured in the direction of the shipyards.

Mrs. Debney put the dough into a buttered steel bowl, and began mixing a fresh batch. "Nobody's helping. Navy moved their people out in helicopters yesterday. We haven't heard a peep from City Hall, or the state government, or anybody else."

"That's incredible," Owen muttered. "They must be stretched damn thin."

"I don't know and I don't care," said Mrs. Debney. "All I know is, I got over two thousand people lost their homes, and hundreds hurt, and more coming in every minute. The whole Bayview neighbourhood is burning down. I need help, Mr. Ussery."

"But—we've only got maybe twenty days' food for thirty-two people, and some medical supplies, just a little—"

"We'll take it all, and thank you. That's six hundred and forty servings, more if we stretch it. And the medical things—bandages, drugs, whatever you got. Anybody a doctor?"

"Yes, and four or five first-aid people. Uh, Mrs. Debney, look—we have to eat too. I don't know how long we'll have to stay aboard our ship."

"You're all welcome to come here. Take potluck, and give us a hand. Especially that doctor and those first-aid people."

"I can't order my people to do that," Owen said. "They want to get home and see their families."

"I understand. Just so long as we get some food and medical help, your people can come and go as they please."

Owen's mouth compressed into a tight line. Don said, "Excuse us, Mrs. Debney," and led him a few steps away.

"Let her have the food. They obviously need it. We'll use the Zodiacs to get our people ashore. Mrs. Debney's people can give us some local support in exchange."

Owen looked around the dim, noisy kitchen, and nodded reluctantly.

"Okay," he told Mrs. Debney. "We'll supply our food and medicine, and our doctor. In exchange we'd like some help with shelter for crew members who can't get home yet."

Mrs. Debney turned the bread dough out onto the counter and started kneading again. "All right. Thank you, Mr. Ussery. Mitchell, you see to it."

"Yes, ma'am. Get right on it."

She smiled. "Well, I won't keep you."

Mitchell, Owen and Don headed back to the stairs.

"I see why you call her ma'am," Don said.

"She's a pretty smart ole lady," Mitchell nodded. "It don't pay to mess with her."

Don rode in one of the Zodiacs north along the shattered waterfront. The wind was still blowing from the west, but blue sky showed through gaps in the clouds; the passengers squatted in the middle of the big inflatable boat, trying to shield themselves from the uv. A black from Hunter's Point sat easily in the stern, guiding the Zodiac with no more protection than a pair of sunglasses and a poncho.

"This is like old times," the man remarked to Don. "I used to run one of these when I was in the navy." He put out a calloused hand. "I'm Chief."

"Don Kennard. Good to meet you."

"Where you headed for?"

"Berkeley."

"Woo. Good luck. Think you can get across the Bay Bridge all right?"

"I hope so."

Don was looking east, trying to judge what the far end of the bridge was like, when a sudden concussion made him turn to the west.

They were less than a kilometre offshore, just east of Potrero Hill. The blocks of houses at the foot of the hill were in flames, and the freeway that sealed the hill off from the waterfront was blackened by smoke. Up on the hill, two clouds of debris were gently settling; as he watched, Don saw another cloud shoot up suddenly. Moments later, the crash of the explosion reached them.

"They're dynamiting the houses," Don said. "Just blowing 'em up, all along the line of that street."

"What for?" asked Chief. "Trying to stop the fires?"

"I think so. Just like the earthquake and fire in nineteen-oh-six. At least it shows that someone's trying to do something. The government hasn't just disappeared, the way it has in Hunter's Point."

"If that's their idea of doin' something," said Chief, "I'd just as soon they forget about us."

The smoke thickened as the Zodiac travelled north across the muddy bay where PIO had stood. Chief manoeuvred cautiously, almost daintily, through a maze of logs, boards, capsized boats, even furniture. The bodies in the water were past counting. Don saw the other passengers' face grow drawn and impassive and knew that his own must look the same. He coughed in the bitter smoke.

In most places it was hard to tell where the water left off and the land began: a seemingly solid mass of rubble would bob up and down as a wave passed through the water beneath it, and many buildings on the old waterfront survived as brick islets. Chief finally found a place where he could bring the Zodiac to shore at a gap in the irregular wall of wreckage. The western approaches to the Bay Bridge loomed through to the smoke nearby.

"Good luck to you all," he said as they scrambled ashore. Don shook his hand again.

"Thanks, Chief. Give my respects to Mrs. Debney."

The streets behind the waterfront had always been grimy and decayed; now they were deserted and flooded. The ten passengers from the Zodiac waded ankle-deep through black water. No one else could be seen, and it was very quiet.

After three or four blocks, they came to a freeway access ramp and walked up it. The freeway itself held a few abandoned cars and trucks—most already stripped— as well as hundreds of people on foot or bicycles, travelling in both directions.

"Never saw traffic move so fast," someone said, and everyone laughed nervously.

The others all had homes in San Francisco; they turned to the southwest. Don said good-by and turned northeast, towards the Bay Bridge. He walked quickly, head down, but already felt the tingle of sunburn on his face and hands.

By the time he reached the shelter of the bridge's lower deck, his feet hurt and he was feeling unexpected awe at the sheer size of the city's highway system. The bridge extended into a smoky distance; the grade was a steady, seemingly endless uphill climb.

It was easier for him, he saw, than for many others. Old people and children straggled among the deserted cars. Many people carried heavy bundles, or pushed wheelbarrows loaded with possessions.

A tall, stocky Chinese man in his twenties fell into step with Don. He looked at the PIO badge on Don's duffle bag.

"You a sailor?"

"Oceanographer." He put out a hand. "Don Kennard."

"Dennis Chang. Hi, good to meet you. I'm a biologist."

"Where you headed, Dennis?"

"Gotta check on my mom and dad. They live in Berkeley." He looked off to the north and northeast, where a long arm of the burning oil slick extended across the bay from Richmond almost to Tiburon. "Look at that sucker burn. Man, that's one of the worst parts of this whole mess—we're losing the energy we need to rebuild."

"They'll just tighten up the rationing," Don said with a shrug.

"Boy, I sure wish I could believe it'd be that easy. I work for an outfit called Neogene. Ever hear of it?"

"Sure. Down in Palo Alto." He paused. "Dennis Chang. You don't work for Neogene, you own it."

"It owns me. Anyway, last year we got a contract with the Energy Department to see if we could design a high-quantity methanogen out of $E.$ $coli.$ Put enough of 'em in a vat and they'll grow until their tiny little farts add up to lots and lots of natural gas."

"Did it work?"

"Not yet. Another eight, ten months maybe. The point is, the people in Washington were really hot to get it developed, because as far as they could tell we were going to be strapped for oil by this summer. Really strapped." He waved at the burning slick. "Now look what we have to contend with."

"Well, if the fuel shortage is going to be that bad, your outfit ought to have top priority."

"Sure, in theory. But it'll take weeks to reorganize. My people will be applying for disaster loans and pumping out their basements, instead of working in the lab. The government's going to be scrambling around with a million other things on its mind."

They plodded on over the bridge, trading disaster stories and gossiping about mutual acquaintances. Don was glad to have company; as he neared home he was beginning to be afraid of what he might find.

It was late in the afternoon when they reached the eastern shore of the bay. The bridge slanted gently down to where the toll plaza had been, between the mud flats and the Army Terminal; now the shoreline was a broad tangle of wreckage. The seiches had jumbled trees, logs, cars and shattered concrete blocks into a low barrier almost a kilometre wide, from the water to the far side of the freeway.

Many of the people who had walked across the bridge seemed to give up at the sight of the obstacle before them. Some turned back towards San Francisco; others erected crude shelters and even started campfires on the pavement. A few abandoned whatever they had been carrying and began to clamber through the wreckage zone. Don and Dennis watched them working their way through the zone and followed what looked like the easiest path.

Over an hour later, the two men reached what was left of the East Shore Freeway. Its eight lanes were choked with overturned cars, uprooted trees, mud, stones, and even houses wrenched from their foundations. Corpses lay half-buried in the mud, and rats skittered among them.

Speaking very little, they went on north to the University Avenue off-ramp. It was hard going for the first kilometre inland, over mud banks and across big, water-filled holes gouged in the pavement.

At the intersection of University and San Pablo stood two black policemen in orange ponchos. They motioned to Don and Dennis.

"Where you fellas headed?" the older policeman asked. They told him. "Better hustle. Curfew is at seven. Lasts until seven tomorrow morning."

"Curfew?" Dennis echoed. "Who ordered it? The governor?"

"The mayor. Haven't heard from the governor all day, far as I know."

"What if you stay out past seven?" asked Don.

"If you're lucky, you get thrown in the can and you stay there till we remember to get around to you. If you're not so lucky, you get shot."

The two men went on up University; at Sacramento, Dennis shook Don's hand and turned north. Alone, Don broke into a slow jog. He wanted to get home quickly.

The streets going up into the hills were deserted, though he saw many faces peering out into the twilight from darkened windows. Two blocks from home, he heard a gunshot and saw a tiny patch of sidewalk in front of him suddenly explode as the bullet ricocheted into the gloom.

Don sprang to his left, into the street, and ran for the cover of a parked car. Bent over, he scuttled on to the next car, and then dashed for the corner. The shot was not repeated.

He ran the last two blocks, and bounded up the steps from the sidewalk to the steep front yard of his house. The living-room curtains were drawn, but a sliver of light showed through. The door was locked; he fumbled for his keys and unlocked it, hoping the chain wasn't latched.

The door swung open. He heard a gasp, and saw Kirstie lying fully clothed on the couch; two candles burned on the coffee table in front of her.

"Don? Oh Christ, but you frightened me!"

"You scared me too." He shut and locked the door, and went to her. "Are you all right?"

"Yes, I'm fine. I must have fallen asleep the moment I got home."

They talked while they improvised a dinner of sausage and stale bagels. She was horrified when he told her about the turbidity current; he shook his head and groaned when she described the fight in the drug room.

For a long time they sat in the kitchen, with a single candle, drinking room-temperature beer and talking quietly. Then they went upstairs and looked out the bedroom window.

"What do we do now?" he wondered.

She turned and looked at him, surprised. "Are you asking me? After all these years of telling me?"

"Kirstie—I'm damned if I know what to do next. After all we've gone through in the last six months with uv and flares, and then this. Did you know the cops are shooting people for breaking curfew? And I didn't even get around to telling you—someone shot at me just down the street as I was coming home."

"The silly bastard shot at me too."

"Oh, for God's sake! You should have told me."

"So should you." She gave him a gentle hug. "I think I like you when you're a little less confident than usual. Makes you almost human."

"Belt up. The point is that it's getting too dangerous here. I think we ought to go back to Vancouver."

"What? After swearing you'd never darken your grandfather's door again? And all the moaning about how there's not enough work for us there?"

"At least you don't get shot at. Well, what do you think?"

"We can't, not yet. I've got Sam's case to see through, and we can't just walk away from all those thousands of casualties and homeless people. I'd feel terrible if we did. Let's tough it out a little longer. All right?"

Reluctantly, he nodded. They went to bed and fell asleep in each other's arms.

Two hours later, light glared in their eyes. Don sat up and saw Kirstie squinting and blinking. Her face and throat were sunburned.

"What—?"

"Power just came back on," he said. "I'll go turn things off."

The refrigerator hummed reassuringly. Don shuffled about, turning out lights and checking the locks. A drunken voice down the street called out: "Happy New Year!" Five or six shots rattled suddenly, and a dog barked frantically.

When he returned upstairs, the bedroom was dark again.

"I turned out the light when they started shooting," Kirstie whispered. "Christ almighty, we can't let all this stuff just go on."

"No." Standing back from the window, he looked out at the bay again. San Francisco was still dark; street lights burned blue or orange all over Berkeley, and many windows glowed yellow. The air was sour with smoke, and the sky still pulsed orange from the fires.

The street lights brightened suddenly, then dimmed and went out.

7

"Bob Tony, it's the end of the world." Ted Loeffler stared past the clicking windshield wipers at the crowded freeway.

"Yeah. Ain't it a bitch?" Allison slumped a little lower in the seat of Ted's station wagon. Rain drummed on the roof and pooled on the pavement. The Hollywood hills were grey-brown blurs on either side as the car crawled through Cahuenga Pass from the San Fernando Valley.

"You see Long Beach when you were coming in?"

"No, but I sure as hell saw Malibu." Mile after mile of mud and wreckage and an occasional house somehow spared by an accident of topography, and above the wave line the rusty beige of the dead chaparral on the mountainsides.

"Half the industry, Bob Tony. Half the fucking movie industry, wiped out in two minutes. Christ, you're practically the oldest filmmaker left in California."

"How's Suzi?" Allison asked. "And Ken?"

"Okay. Scared shitless, but okay. The flooding, the slides, you should see it on TV. Suzi nearly went out of her tree when you called, she was sure I'd get washed away before I ever got near the airport. Ken was pissed off 'cause I made him stay home. He wanted to see the sights." Ken was the Loefflers' thirteen-year-old; Allison was fond of the boy, who reminded him of himself.

"Is that what all these people are doing—sightseeing?" Allison wondered.

Ted laughed, showing big yellow teeth. "Looking for an open gas station so they can gas up and go looking for a quart of milk. Absolute chaos. Thank God they got the power right back on. We got three freezers full of stuff, another day and it would've been garbage."

"Listen, Ted. We have to suspend *The Longrangers*. For the duration."

"This is not a shock." They were passing the Hollywood Bowl, and it was raining harder than ever.

"No. And it's going to be a long duration. Maybe years."

Ted's long, homely face twisted. "Looks that way, kemo sabe."

"You know, Ted, this is no standard California disaster. This is it, the big one. By the time the government gets a grip on things again, a lot of people will be dead. Any looting here?"

"Sure. Watts, Compton, all the black areas."

"What happens when they get hungry again? And other people get hungry? Blacks aren't the only people with a little enterprise. And no food in a city of eight million people?"

"I've got a gun."

"Every son-of-a-bitch in L.A. has a gun except me, and I'm working on it."

"Okay, okay. You got a plan, so tell."

"I think we can hole up at the ranch and ride this out. We've got some resources now, and I'll be getting more. The neighbours are scattered and pretty self-sufficient, too, and shouldn't be a problem. Monterey and Carmel are wrecked all to shit, but the army's already patrolling. Remember Ernie Miles from Fort Polk? He's the co at Fort Ord now, and he really moved fast yesterday. Declared martial law from Monterey to Salinas, got his troops out there, and kept things calm. He's a good guy to know. He had his MPs on duty at the airport, and they didn't want to let me charter the plane. But I got him on the phone and he personally authorized the flight."

"I love him, I love him. Well, look, let me talk to Suzi, okay? It sounds like a basically good idea. Not as good as making sixty million dollars, but good."

Allison turned on the car radio. It already felt like luxury to hear a news broadcast; all of central and northern California had been blacked out since the waves, but Los Angeles still had power. For now.

The waves were already old news; now the stories were about floods in the hills, fires in Long Beach and Watts, the countless injured people overcrowding the hospitals. Most of the news from the east was about governmental determination to cope with the disaster. Tsunamis had also hit several places along the east coast: a hundred people were reported missing on the south shore of Long Island, parts of New York City had been flooded, and Boston's waterfront was wrecked.

Allison felt a sombre satisfaction at the economic news. Several major banks had suspended operation for at least a week. Gold and silver prices were shooting up, with gold at close to a thousand dollars an ounce—up three hundred dollars in a day. With almost a thousand ounces of gold carefully hidden in his house, Allison had become suddenly richer. The New York stock market hadn't opened today; a full-scale panic had erupted in the stock markets of Tokyo, Hong Kong and London.

Ted turned south on La Cienaga. Most of the art galleries and boutiques were closed, early victims of the depression, but the street still had some class. In the seven-hundred block stood a four-story block of marble and black glass; Ted pressed a button on the dash, activating an automatic gate, and drove into the building's underground garage.

"We're in luck," he muttered. "Last time the gate wouldn't open. The flares burned it out." He parked in his usual slot, next to the company sedan, a new Nissan. Not many other cars were there; fluorescent lights flickered on bare, oil-stained concrete.

"Thanks, Ted. You go on home, look after Suzi. I'm going to make some phone calls. Then I'll take the Nissan home."

"What about dinner? You want to come over for dinner?"

"No, no—Suzi's got enough trouble without me. I'll eat at home. But I'd like you both, and Ken—all of you—to come over tomorrow morning. Ten o'clock. Okay?"

"Sure, Bob Tony."

Allison gripped Ted's hand. "Thanks. See you then."

The Pontiac growled back through the electronic gate while Allison took the elevator to the third floor.

He took pride in running a multimillion-dollar production company from a six-room office suite. The decor was lived-in elegant, with some lovely Ben Shahn originals hanging above battered Edwardian armchairs. Allison let himself in and walked to his office without bothering to turn on the lights. The office was eclectically furnished: an antique roll-top desk, three wingback chairs, a whole wall of VTR equipment including a large TV projection screen, and a word processor. Rain slithered down the big windows overlooking the street.

The submarine gloom appealed to him. He sat at the roll-top and scrawled a few notes to himself; then he picked up the phone. First the logistics call: for transport, fuel, food and weapons. His contact was hard to reach, and harder to bargain with. When negotiations ended,

Allison had promised a half-million dollars in gold for two hundred thousand dollars' worth of supplies and equipment. For the first time, he felt grateful for gas rationing; without it, black marketeers like his contact would still be dealing in nonessentials like cocaine.

Next he reviewed the mental list he'd made the day before, on the drive back from Carmel to the ranch. The Loefflers were at the top of it, thanks to Ted's organizational ability; Allison expected them to agree. Two more couples remained to be contacted. From what he'd seen so far of conditions in L.A., they were likely to accept his offer as well. He began to punch the number of the first couple.

An hour later, as the rain began to slacken, Allison made one final call. A child's voice answered:

"Hello, this is Sarah Allison speaking."

"Hi, love. It's Dad. How are you?"

"Daddy! Hi, Daddy! Mommy, it's Daddy. We didn't have any lights yesterday," she told him proudly. "So we had cold hot dogs for dinner."

"Sounds yummy. Listen, love, can I talk to your mom for a second?"

"Okay. Here's Mommy."

Astrid sounded cool but tense. "Where are you?"

"Up at the ranch. I've been trying to get through to you guys since yesterday. How are things?"

"As well as we might expect. The power just came on a few hours ago. It's been freezing cold."

"Same with us."

"It must be tough to live in a palace with no lights."

He would not let himself be baited. "Have you got enough food? Enough money?"

"We have a freezer half full of soggy meat. If the power stays on long enough for me to cook it, we'll be all right. I don't know about money. Most of the markets in Santa Monica are locked up tight. The open ones are charging three times what they were last week. And the Honda needs a brake job, so I can't even get out of here except on foot."

"Jesus. Okay, listen. I'll call Ted Loeffler and ask him to get out to you with some money and the office car, the Nissan. You're welcome to it for as long as you need it."

"Why, thank you, kind sir. Sarah, be still, you can talk to him in a minute, okay?"

"Anything else? Sarah need anything?"

"She's fine. Mostly we've been playing Fish and Crazy Eights. And eating cold hot dogs."

"Listen, Astrid, this line is getting worse. Can you still hear me?"

"Perfectly."

"What? I can hardly hear you. Look, I'll get in touch with Ted. You guys take it easy, and I'll try to call again tomorrow. Give Sarah a kiss for me and tell her I'll have a long talk with her next time."

"And give Shauna Dawn a kiss for me," Astrid said. She hung up abruptly. More slowly, Allison did also.

By a quarter to eleven the next morning, all of Allison's guests were sitting together in a corner of the big living room of his house on Encantada Drive. Rain pattered steadily on the long-unused sun deck outside; across the room, logs burned in the fireplace. The air was pleasant with the smell of coffee.

The conversation, as people had arrived, had centred on everyone's difficulties since the waves: power outages, shortages of food and gas, looting in local stores, businesses collapsing. Allison let them talk for some time, pleased but not surprised that each family's problems had alarmed them without panicking them.

"Well," he said at last, "it sounds as if we all agree that L.A. is a bad place to live just now."

"What do you mean, 'just now'?" grinned Dave Marston. He was a solidly muscled man in his late thirties, a professional stunt man who had worked on two of Allison's films.

"Your point is well taken," Allison smiled through the laughter. "But I think it's gotten a little past the stage of putting up with smog and no garbage pickups. In catastrophe theory, we're at what's called a cusp, the point where everything breaks down."

Bert D'Annunzio shook his head. He was a small, dark man, an ex-marine who was now doing well as a technical adviser on war films like *Gunship*. "This isn't theory, Bob—this is reality."

"You're right as usual, Bert. So for us the question is, how do we tough out the next few weeks or months? Los Angeles is a dangerous place now. We're going to see riots, serious food shortages, maybe epidemics, and probably a complete economic breakdown."

"That's already happened," said Bert. "The New York Stock Exchange is closed for the rest of the week, at least. My broker says if it ever does open again, everything's going to crash. He told me to forget about anything we own except gold and silver and food." He hugged his wife Aline. "I sure hope you love me for my good looks, honey, 'cause there ain't anything else left to love." Aline, a quiet, pretty blonde, smiled at him—a little nervously, Allison thought.

"So you're suggesting we all move up to your ranch in Escondido Canyon," Ted Loeffler said. Good, thought Allison; Ted always keeps us moving along.

"Right. Ted and Suzi have been there before, and Bert and Aline." He focussed on Dave and Diana Marston. "It's hundreds of acres of rolling hills, stuck up a canyon out of sight. It's got a compound of buildings, a good water supply and limited access. It's right near Fort Ord, and I'm a friend of the commanding officer there—Ernie Miles. So it's well protected, about as secure as any place in the country. And it's got a smart, loyal staff, a Chicano couple.

"What it doesn't have," Allison went on, "is enough people to keep it going on a self-sufficient basis. That's why I thought of you people. Ted's a super organizer, a guy who gets things done. Suzi has crafts ability, pottery, leatherwork. Dave's a jack-of-all-trades and a good shot, but I'm really after Diana." More laughter: Diana Marston was a local celebrity thanks to her gourmet cooking show on the Los Angeles PBS station. She smiled and blushed.

"Bert's a weapons expert and a hell of an outdoorsman. Aline is another good organizer, a born quartermaster."

"You keep talking about weapons and military stuff," Suzi Loeffler said. "Do you think we'll all have to, have to fight people?"

"I hope to God not," Allison smiled. "But if we get in a bind, it might help to know something about fighting."

"If we accept," asked Suzi Loeffler, "can we bring other people too? Relatives, you know, or friends?"

"Immediate family only. Your kids, but that's it." Allison shrugged. If we get into nephews and nieces and cousins and neighbours—"

"I understand," Suzi nodded. "Just getting it straight."

"Okay," said Bert. "And when do we go?"

"Tonight, about seven o'clock."

It had the effect he'd expected: hands to faces, widened eyes, a long moment of silence.

"All right," Dave said. "Makes sense. What do we bring?"

The planning went on for hours. At two in the afternoon, the phone rang. Alison answered it, then took Bert aside for a moment.

"Have you got a gun with you?"

"In the car."

"Some people are coming over in about an hour with a lot of stuff I've ordered. They're getting paid in gold. I just want to make sure no one gets ripped off, least of all us."

Promptly at three, a new Range Rover and Dodge van pulled into the driveway, while a Volvo diesel sedan parked across the street. The drivers of the Range Rover and the van got out and stood in the shelter of the garage, where Allison was waiting for them. They were young, tough-looking men in rain parkas, jeans and hiking boots. One of them handed Allison a neatly typed invoice. Allison scanned it briefly, then went out in the rain to check the trucks' contents against the list. Canned and dehydrated food, drugs and medical supplies, tools, jerrycans of gasoline.

"Okay," Allison said. "I'll be right back."

When he returned from the house, he was holding a leather shoulder bag. It thumped when he put it on the trunk lid of his Nissan. Opening it, Allison began counting out Krugerrands. At a thousand dollars an ounce, half a million dollars in gold weighed just under thirty-two pounds.

"Aw*right*," smiled the invoice man. "All present and accounted for."

"Now," said Allison, "I'm going to carry it to the Volvo. You two stay about fifteen feet behind me. Once I hand it over, you get in and leave at once. No funny stuff."

"Hey, don't you trust us?"

"I trust you a lot. I just believe in consumer protection. So a friend of mine will be watching you, and he's very well armed."

The two men glanced at each other. "Okay, it's cool," said the invoice man. "We got some backup too, you know? Nobody gets burned."

"Great." Allison picked up the bag. Hatless, but wearing sunglasses, he strode out into the rain, across the driveway, and into the street. Both windows on his side of the Volvo rolled down. A man in the rear seat took the bag. The driver grinned and waggled a .38 revolver in his lap, where Allison could see it.

"A pleasure doing business with you," Allison said to the man in back.

"Likewise," said the man. "Nowadays you can't be too careful."

The invoice man and his companion got into the Volvo; the driver backed downhill into the next driveway, then accelerated towards Sunset Boulevard.

Bert, holding a revolver, stood up behind a laurel hedge.

"Nicely done," he said. "That took balls. Everything okay?"

"Sure. A little tense there for a minute, but I knew you were watching. Thanks."

Bert cleared his throat. "Uh, Bob—did you really pay those suckers half a million in gold?"

"That's right. And if they can figure out a way to eat it, or shoot it, or live in it, they're smarter than I am."

"Jeepers. Seems awful steep to me."

"Listen," said Allison. "From now on, wealth is goods only. No abstractions, no gold, no paper, no jewels—just food and fuel and shelter and weapons. I just ripped those guys off something cruel."

Late in the afternoon, Ted Loeffler drove the Nissan to Santa Monica, with Allison following in the new Range Rover. Ted had phoned Astrid to say he'd leave the Nissan outside her building, with the keys and a thousand dollars under the driver's seat. He couldn't stay to visit; the neighbour who was following to pick him up was in a hurry. She'd understood and thanked him.

It was almost dusk when they turned off Santa Monica Boulevard onto Yale Street. Astrid's was a fairly new five-story building; her apartment was on the second floor. Lights burned in the windows, but they had an almost orange glow: voltage had just been stepped down into a brownout.

Ted parked across from the building, and honked twice. Getting out, he waved to Astrid, a dark outline, and climbed into the waiting Range Rover.

"I sure hope this is the right thing, Bob Tony."

Allison drove down to the corner, turned left, and left again into an alley. "I know it looks shitty, but the kid's safety comes first."

"Sure."

"Ted, after this I owe you a big one."

Ted didn't answer. Allison parked at the rear of the building, got out, and went through the rear entrance into the recreation room.

A door led to the lobby. Allison peeped through, heard footsteps on the stairs, and then saw Astrid hurry across the lobby in a glossy yellow raincoat. The coat made it easy to see her cross the street and slip into the Nissan.

Allison walked casually into the lobby. Once out of sight of the street, he raced up to the second floor and rapped on Astrid's door.

"Mommy?"

"No, Sarah, it's Dad. Open up, I've got a surprise for you." Astrid would be searching in vain for the keys to the Nissan; he would not have much time before she gave up and returned.

The door opened. God, Sarah was beautiful. "Daddy!"

He picked her up, dizzy with the joy of holding her, smelling her, feeling her wiry little arms around his neck.

"Where's my surprise?"

"Downstairs. Come on, we have to hurry." He held her on his hip, just like the old days, as he took the stairs two at a time. She giggled excitedly at the jouncing until he shushed her. A quick turn from the lobby into the rec room, not even a glance from under his wide-brimmed Stetson to see if Astrid was still across the street. Christ, what an adrenalin rush. Fun.

Then they were in the alley, in the truck. Ted was behind the wheel; the Range Rover lurched forward.

"Where we going?" Sarah asked.

"On a surprise trip up to the ranch. We're going right away, and we'll be there in the morning when you wake up."

"What about Mommy?"

"You know she doesn't come to the ranch, silly."

In the dashboard lights, Ted's face looked taut and grim. "Bob Tony, you really do owe me a big one."

Allison reached over and patted Ted's arm. For an instant, as he chattered with Sarah, he imagined what Astrid must be going through: coming back to find the door open, the apartment empty; asking neighbours if Sarah was with them, calling police who wouldn't come, calling anyone she could think of and getting no useful answer.

Well, very heavy, sure, but so what? Astrid was part of the past, the dead past. They were driving through the rainy night into a strange and terrible future where private sorrows dwindled into less than the chirping of crickets. He cuddled his daughter. He would get her through that future at any cost, protect her from any danger.

The convoy was moving north on the San Diego Freeway by a little after seven: Allison in the Range Rover, with Sarah asleep on the back seat; the Dodge van with the Loefflers; the D'Annunzios in their Vanagon; Dave and Diana Marston in their GMC Jemmy. All had CB radios, which were almost useless: endless jabber filled every channel, barely audible under waves of static.

It was still raining when they crossed the Santa Monica Mountains into the San Fernando Valley; the northbound lanes were crowded, and traffic was slow. The Valley looked utterly ordinary, except for the orangey dimness of the street lights. Traffic rumbled along, stores were open, police cars cruised silently. Allison looked out at the countless bungalows and garden apartments, the taco stands and Polynesian restaurants and shopping centres, and said good-by to it all. For a few more days or weeks, places like this would sustain the pattern of normality. Then they would go under. Towns and cities to the east would fail soon as well, overwhelmed by refugees and the collapsing economy. Food would be scarce in a month, maybe less; he'd read not long ago that the uv damage to crops had left North America with only a twenty-six-day supply of grain.

Allison felt the drag of the .45 automatic holstered at his waist. It was one of Bert's; Allison had accepted it more out of the logic of their circumstances than out of felt need. It was somehow comforting to be armed, even if he hadn't yet fired his gun even in practice.

The convoy turned west onto the Ventura Freeway; driving was suddenly easier, with almost no other traffic to contend with. Wondering whether the road might even have been blockaded, Allison turned on the cb. Static and fragments of chatter crackled from the loud-speaker: then an urgent command.

"—get everybody right outa there, right now. The police are up there now, tryna get 'em moving. They figure it'll go right across Ventura and up Balboa Boulevard. You know how many houses there are in that area? You know how many people? You get your people out. . . . Any minute, any minute. It's comin' over the top of the dam already."

Allison got on his cb. "This is Escondido One. Anyone pick up something about a flood on Ventura Boulevard?"

"Escondido Three." That was Bert. "Uh, yeah, it's the Encino Reservoir."

"Well, we're nearly at Balboa Boulevard. We should be able to get past in time. It's not going to reach the level of the freeway, anyhow."

"Uh, no," said Bert, "but we could get in a real jam if people *use the freeway as high ground."*

"This is true. Okay, well, as they used to say, let's go for it."

The lights along the freeway went out, and most of the lights on the streets below. Driving in the far right-hand lane, Allison looked down and saw chains of red taillights moving north. The truck shuddered, as if it had gone over a bump, and seconds later Allison saw the taillights in one street begin to wink out, from south to north. Down there in the darkness, a flood was rolling past. A grinding rumble overwhelmed the noise of the engine.

"Daddy, what is it?"

"Hush, love, it's just raining really hard."

"I can't hear you!"

"It's raining, it's raining!" Allison shouted. "Now hush and let me drive!"

The headlights could scarcely penetrate the rain. Allison slowed down when he saw a cluster of taillights up ahead. They weren't moving; in a few moments the convoy was on the eastern edge of a small traffic jam.

A sports car and a pickup had collided, blocking three lanes. The unconscious driver of the sports car was trapped inside, his head on the steering wheel. No one was trying to help. The pickup seemed to have been abandoned. A Trans Am and a Toyota tried to squeeze into the one clear lane, and sideswiped each other. The driver of the Trans Am got out with a gun in his hand, rested his arms on the roof of his car, and began firing at the other one. The shots did not sound very loud. Allison, behind several other cars but able to look over them, saw the Toyota glance into the guardrail and stop, plugging the one remaining lane. When the shooting stopped, he could hear screaming.

Bert was suddenly there, beside Allison's door. "Gotta move that car, Bob."

"Right. Sarah, love, you stay put, understand? We have

to go give those people a push."

"Was that man shooting? It sounded like shooting. Are they making a TV show?"

"Just stay right there till I get back."

Bert and Allison jogged up between the stalled cars; none of the other drivers seemed willing to deal with the Trans Am and his gun.

The gunman was just getting back into his car. The screaming was coming from the Toyota. Bert walked up to the gunman's window.

"We're gonna push that car out of the way so you can get through. Want to give us a hand?"

"Fuck no. Not gonna give that son-of-a-bitch any more fuckin' help, man." He was a pale young man of twenty or so. No one else was in the car.

The driver of the Toyota was dead. Most of his head was covered with blood and splinters of glass. A woman on the seat beside him was howling, her face in her hands, and two small boys wailed in the back seat.

"Jesus, Jesus Christ," Allison muttered. He opened the driver's door, and saw the car was stalled in first gear. He put one foot awkwardly on the clutch pedal and reached across the corpse to shift into neutral. The dead man smelled of aftershave.

"What are you doing? What are you doing?" the woman screamed.

"Helping," Allison answered. The rain was cold on his neck, and trickled through his beard. With Bert pushing from behind, he managed to steer the Toyota a few yards past the bottleneck. The woman and her children kept screaming.

"Don't leave us! Mister, please, don't leave us. My God, he's hurt, he needs help. Please, get the doctor, the police."

"The police will be along any minute. It'll be okay," Allison said. Before her hysterical pleading could soften him, he turned away and followed Bert. The Trans Am was idling in the gap, waiting for them to get out of the way. Bert, in the lead, paused and rapped on the driver's window. The young man rolled it down.

"Yeah?"

Something flashed orange in Bert's hand; the boom of the shot was sudden. Allison saw the window on the right-hand side of the Trans Am blow out, a burst of glitter in the headlights.

Bert turned to Allison, holstering his pistol under his poncho. "Let's get this asshole out of the way."

"Christ, Christ, Bert. You just blew him away."

"What's the matter, think he didn't deserve it? Come on, push this thing."

"You're making me accessory to murder, Bert," Allison said, but he pushed.

"Weren't you ready to shoot those schmucks in the Volvo this afternoon if tried to rip us off? This jerk had it coming."

Bert opened the Trans Am's door and twisted the steering wheel to the left, guiding the car past the Toyota and onto the side of the road. Almost at once, cars began to stream through, honking; people leaned out, grinning at the men and shouting "Right on!" "Thank you!" Not far to the east, the growl and rumble of the flood was softening.

A few minutes later Allison was back in the Range Rover, driving west through heavy rain. Sarah had finally fallen asleep, despite the buzz and sputter of the CB.

He thought for a long time about what had happened. Bert, he decided, had been a very smart choice. He himself had been slow, and shocked by the second shooting, but he had swallowed his objections and co-operated. For all his talk about economic and social collapse, he was just not yet fully emotionally aware that the old rules, the old laws, were as dead as the two drivers back there.

Allison promised himself that the next time, whenever it came, would find him ready. He only hoped Sarah wouldn't have to see it.

8

It was extraordinary, Kirstie thought, how quickly one adjusted to arbitrary new routines. Electricity was now on, at best, two hours a day, usually in the early morning. That meant they had pumped water, so the toilet could be flushed and the bathtub and sinks filled. Whatever needed cooking was cooked then and either eaten cold or rewarmed in the fireplace—a smoky, clumsy business she preferred to avoid. Don had managed to find two battery rechargers; they were plugged in the moment the power came on, to ensure that the radio and flashlights stayed functional.

Amid the early-morning bustle, they heated water on the stove, took hasty sponge baths, and washed the last day's accumulation of dishes and pots in the same water. Sometimes they washed a few clothes, using cold water and a sliver of hand soap; in this cold, damp spring, in an unheated house, things took forever to dry. Kirstie sometimes found herself wishing they could move down the hill, where water was available almost all day long by gravity feed. But the municipal authorities were adamant: hill people were to stay on the hills or move out of the city. Since transportation was almost nonexistent, that meant the city's former elite were now tied to their property like serfs.

Food was the major problem, the continuing outrage. The government had patched together a rickety distribution system for the Bay Area, but had little to distribute through it: rice, beans, some canned goods. Meanwhile a flourishing black market had sprung up to supply meat, milk, fruit and fresh vegetables—all of poor quality and available only for gold, silver, or usable goods like tools and gasoline. The Kennards were perpetually hungry; they had little to trade, and their savings were worthless.

Money had disappeared from the economy within three or four days. First the banks had closed and were not expected to reopen soon. For a week, companies had gone bankrupt; after that, their owners and officers didn't bother and just walked away. If millions of people had lost billions of dollars through damage to their homes and businesses, they had saved billions simply by not paying their creditors. The economy, built on two generations of consumer debt, had not so much crashed as evaporated.

Many government agencies were nominally open, but their employees did not turn up to work. A few, mostly in agriculture and transport, paid their employees in agency scrip which could be exchanged for some resource the agency possessed. So a day of work might earn a gallon of gasoline, which one could then trade on the black market for a case of canned tuna—perhaps, if one felt like speculating, for a couple of cartons of cigarettes.

The University of California was one of those agencies, sustaining its employees out of a dwindling stock of gasoline, tools, lumber and services. Kirstie had been promised some support until the end of her appointment in June, but did not expect it to last that long; she had, in any case, no students.

With Pacific Institute of Oceanography gone, Don now spent part of his days working for Berkeley relief organizations, and had already left for half a day's work on a salvage crew. It was an early March morning, unusually clear and sunny. Kirstie wished she could stay inside and enjoy it; instead she put sunblock on her face and hands, tied a big straw coolie hat to her head, and left the house. The next-door neighbour waved from her living-room window, and Kirstie waved back.

That was something: the neighbours looked after one another now, protected one another. In the past month, the Kennards had gotten to know almost everyone for blocks around. First it had been simple self-defence: disarming the half-crazy teenager in the Tudor house who had been shooting at everyone. Then it had been a rapid growth of what Don called "housewives' communism," as people pooled their resources and lent one another a hand. Lately it had formalized into block committees and local councils—locals for short. They were made up of people in neighbourhoods who looked after each other and negotiated for help with other locals or the remaining government agencies.

Kirstie walked quickly down the hill to Telegraph and then on to the campus. In the Physics Building, four or five families were tidying up the first-floor lounge where they had lived since the waves. They recognized her, and waved as she passed; she waved back, and ran up to Sam Steinberg's office on the third floor.

He was already there, hunched up in a shabby old windbreaker with his feet on his desk. Einar, in a red-and-white striped soccer shirt, was scribbling on the chalkboard. It was cold in the office, and the only light came from the west-facing window.

"We've been waiting for you," said Sam. He held up an opened envelope. Kirstie took it as she sat down and read the letter it held.

"That's absurd," she said. "Why should they postpone your renewal appeal indefinitely?"

"My sources tell me the university is about to close down. Indefinitely. Why fire me when we'll all be on the street in a few days?"

"Close down Berkeley?" Kirstie shook her head slowly. "Just lock up one of the best universities in the world and walk away? I don't believe it. Who told you?"

"Doesn't matter. It's true, though. Thanks anyway for all the help you've been. I'm grateful for it."

"If they close down, what are we going to do?" Kirstie murmured. "We're barely scraping along as it is."

"Go to work for the Berkeley local."

"Oh sure, but how much longer will they last? Don brings home some pretty grim rumours."

"All of them true." Sam rubbed his hands together, trying to warm them. "But starving slowly beats starving fast." He glanced at Einar's chalkboard equations and seemed to lose interest in the university and the local. "Oho. Very pretty ... very nice. Tidy rather than elegant—and equation six leads to—"

"A drop in energy output of about one per cent, for five thousand to fifty thousand years before reignition. But the flare activity should last only one or two hundred more years before it becomes normal again."

"What is this you're talking about?" Kirstie asked.

Einar smiled at her, his breath frosty in the cold room.

"My solar model. What it shows is that the sun has gone out. Turned itself off."

"Ah. And what's that shining outside then?"

"The sun. It's just starting to cool."

"It looks from Einar's model as if nuclear fusion isn't a constant process in the sun," Sam explained. "It runs for a while and then switches itself off. When that happens the sun begins to cool off and shrink, pulled in by its own gravity. Eventually the shrinkage gets fusion going again.

So the sun puffs up and down."

"And how long did you say we have until it puffs up again?" she asked Einar.

"Five thousand to fifty thousand years. Then fusion for at least fifty thousand years, maybe much more. And so it goes."

"Don't look so surprised, Kirstie," said Sam. "It's not exactly a bolt out of the blue. We've suspected something like this for years, ever since they tried catching solar neutrinos and there weren't any. Einar figures the sun's been turned off for several thousand years, and the effect has finally started working its way to the surface."

"Are you saying that it might get really cold for a long, long time?"

"Yes," said Einar. "Do you know the old Norse mythology? At the end of the world, the World Serpent under the sea comes up again and makes huge waves. Fenrir the wolf runs free, killing people. Then come three years without a summer, the Fimbulwinter, and then the ice giants come to fight the Aesir at Ragnarok. The giants win."

The three of them walked down to the civic centre, staying out of the sunshine and happily talking shop. Kirstie told them about the new climatic regime that seemed to have settled over the northern hemisphere.

"I've done some rough calculations on the amount of snowfall this past winter. It's rough because I don't have anything like complete data, especially for this last month, but it doesn't look as if the snow could *begin* to melt over the summer. Next winter we'll see more snow on top of it, and still less melting the following summer. Between what Don's told me about that Antarctic surge, Einar's solar model and my snowfall calculations, I'd say we were well into a new ice age."

Einar grunted. "Maybe Iceland will be a good place to

be, then. We are used to it. And we have plenty of volcanic energy."

"Any kind of energy would help just about now," Sam grunted. "I am getting damn tired of freezing indoors and walking outdoors."

Two portable generators, guarded by policemen with shotguns, hammered away behind City Hall. Inside, the offices looked almost normal: typewriters clattered and fluorescent lights glowed. But the people looked tired and dirty. Most of the men wore new beards; most of the women had cut their hair short to make it easier to care for. The place smelled like a locker room.

The receptionist was a big, burly man with a nightstick on his desk. He nodded as they approached him.

"Hi, Sam. Einar. Got a meeting?"

"Nope," said Sam. "We're looking for full-time jobs."

"Full-time! What a compliment to our working conditions and wages and fringe benefits. Go see Bernie. I hear he's looking for people." He pointed with the nightstick to the far corner of the crowded office behind him.

Bernie turned out to be the young medical student who had been working in the school on Francisco Street after the waves. He looked thinner and older; his desk was piled high with paper.

"Sure, I remember you," he said to Kirstie. "And you guys. I've seen you around since then. And now you need a full-time job, okay. Got any medical training?"

"No. I'm a climatologist. Not very useful, I'm afraid."

"Any experience with guns?"

"Not really."

"Okay, so we can't use you as a medical aide or as a guard. Believe me, we need both. How about scrounging?"

Kirstie felt awkward and ignorant. "I'm sorry?"

"Scrounging. There's a lot of stuff still lying around, okay? You go into stores, warehouses, abandoned houses, wherever, and bring back anything that might be useful. If we don't get it, the black-market guys will. They're starting to give us some real problems, almost as bad as the feds."

"That sounds a bit like what my husband's been doing, down in the wreckage zone, only they call it salvaging."

"That's different. In the zone, the stuff has been completely abandoned and usually has to be dug out of the mud and crud. Scroungers stay out of the zone. You usually have a team of three, four, five people, and a push-cart, okay, only really it's modified U-Haul trailer. We got a bunch of 'em.

"And what does it pay?"

"The team splits twenty-five per cent of the haul, okay? If it's not practical to take home, like a gross of plastic plates and a barometer, we pay in beans and rice, maybe a little flour, but we bargain hard."

"Well." She looked at Sam and Einar. "Would you lads like to become fellow scroungers?"

"Sounds all right," said Sam. Einar nodded.

"Good," said Bernie. "Now I can tell you that you have to be really careful. The feds say it's looting and sometimes they shoot scroungers. Some of the black-market guys don't like it either." He scrawled something on the back of an old memorandum. "Show this to the people in the basement, and they'll issue you each a gun. You can start work this afternoon."

"I can see why they think we need guns," Kirstie said to Don that night. "Some people didn't like us at all." She turned over in bed, groaning; her muscles were sore, and the crude harness, in which she and the men had pulled the trailer, had rubbed her shoulders raw. "Not that we got anything worth fighting for."

Their total haul, for over four hours' work, had been three bales of peat moss and a case of motor oil from the shed behind an abandoned house in north Berkeley. Scrounge pay had been a pound of rice for each of them.

"You're right." Don lay beside her in the darkness. "More and more people picking over less and less. It can't go on much longer."

"It doesn't make sense," she complained. "I know about the waves, and I know about the blizzards in the Middle West, and the economic collapse, but even so—this is supposed to be one of the richest countries in the world. Surely we ought to be able to do better than this."

"Energy," said Don sleepily. "All the machines are there, but we have to pull trailers with our own muscle. We can't build anything, we can't run anything, we can't grow anything. Not enough energy."

"If only those bloody oil tanks in Richmond hadn't burned."

"Must be more stockpiles." He was silent for a time, and she thought he had gone to sleep. Then he said: "We were down by Alameda today, by the naval air station. The feds had a big barge sitting just offshore. I think they must have been pumping oil out of storage there. There must be a lot of oil around, out of reach—ah."

"What is it?"

"Remember that supertanker, the *Sitka Carrier*? It went down in Monterey Bay when the tsunamis hit. Half a million tonnes of gasoline and diesel fuel. If you could get down to it, you could rig up a valve and pump the stuff up to a tanker or barge on the surface. Half a million tonnes would last a long time."

He got out of bed and walked to the window. For a time he looked out, saying nothing. "It'd be a lot of work, but just maybe we could pull it off."

"Don—I don't want to spoil your party, but even if you did salvage it, what would we do when the oil and gas ran out? Good God, close to three million people are still living around the Bay Area; they could go through that much in no time. Then we're back to scrounging again."

"Not if Dennis Chang gets back in business."

"And who the hell is Dennis Chang?"

"A guy I know. He's trying to produce methane on a large scale down in Palo Alto. Hey, Kirstie, how'd you like to go for a cruise?"

"You've gone bonkers."

"You're not going back to scrounging tomorrow. We're going down to City Hall to sell the local on a long-term investment."

"I don't like your tone of voice. You sound like your grandfather. Now come back to bed; I'm getting cold by myself."

When trucks moved at all these days, they moved in heavily armed convoys. Two nights later, eight trailer rigs moved out of Berkeley loaded with clothing, drugs, vitamins, tools and assorted trade goods, bound for the farm communities south and east of San Jose. Don rode in one of the trucks, listening to the driver and his guard exchanging horror stories about hijackers. It seemed slightly unreal to be travelling so fast; in less than half an hour the convoy reached Fremont. Don's driver stopped; Don got his bicycle out of the rear of the truck. A few seconds later the convoy was gone in a rush of diesel fumes, and he was alone in the darkness.

Visibility was good; the sky was partly cloudy and a full moon hung in the south, bright enough to cast shadows. The air held the now-familiar stink of the shoreline, a mixture of smoke and decay. Seeing water on the road ahead, Don braked and then stopped completely.

The low-lying shore around the approaches to the Dumbarton Bridge was flooded. Water glinted in the gaps between ruined town houses; cars seemed to be floating. The area must have subsided dramatically since the seiches; that had happened in many infilled areas now reclaimed by the bay.

Something about the flooded area bothered him. Dismounting, he walked his bike through water almost knee-deep. As the road rose onto the bridge, he came back onto dry pavement again; turning, he studied the flooded stretch, until he understood what he was seeing.

The seiches had saturated many infills, liquefying them to the point where they could no longer support any weight. Buildings on such sites tilted, collapsed, even sank below the surface. But the town houses near the bridge stood upright, showing only the month-old damage of the seiches themselves. They had not collapsed, because they were not on infill; yet now they stood flooded to a depth of half a metre or more.

The tides, Don knew, had been unusually high lately, and had sometimes reached the freeway along the Berkeley shoreline. He had assumed that was because the waves and seiches had eroded the shore, but now he was not so sure. After all, the Antarctic surge had dumped billions of tonnes of ice into the ocean almost instantaneously; that had triggered the tsunamis. By now, according to his brother's theory, the ice would have spread far north, while more ice followed it. By July or so, in the dead of the southern winter, the ice would weld together into a floating shelf circling Antarctica. In the meantime, much of it was melting—melting enough to raise sea level by half a metre in a month.

He shook his head in wonder. Half a metre of sea water, distributed all over the world's oceans, represented an enormous quantity of melted ice. It also meant the loss of much of the Southern Ocean's stored heat, gone into melting that ice. If all the ice in Antarctica melted, sea level might rise by sixty metres. That seemed highly unlikely, but a rise of ten or twelve metres did not.

A ten-metre rise would drown every seaport in the world and turn many river mouths into brackish estuaries or silt-clogged swamps. The increased area of the oceans would have unpredictable effects on climate; the increased weight of the oceans would strain the earth's surface.

Don got back on his bike and pedalled across the empty bridge. He thought he ought to to feel depressed and defeated by his own hypothesis; instead he felt excitement and the anticipation of a challenge.

Neogene was just another low sprawl of cinder block along a broad suburban road lined with high-tech industries. Don left his bike in the empty parking lot and tried the front door: locked. Walking around the building, he saw the glow of a light behind curtained windows and found a nearby door that opened unexpectedly. Taking a flashlight from his backpack, he walked in.

Light fell through an open doorway into the dusty corridor. Don walked towards it and called out, "Hello, this place." He stepped through the doorway.

Dennis Chang, pale and unkempt, sat at a table at one end of a long laboratory. A Coleman lantern threw white light over the papers strewn on the tabletop.

"Hi, Dennis. It's Don Kennard; we met on the Bay Bridge."

"I'll be damned. Hello. Come on in." Dennis got up, shook Don's hand, and sat him down in a battered old armchair. Then he lighted a Bunsen burner and put a flask of water on to boil.

"You've got natural gas?"

"Unnatural gas, brewed by my little monsters. They're producing enough to keep part of the lab warm and to heat enough water for Mei Ming and me."

"You're living here, then."

"Just the two of us. Our staff are scattered all over the place. So it's a mom-and-pop operation, just like my folks' grocery store. Mei Ming's gone to bed, or I'd introduce you. Hell, you'll stay the night and meet her in the morning. You even get a hot shower if you want one."

"My God, that sounds wonderful."

They talked easily for a time about how things had gone in the past month. Over his second cup of tea, Don asked:

"What would you need to get back in business?"

"Five or six technicians, people with experience in recombinant DNA. Some tradesmen—plumbers, sheet-metal workers, carpenters. Maybe three or four molecular biologists. A couple of clerical types. Why, you want to finance me?"

"Could you be in mass production of methanogen by this autumn, if you had that many people?"

"Mass production meaning how much?"

"Enough to supply the basic energy needs of the Bay Area—call it three million people."

Dennis guffawed. "Wow, from mom and pop to A & P. Yes, by God, we could if we had some extra help at a couple of crucial points. We've got one big technical problem to solve—the gene for methane production doesn't always take, so some cultures don't produce for more than five or six generations. It's nothing we can't fix, but it'll take awhile. This lab alone could produce ten thousand cubic metres a day. And you could export cultures to anywhere. Feed 'em garbage, dead grass, wood chips, and they'll turn it all into methane."

"Good enough. How would you like to make a deal with some of the Bay Area locals, Dennis?"

It took four more days to talk to the Berkeley local, obtain a sailboat from Mrs. Debney's salvaged flotilla, equip it, and sail out of San Francisco Bay.

The boat was an eight-metre sloop, the *Naiad*. It reminded Kirstie of boats she'd sailed with Don in the Caribbean and Mediterranean, and it cheered her up just to be aboard as Don piloted it through Golden Gate.

"This is fun. I'll feel damn guilty if we don't find your oil tanker," Kirstie said.

Don smiled. "We'll find it."

Naiad ran down the coast with the wind from the northwest, and that night lay at anchor off the tip of the Monterey peninsula. The sea was choppy. In Pacific Grove and Monterey and Seaside, a few lights twinkled: candles, mostly, though now and then car headlights flashed out.

"Somebody's still got gasoline," Don said as they sat on deck drinking beer. "Probably soldiers. They seem to have a real grip on things here."

"I wonder what they'll think when they see us out in the bay tomorrow," Kirstie said.

"We'll see. I wouldn't like it if they tried to interfere. Soldiers make me nervous."

Next morning at dawn, in wind-driven rain, *Naiad* crossed the bay towards Moss Landing. The tanker moorage was about nine kilometres offshore, according to Don's charts, in about a hundred metres of water. The *Sitka Carrier* had been overwhelmed at the moorage and probably driven some distance towards shore before hitting bottom.

Still, when he looked at the actual area where the tanker might be, he wondered if it could be found after all. First of all, the charts were now obsolete: the coastline was sharply changed. Sandbars loomed up where water should be deep. Surf broke around rocky islands which had once been part of the shoreline and now stood well out in the bay. The area within which the tanker lay was perhaps five or six kilometres wides and ten long.

He took some heart from the oil slicks streaking the water; they were certainly diesel fuel, and not noticeably decomposed by long exposure, so the tanker could not be completely buried. If the currents in the bay had not changed too much, he should be able to trace the slicks to their source.

After three hours of tacking back and forth across the eastern reaches of the bay, they found themselves just north of a heavy slick that trailed away to the south.

"This must be it," Don said. "The current still runs south along the shoreline, and the speed must be a couple of knots. That means we should be right above the tanker."

Kirstie secured the wheel and dropped anchor. "It's not the nicest place you've ever brought me diving."

The water was cold, a soupy beige with little visibility. He and Kirstie followed the anchor cable down and reached bottom at eighty metres. Visibility was still bad, not much more than a metre or two, but each carried a powerful lamp strapped to one wrist and swam in a fuzzy yellow glow.

Since compasses were no longer reliable, they had improvised a survey pattern: tying a thin line to the anchor cable, they reeled it out about a hundred metres. Then they turned to their right and began a slow sweep, swimming just above a lifeless bottom of mud and jumbled stones. The sweep revealed nothing. Don and Kirstie floated unmoving for a few seconds, until the current began pushing them; they turned and followed the current's direction, unreeling another line tied to the first.

Don actually touched the hull before he saw it; coated with mud, it blended in with the murky water. But just below the mud was cold metal. Kirstie squeezed his arm and pointed to her left; he followed her. They swam for a long time, along the length of the hull, and then, as it began to taper towards the bows, they ascended.

The *Sitka Carrier*, they saw, had capsized and struck bottom upside down. Its superstructure lay crushed and inaccessible; its hull must be largely intact and holding its cargo. Thirty metres from the bottom, the hull curved sharply away from the vertical and rose more gently for another fifty metres until it reached the keel. The water here shone differently in their lamps; oil droplets gave it a brownish tinge.

The breach in the hull, when they found it, was unexpectedly small—a torn weld perhaps six metres long and no more than ten centimetres wide. Diesel oil rose from it in a black, shimmering sheet that vanished into the gloom above. Cautiously, Don and Kirstie circled the breach and searched for others. Apart from a few small cracks, they found none.

Don secured a powerful magnet to the hull and attached a cable to it. An inflatable buoy clipped onto the cable; compressed air lifted it to the surface. They followed it up and found themselves a couple of hundred metres from *Naiad*.

Back on board, Kirstie tugged off her mask and yelled with delight. "We did it! You clever bugger, we did it!"

Shivering, exhausted, smeared with oil, they hugged each other. Without getting out of their wet suits, they stood in the rain eating cold beef stew out of cans and then moved *Naiad* closer to the buoy. After a brief rest they went down to complete their survey and found no other major leaks.

"I can't believe our luck," Don said as they ate supper that night, anchored some distance off Santa Cruz at the north end of the bay. "Not only are there just those little leaks, but they're all from diesel tanks. It'd be tough to run a salvage operation in a cloud of gasoline vapour. And it's in shallow water but well offshore. No trouble with anchoring or pumping, and a good distance from the soldiers."

"Still worried about them?"

"A little. I'm worried about getting the hardware in place. There's not much available in the Bay Area. We can get hold of a barge or two. But we'll need a good-sized ship, a lot of fuel and a submersible."

"What about *Ultramarine* and *Plummet*?"

"*Ultramarine* is set up for research, not salvage. And *Plummet* really took a beating. I'm not sure she could be repaired. She's more for surveying and sampling than hard work, anyway. Don shook his head. "No. I know where to get what we need, but it won't be fun."

"Where?"

"In Vancouver. From old Geordie."

9

"God damn it, Bob Tony, I can't take much more of this shit." Shauna sat tensely on the bed, smoking her fourth cigarette in an hour.

The bedroom was dark, except for a single candle burning on a dresser. Rain rattled on the skylights, and occasionally a blue flash of lightning glared through them. It was almost five in the morning, not long before dawn; Allison was undressing for bed and thinking tiredly that he would have to rig screens over the skylights if the group switched over to a completely nocturnal lifestyle.

"What's the problem, kid?"

"Living like this. Sitting in the house all day, listening to Diana and Aline and Suzi. Telling Lupe one thing and finding out someone's told her the exact opposite. Trying to get Sarah to act like a human being, and then having somebody sabotage me. Eating crappy food and wondering what the hell is happening out in the civilized world."

"Kid, did I ever say this would be a house party? No, wait a minute. You had your say, so let me have mine. Okay, you sit in the house all day? Get out to the barn and help with the animals, or work in the greenhouse. You don't like what the women are talking about, change the subject or go find someone else to talk to. If Lupe doesn't know what to do, you tell her to check with you. But that means you have to pay attention to what's going on in the kitchen.

"And as for that dig about Sarah and somebody sabotaging you, you can be up front with me. I don't like the way you're treating her. She's my kid, not yours, and I'm responsible for her. She's had a hell of a time, and I think she deserves a few breaks instead of all this drill-sergeant shit you lay on her. As for the food, I agree it's pretty boring even with Lupe and Diana working on it, but be glad we've got it. And as for the civilized world—kid, this is it."

"The hell it is."

"Come on, you're not stupid. What happens when we splurge a little extra gas on the generator and turn on the TV? The radio? Nothing, right? They just crackle. When was the last time the mail was delivered here? How long since we've seen a Highway Patrol car in the canyon? Shit, the *army* doesn't even come up here. And you want to pretend that things are okay out there? Get serious, kid."

"It can't be all that bad," she snapped. "Jesus, it was just some big waves, not the end of the fucking world. We aren't exactly fighting off the invading hordes or anything. We're just—sitting here."

"That was the whole idea. Kid, kid—" He sat beside her on the bed. "It hasn't even been a month yet. Sure, we don't know just what's going on. But we can get a pretty good idea from what we don't hear, you know. I'll tell you this: by summer things'll be a lot better. The government will be back on its feet, the power will be back on, and we'll be smelling like roses." He paused for two beats. "It's late. Let's go to bed."

Grudgingly, she butted out her cigarette and slid under

the covers. Allison was about to do the same when someone started pounding on the front door downstairs.

"Oh Christ," Shauna quavered. "Oh Bob, what's that?"

Allison pulled his jeans back on, and took his .45 from the night table.

"Stay put. And keep quiet. Don't wake Sarah." He glanced into the adjoining room, where Sarah slept now. She hadn't stirred.

Barefoot, in pitch darkness, Allison glided downstairs and along the hall to the front door. The pounding started up again. Peeping through a side window, he saw a man, evidently alone, standing on the porch. Silently, Allison turned the lock and slid back the two bolts; then he jerked the door open and brought the pistol up into the man's face.

"*Freeze*," he hissed. The man's hands went up. "What do you want?"

"Please—is that Mr. Allison? I'm Ray Wilder. You know, from Brotherhood House."

Allison relaxed a little. Ray was the young Bible-basher he'd picked up on the canyon road on the morning just before the waves. Having escaped death in Monterey, Ray had plodded back up the canyon praising Jesus. Since then he'd dropped by the ranch a few times, to borrow tools or ask Hipolito for advice on livestock.

"Come on in, Ray. What the hell's the idea of turning up at this hour?"

"I'm deeply sorry to trouble you, sir. But we need help. Our cow was stolen tonight. Someone got into the barn and led her away. We followed her tracks up the road towards Mr. Burk's people."

"You followed her tracks in this downpour?"

"Well—her droppings, actually. But when we got to Mr. Burk's property line, one of his friends was there, carrying a rifle. He told us to go away."

Allison sighed. "Well, it doesn't sound good, but what

am I supposed to do about it at five in the morning?"

"Could—could you and some of your friends come back with us to Mr. Burk's? Just to show them that their neighbours are sticking together?"

"Hell, I don't know." Allison felt a cold breeze behind him, and turned to see Bert D'Annunzio walk silently in from the back door. He was carrying an M-16 rifle.

"What's the problem?" Bert asked. Allison explained. As he did, Shauna came downstairs and stood listening at the foot of the stairs. Allison noted amusedly that Ray kept his eyes chastely away from her.

"How serious is losing your cow?" Bert said when Allison was through.

"She's the only one we have left, sir. She still gives a little milk, the only milk our children have. Without her we'll be in trouble."

"Ray, would you excuse us for a minute?" Allison said. He led Bert and Shauna off into a far corner of the big living room.

"What the hell are we supposed to do about this?" he asked them softly. "We're not cops."

"Maybe we'd better be," said Bert. "Are you sure *our* animals are okay?"

Allison felt dizzy. "Oh-oh."

"In fact, they are. When I heard the pounding, I thought it might be a distraction and checked out the barn. Everything's okay, this time."

"Well, Bert, what do you suggest?"

"Maybe we better get acquainted with these neighbours. Didn't you tell me there's four or five families?"

"As far as I can tell. They've been up there since before we bought this place. The guy in charge is named Frank Burk, but I only know that from talking to Ray Wilder. Burk's people stick to themselves."

Bert grinned. "Cows stick to them too. Maybe we can unstick this one."

"How?" asked Shauna. "If they don't want to give the cow back, what are you supposed to do?"

"We can take it back."

"I think your idea is the shits," Shauna said. "You want to go up against guys you don't know anything about, except that they've got guns, just to do a favour to some religious nuts who never did a thing for us."

"People shouldn't steal their neighbours' cattle," Bert said calmly. "And if they get away with it once, they'll try it again. That means our cattle."

"We've got to do something, I agree," said Allison. "As a matter of fact, the way Ray just barged up to the front door showed me how weak our security is. We're lucky he didn't decide to take one of our cows to make up for theirs."

"We'll have to move fast," Bert said. "Get this sorted out in a hurry. If we hustle, we could be there and back before the sun's very far up."

Shauna sat back in an easy chair, looking annoyed as she fished in her bathrobe pocket for another cigarette. "This is stupid. You guys are acting like a posse in some old Hopalong Cassidy serial."

"Shane," said Allison, deadpan. "Shane. We try to keep this a class act, kid. Okay, Bert. Go get Dave."

"What about Ted?"

"Leave him out of this. It's not his kind of scene. This is our show, I'm afraid."

"You don't look afraid," said Shauna, standing up. She rubbed her neck tiredly, under the mass of thick, dark hair that fell over her shoulders. "I'm going to bed. Don't you dare wake me when you get back."

Dave Marston, Bert and Ray Wilder sat in the back of the Range Rover; Allison drove, and Jeremy Lamb sat beside him. It was the first time the truck had been out in weeks, and Allison enjoyed the feel of it, the noise and power.

"We truly are grateful for your help, Mr. Allison," Jeremy Lamb said. He was a tall, well-built man in middle age, with grey hair framing a picturesquely craggy face. He wore an expensive trench coat over a dark business suit; Allison thought he looked as if he were on the way to a prayer breakfast.

"Thank me when your cow's back home," Allison said with a smile. Lamb smiled back. He was a lot easier to take than Ray Wilder, thought Allison. He didn't wave his religion around and seemed more like an administrator than a charismatic leader.

The rain had tapered off, though lightning still flashed in the east. Morning was a blue-grey gloom that showed the steep slopes of the canyon's upper end. Trees, mostly pines, stood scattered on the hillsides, and showed some new green at the tips of their branches. uv hadn't hurt them as much as the oaks and grasses.

The road wound along the south side of the canyon, past a narrow meadow, and entered denser stands of pine. A heavy gate of new lumber barred the way; Allison braked and got out.

"Hold it right there, bud."

The voice came from somewhere in the woods beyond the gate. Allison scanned the trees but saw no one; the guy must be less than a hundred feet away, but his concealment was perfect.

"We'd like to talk to Mr. Burk," Allison said.

"Who are you?"

"Robert Allison. I live down the road. The other people here live with me or at Brotherhood House."

"What's on your mind?"

"Like to talk about a missing cow."

"Somebody already asked us about that. We don't know anything. Now turn around and leave."

Allison began to feel annoyed. He walked up to the gate

and rested his forearms on it. "I'm not leaving here without talking to Mr. Burk. And if he doesn't come to me, I'll go to him. Don't waste my time."

The unseen sentry didn't reply, but a moment later Allison heard the fuzzy crackle of a CB radio. He felt growing respect for Burk's organizing ability.

"Okay, Mr. Allison. You can come in, alone, on foot. You can keep your side arm."

Allison nodded and went back to the truck to tell the others what was happening.

"Give him a deadline," Bert said. "Like nine o'clock to give the cow back."

"Or what?"

Bert glanced through the window at the gate. "Or we'll take out his man here."

"Bert, hey—let me do this without a heavy intimidation number, okay?"

Allison climbed over the gate, seeing a heavy padlock on the other side.

"Go on up the road," the sentry called out. "You'll be met."

The road was rutted and winding. The woods to the north had long ago been cleared to form a meadow that stretched from the road to the creek. On the east side of the meadow stood an old-fashioned three-story farmhouse; it faced the road across a sizable vegetable garden growing under sheets of clear plastic nailed to waist-high wooden frames. A shoulder-high chain-link fence, topped with strands of barbed wire, surrounded both the garden and the farmhouse. To the south of the road, on Allison's right, the woods thinned out; he glimpsed three or four log cabins half-hidden among the trees.

A tall woman, with a revolver holstered on her hip, stood at the gate into the fenced area. She wore jeans and a brown leather jacket, and a sort of burnoose that shadowed her face.

"Mr. Allison. Hi. Come with me."

He walked with her down a gravel drive to the big farmhouse, which he could now see was part of a compound including several sheds and a long barn. Crossing a wide, screened-in porch, the woman unlocked the front door and ushered Allison into an unlit living room.

"In there, please." She pointed to a door standing ajar across the living room. Allison knocked twice on it, then entered without waiting for an invitation.

A man in camouflage fatigues sat at a roll-top desk, drinking coffee. He was somewhere between forty and fifty, with close-cropped hair and a seamed face. With an abrupt gesture, he motioned Allison to an armchair and poured him some coffee.

"My name's Frank Burk," he said in a deep, hoarse voice. "I'm a fan of yours."

"Oh?" The compliment put Allison off balance.

"I thought *Gunship* was one of the best movies in years. One of the best ever. It was honest, it was fair, it was almost as exciting as the real thing." He grinned, showing small grey teeth. "Brought back a lot of memories."

"I'm pleased to hear it. But I don't give autographs."

Burk's laugh was an unnerving cackle, octaves higher than his speaking voice. "I hear you're representing our neighbours."

"Mr. Burk, they need their cow."

"Call me Frank. Let me explain something, Bob. I wouldn't have their cow as a gift. We're in no position to feed one."

"You have kids here."

"Sure. They drink powdered milk. You see, we saw this coming—not the waves, but the whole social collapse. We've been preparing for it for years. Personally, I figured on nuclear war. That's why I chose this place, out of the fallout zones. And I figured livestock would be a liability. We raise rabbits for meat, keep a few chickens, and grow some vegetables. But we planned to live on canned and dehydrated food for a long time. We intend to survive on our own and we don't need to rob our neighbours. Leave us alone and we'll leave you alone."

"So you're what they used to call survivalists."

Burk grinned again. "Aren't you? And the Brotherhood?"

"Okay, maybe so. But why are the Brotherhood people so sure that you took their cow? They say they followed her droppings right up to your gate."

"Maybe cowshit is more persuasive than bullshit," Burk cackled. "Hell, Bob, for all I know their damn cow wandered up the road and then turned off into the woods. But I'll tell you something—she won't last long if she's outside in daylight. She'll go blind by sundown, and the coyotes will finish her off at night."

Allison began to feel foolish. Burk was much more his kind of man than Ray Wilder or Jeremy Lamb; he felt as if he had been suckered in on the side of the wimps.

"Well," he said. "I'll tell Mr. Lamb what you've told me. Thanks for your time."

Burk stood up and extended his hand. "It's been a real pleasure meeting you, Bob. Take care of yourself and your people. Nobody else will."

Allison let himself out the front door and walked across the porch. The tall woman was nowhere around. He studied the vegetable garden admiringly: the sunshields faced south, leaving plenty of open space for rain and cultivation. The sun was up now, somewhere behind the overcast, and he should be getting under cover; but he walked into the farmyard behind the house to see what else Burk and his people had done.

In the yard was a fresh cowpat. "Uh-oh," Allison muttered. He walked farther into the yard, until he could glance into the open barn door. A rivulet of blood ran over the concrete floor of the barn and lost itself in the mud. Inside, working by the light of a Coleman lantern, three men were butchering a cow. They didn't notice him, and he walked quickly out of the yard. The tall woman was standing on the porch.

"I didn't expect you to be finished so soon," she said. "I'll walk you back to the gate."

"That's okay; I can find my way."

"It's no trouble," she insisted. Allison ignored her all the way out to the gate, while he angrily thought that cowshit was indeed much more persuasive than bullshit.

A month after the waves, the wrecked areas of Monterey were still uncleared moraines of rubble, turning green in places with uv-resistant weeds. The surviving neighbourhoods, south and west of the rubble, were not much better. No store was open; all had long since been emptied by the army or by looters, and many had been gutted by fire. Squatters had moved into some storefronts, patching the lost windows with plastic or cardboard. Now that it was after five in the afternoon, and mostly cloudy, a few children were venturing out of apartment buildings and houses to play in the littered, potholed streets. Like the adults who watched them from behind glass, the children were scrawny, ragged and deeply tanned. The only other people on the streets were soldiers, most of them blacks, patrolling in teams of three. They watched expressionlessly as Allison and Bert drove past in the Range Rover; the truck carried an orange plastic pennant on the antenna, a passport bestowed by a patrol in Carmel when Allison had told them his destination was Ford Ord.

The waves had wiped out Highway 1 from Monterey to the village of Marina, north of Ord. The fort's dunes and firing ranges were gone. For a mile inland from the surf, the shore was a sandy plain studded with half-buried cars, boats and odd bits of wreckage—all of it blackened by oil.

"Really stinks when you're downwind," Bert observed.

"Ray Wilder tells me it's from a tanker called the *Sitka* something. I think I must've seen it the morning before the waves hit. Big son-of-a-bitch, off in the middle of the bay." Alison glanced out at the water. "About where that sailboat is. Christ, who would be crazy enough to go sailing through an oil slick?"

"Maybe it's somebody thinking about salvaging the tanker."

"Good luck. I'd be surprised if there was any oil left in that damn thing. The whole goddamn shoreline is filthy."

At the new main gate, six black MPs inspected them, then waved them through. The post, as they drove up North-South Road, looked almost normal. The lawns in the dependents'-housing area were dead, but house plants in the picture windows were vividly green. The school was deserted. Except for MP patrols in Scouts, the streets were empty.

The centre of Fort Ord was busier: soldiers and their families were in the PX, the snack bar and even the library. The bank was opened; Allison had heard that it now dealt only in army-issued scrip. Everything was in good repair, but buildings and cars looked shabby: months of UV had blistered and bleached their paint.

General Miles's office was in a stucco-and-tile building not far from the officers' mess. Miles was cheerful, friendly and drunk. He offered them Scotch or rye, and did not mention Perrier water. Both men took Scotch and settled onto a leather couch, across a coffee table from Miles's armchair.

"You're looking pretty damn good, Bob. Pretty damn good," Miles boomed after Bert had been introduced. "Haven't seen you since the big day. Boy, that was a hell of a week, wasn't it? Huh?"

"It sure was, General."

"How d'you like living under martial law?"

Allison hadn't noticed that he was living under any sort

of law at all, but he leaned forward, solemn and intent. "General, it was your decisiveness that saved this whole area. We all owe you a debt of gratitude. Otherwise we'd have gone down the drain like L.A. or San Francisco. I mean that sincerely."

"Well, I appreciate that, Bob. Hell, I'm just trying to do my job. Not getting any easier, either. I keep asking for help, and they keep telling me to hang tough, hang tough, I got it better than most." He finished his drink and poured another. "Got it better than San Diego, I'll admit that."

"What's the story there?" Allison asked.

"They had some kind of radiation spill when the waves hit. Some people think it was a nuclear reactor on shore, some think it was one of the nuclear subs that got sunk. Whatever, they ended up with about a quarter-million dead from radiation alone. Not counting the hundred thousand dead in the waves. Fallout reached all the way to Tucson."

Allison and Bert stared at each other.

"Things're screwed up all over the west," Miles went on in a slurred drone. "Some kind of war going on in Seattle, with regular troops and National Guard units fighting each other. No goddamn organization at all left in San Francisco. All they got is these local councils, sort of vigilante outfits, and some individual army units still runnin' a couple of neighbourhoods."

"What's it like back east, General?" Bert asked. "We haven't heard a thing."

"I haven't heard much either. The president's still in Washington, but the government doesn't seem to amount to much outside of the army and air force." Miles rambled on in a monologue full of rumours, digressions, bad jokes and nostalgia. At last Allison found an opportunity and explained why they had come. The general listened, nodding and grunting, and then said:

"Can't have that. Not for a minute. We'll kick his butt. Only thing is finding the men to do it."

"I don't follow you," Allison said.

"We got a little AWOL problem here. See, a lot of my boys are getting worried about the folks at home, you know? So they're packing up and moving out, a couple dozen every night, sometimes more. The ones that stay are gettin' hard to handle. They sit around smokin' dope and gettin' kinda wild. I'd like to shoot a couple, but the next thing, they'd frag a couple of officers or just take over. So I don't have the reliable manpower I had a month ago. Some of them are gone, some of them are stoned, and lots of 'em just aren't obeying orders."

"My God, Ernie," Allison said urgently, "we just need like a platoon for a day or so, to sort out these guys and arrest the leaders."

"Oh—that's all? Well, hell, we can manage that. Sure." He yelled for an aide, who popped through the door instantly. "We got a company of trainees that's up to strength and not assigned to anything too serious?"

"Uh, two or three, sir. A-one-one is probably the best. Lieutenant Mercer's the OIC."

"Okay, fine. They're goin' out on police duty tomorrow. These guys here will give you the details."

His handshake was hard and too long; his breath reeked. Allison met his eyes and saw blankness.

Company A, First Battalion, First Brigade arrived at the ranch at dawn the next day, in a big cattle truck with a canvas canopy. Shauna watched them from the bedroom window; they stopped where the driveway met the road. The sky was clear for once, and the first shafts of sunlight struck down the valley from the Salinas Range, across the brown-and-yellow hills. A young officer and an older sergeant, both blacks, left the truck. Halfway up the drive they were met by Allison, Bert and Dave Marston, all carrying side arms. The five men talked for a few minutes; then the whites walked up to the garage and came back down in the Range Rover. The two blacks got in beside Allison. The trucks moved on.

Shauna rubbed her neck. The bump under her left ear felt bigger: a mole or a wart, or even a cyst. Maybe she should get an army doctor to burn it off. It didn't show or hurt, but it bothered her sense of herself.

Wrapped in her shapeless old bathrobe, she went downstairs. The Wives—she always capitalized them—were chattering away in the kitchen. Sarah was helping to feed the D'Annunzio twins. The excitement in the air only made Shauna nervous.

"This ought to shut those guys up for good," Aline D'Annunzio was saying.

"I just wish our brave husbands had stayed put," said Diana Marston. "If that Burk character decides to start shooting—"

"Will he?" asked Sarah. "Hi, Shauna! Shauna, will he shoot anybody?"

"No. Don't be silly." She poured herself a cup of coffee. "Good morning," she mumbled, and took her cup back upstairs. God, how could they all mob together like that? She wished they would all go away. Okay, folks, disaster's over. Thanks a lot for everything. It's been real. A month of this was enough. Another month would drive her crazy.

The lieutenant's name was Odell Mercer; he came from Los Angeles and, like Allison, had graduated from Hollywood High. His senior NCO was a master sergeant, Calvin Hoops, who was from Texas and said very little. Allison drove slowly up the road; the cattle truck stayed close behind.

"There's Brotherhood House," he said as they drove past. Two women were hanging out laundry, seizing the sunny morning; others, men and women and children, came out of the big house and the barn when they heard the trucks.

"You religious yourself?" Mercer asked. His voice was deep, soft and sibilant.

"No."

"Me neither. Something like this happens, everybody gets religion or gives it up. I gave it up."

Allison glanced at Mercer with wary interest. He was a handsome kid, athletic and graceful, a sharp contrast to his burly but potbellied sergeant. But where Sergeant Hoops was cheerful and relaxed, Lieutenant Mercer looked dangerous. Allison decided to do nothing to annoy him.

Near the little meadow half a mile before the gate, Allison braked to a halt. Burk's settlement could not be seen, but the lay of the land was clear. "Okay, the main buildings are about a mile from here on the left. Four or five other cabins are scattered around on the right side of the road, up in the trees."

"Any problems with the road?" asked Mercer.

"The gate is padlocked, and they keep at least one sentry on it, with a CB radio."

"Well, well. All the latest technology. Okay, we'll just go on up and tell 'em to open the gate."

Two men carrying rifles stepped into the road from the trees. They wore dirty beige jackets and pants, and crash helmets with tinted visors that covered their faces. Allison stopped the truck without turning off the engine. Mercer and Hoops got out, followed by the whites.

"We're here to see Frank Burk," Allison announced.

"You seen him already. You're trespassing. Turn around, and don't come back."

Mercer shook his head almost pityingly and stepped forward.

"You are in the Martial Law Zone," he said, "and you are attempting to interfere with a military officer in the performance of his duties. The least you could get for that would be deportation out of the Zone, with confiscation of all your property. Now, open that gate and stand aside."

The two men stood silently for a moment; then one of them slowly walked back to the gate, unlocked it, and swung it open. The other walked to the side of the road and leaned against a tree.

Mercer walked back to the Range Rover, his face impassive. Everyone climbed back inside; the cattle truck, a few yards behind, started up. Allison put the Range Rover in gear.

"That was really well done, lieu—"

The windsheild flared into thousands of branching cracks, and disintegrated in a spray of fragments.

"Drive on! Get going!" Mercer barked. Allison jammed his foot on the gas pedal and the Range Rover barrelled towards the gate. The man who had opened it was trying to swing it shut, but was too slow: the Range Rover's right front fender struck the half-open gate, knocking the man down.

Allison hadn't heard the first shot, but he heard several more. In the rearview mirror he saw the cattle truck, almost on his bumper. Another burst of rifle fire chattered behind: the soldiers, returning fire.

"Go straight to the main building," Mercer commanded. "We gotta take it over before they get organized."

The gate at the end of the farmhouse drive was closed, and Allison smashed through it with glee. The Range Rover and the cattle truck roared into the farmyard, and Mercer catapulted from his seat with Hoops right behind him.

"First Squad—secure the barn and outbuildings," Mercer yelled. "Second Squad—secure the farmhouse. Get everyone out on the porch. Search 'em. Seize any weapons you find."

Allison watched as the soldiers spilled out in all directions. A third squad took up positions surrounding the compound and facing outward.

"Bob Tony—" Bert's hand was on his shoulder. "We got a problem. Dave's been hit."

Allison turned and saw Dave Marston sitting in the rear of the Range Rover, next to the back window; it too, Allison noticed, had been shot out. Dave was bent over, elbows on his knees with one hand holding up his head and the other clutching his middle. "I feel kind of funny," he said breathlessly.

Bert and Allison helped Dave to lie down in the rear of the truck. Bert delicately unbuttoned Dave's jacket and shirt.

"Oh yeah," he murmured casually. "No big deal, Dave. It's just a graze. You can show it off to Diana." A first-aid kit was in his hand; he pressed a bandage to Dave's belly. "Feel anything when I press?"

"I don't know. It's all kind of . . . numb and . . . tingly, you know? Hey, am I bleeding?" Dave's face was strangely pale despite his tan, and his lips had turned blue.

Bert glanced up at Allison, then at the bench where Dave had been sitting. The black vinyl seat was splashed red. Bert pulled another bandage from the kit and gently drew Dave over onto his right side.

Allison felt himself go dizzy. Blood and excrement pumped from the fist-sized wound at the top of Dave's buttocks. Bert put the dressing over it; it turned a sodden red almost instantly.

"What's that, Bert?" Dave mumbled. "What you doing?"

"Gotta get you cleaned up a little. Don't worry."

"Boy, I sure feel weird," Dave said.

Allison stood by the rear door of the Range Rover, watching blood drip from the seat onto the floor. Dave's eyes met his.

"Don't go away, Bob."

Allison reached in and squeezed his hand. Christ, it was stone cold. "I'm right here, old friend. It'll be okay."

He had no idea how long he stood there, holding Dave's hand while Bert pressed dressings futilely against both wounds. Finally Allison realized Dave was dead. His next thought was that it could just as easily have been himself.

Soldiers had rousted out everyone in the compound buildings: five women, three teenagers, four children. No grown men were among the people on the screened-in porch.

"Isn't this the dumbest thing you ever heard of?" Mercer said to Allison. "All this yellin' and shootin' to protect a fuckin' side of beef?"

He walked to the porch and looked up at the people standing there. Allison followed him.

"Awright, listen up! Who's in charge here?" Mercer demanded.

"I am." It was the tall woman who had escorted Allison the day before. Without her burnoose, Allison could see she had red hair cut almost as short as Frank Burk's, and a deeply freckled face.

"What's your name?"

"Helen Burk. I'm Mr. Burk's wife, and I protest the way you and your men have invaded our home."

"Get down here, Helen," Mercer said.

"What are you going to do?" she asked, walking slowly down the steps. Mercer ignored her. She looked at Allison. "Why are you doing this to us?"

"Because—" His voice was harsh in a dry throat. "Because you stole the Brotherhood's cow, you lied to me, and now you've killed one of my friends and maybe some young men who were only trying to protect us. To protect us from bandits."

Her eyes met his and would not look away. "Please, Mr. Allison. Please don't let them hurt us. Please, the kids." The fear in her voice set off the children. Even after they were sent back inside, their wails filled the air. Mercer kept Helen Burk in the yard. He turned to face her.

"I expect your menfolks will be in the neighbourhood any minute. Maybe they're even watching us now. Where from?"

"I don't under—"

"*Yes you do.* Somewhere right near here, there's a little spot where they can see this place. I want you to stand where they can see you and hear you. Do you understand?"

She nodded quickly and walked out through the dead grass of the meadow towards the road. Mercer walked beside her, his .45 in his hand. To their right, trees stood close-ranked along the edge of the meadow. Thunder rumbled not too far away. Allison saw Mercer lean towards Helen Burk, almost intimately.

"Frank? Frank, if you can hear me—they got all of us. We're all okay. We're okay." Mercer prompted her again. "They want everyone to come out, unarmed. Hands on your heads. Or they'll kill us. Oh, Frank do it, please, please. He'll do it, he will. Please—"

After a pause, men came slowly out of the woods: six of them, all in their thirties or forties. Hands on heads, they walked across the meadow towards Mercer and the woman. Allison recognized Burk and the two who had tried to block the road; the others he had glimpsed occasionally in the past. Neighbours, he thought. But they'd preyed on other neighbours, and killed Dave Marston.

—Mercer was falling backward, arms flailing. The woman beside him looked startled. The six men, off to one side, hesitated. An instant later shots banged, echoing off the farmhouse and the trees.

Allison raised his .45 and fired twice at one of the men. They were running, throwing themselves back towards the woods. Helen Burk bent over with a gasp and fell. More shots blew little clouds of dust above the clumps of yellow grass.

"Stop it! Cease fire!" screamed Bert. He strode across the yard and yanked a rifle barrel up into the acrid air. Allison ran out into the meadow, with a few of the soldiers behind him. Bert was snarling at the others to stay put. Inside the farmhouse, children screamed.

Mercer got up and dusted himself off. Helen Burk was convulsing, knees drawn up to her chest; she wheezed and panted. Three of the six men were dead. The others, including Burk, had made it back into the woods and vanished.

"Who started shooting?" Mercer asked.

"I don't know," said Allison. "I—we saw you fall, and someone was shooting, it was just automatic."

"Fuck." Mercer spat in a hole near his feet, then reached into it and yanked out a square of mud-smeared green plastic. A sharpened stick jutted from the bottom of the hole.

"A punji stick. Must be my lucky day 'cause I didn't step right down onto it. These assholes thought they was playin' war games. Punji sticks—hey, you want to finish off this poor woman here?"

"Me?" Allison said.

"You shot her. I saw you. Thought for sure you'd get me. Now, you going to put her out of her misery?"

"Jesus, lieutenant."

"Man, she's not going to live, but she'll take a while to die. If you can't do it, I will."

Allison lifted the .45 and took a few stiff steps over to the woman. Her freckled face was oddly pale, with blue around the lips. Just like poor Dave, he thought. She was starting to groan: "Frannnk . . . Frannnk."

"I'm sorry. Very sorry," Allison whispered, and shot her in the head.

Mercer was already walking back to the farmyard: "You, you, you—get out there and bring in those bodies.

Sotelo, you get in that house and tell everybody to shut up. You five, go get some shovels and start digging. Rest of you fan out and try to catch those three dudes who got away. Hurry it up. Gonna start raining soon."

"Hey, tough break, Bob Tony," said Bert as he patted Allison's shoulder.

"They were asking for it. Punji sticks, for God's sake. They've got sharp sticks smeared with shit all over the place, like Vietnam or something. Completely paranoid."

"Absolutely," Bert agreed. "You were defending the lieutenant from attackers. No military court would dream of punishing you."

Allison smiled, then laughed. The idea of a trial of any kind seemed absurd. Justice was dead; now there was only self-preservation. These would-be survivalists had been foolish and unlucky. They'd prepared for the end of the old order, but not for the beginning of the new. They'd thought that violence would protect them during the brief period before other people obligingly died off, like some disaster novel; then they'd inherit the earth. Allison knew better, had known it since Bert had shot the driver of the Trans Am: the violence would never stop. It was the inheritance tax paid by the survivors. So be it.

The day was long. Mercer had the surviving civilians trucked out to Fort Ord for interrogation; they would then be deported out of the Martial Law Zone. Their property would be administered by the army for the duration. "Lots of good stuff here, too," Mercer remarked to Allison after a quick inspection of the cabins. "Plenty of dehydrated food, lots of guns and ammo, probably a big fuel dump somewheres. If they'd left their neighbours' cow alone, they'd have been all set."

Jeremy Lamb was not very horrified when Allison came by to tell him what had happened.

"We shall pray for them all, especially the children. It is

terrible to hear of such things. But this is the time of Tribulation; we must accept what is measured out to us. We thank you for your help, Mr. Allison. I wish we had some way to repay you."

"You have a way, I think," said Allison. "Three of the men are still loose. One of them is Frank Burk. As long as they're in the valley, we're not safe. But if we could keep these soldiers here for a while, they'd track those guys down and keep the peace. It's just a matter of being able to feed and house the soldiers."

Lamb looked thoughtful. "My friend, a few months ago I would not have agreed. I would have been afraid of the harm your soldiers might do. Now I see the need more clearly. But to support so many—"

"I know it wouldn't be easy, but they could save us from more serious problems."

"Yes, yes. . . . Perhaps we might send a petition to General Miles."

"You shot her," Shauna said blankly.

"I wasn't *aiming* at her. The men were right near her, and when Mercer fell down I thought they'd pulled something on us. In a way they had, with that goddamn punji stick. But I could just as easily have hit Mercer himself. A forty-five isn't very accurate."

"My God, my God, Bob. You'll go to jail."

"No. I was defending an army officer. Ernie Miles might order a hearing or something, but that's all."

"How could you do it?"

"By aiming and firing," Allison said. "The same way they blew a hole in poor Dave."

"Is that the idea? Dave gets killed so you can shoot some unarmed woman. If you guys had stayed here where you belonged, and left everything to the soldiers—"

Thunder crashed outside. Rain pounded on the bedroom skylights. Shauna walked back and forth, rubbing her neck. It was not yet sundown, but the room was dim except for blue flashes of lightning.

"I can't take much more of this, Bob. It's getting way too heavy."

"Name a better place, kid, and I'll take you there."

"God damn you, I know there isn't anyplace else."

"Kid, you can't do mad scenes. Sit down. Listen." Grudgingly, she obeyed. "Sure, it's a shitty time. I didn't exactly get off on killing her. It had to be done or she would have gone on suffering. There's no other way to cope with this, kid—just, you know, do what has to be done. Because if we don't, we're finished."

He was relieved when her beautiful face loosened into weeping: "I just want it to *end*. I just want everything okay again. Ohh, Bob, why is everything so fucked up?"

Late that evening, Allison and Mercer drove back from Fort Ord. Ted Loeffler and Bert D'Annunzio were waiting in Allison's study with Lamb and Ray Wilder.

"It's official," Allison smiled. "We get Lieutenant Mercer and the two platoons assigned to the valley. It'll be tough, because we'll have to support them, but I think we can manage with the Brotherhood's help. We'll use Burk's empty cabins as their main base, with smaller groups at your place and ours, and down near the mouth of the canyon. Once we've nailed Burk and his two friends, things ought to settle down."

Ray Wilder looked doubtful. "I wonder, sir, if it's wise to put soldiers so close to civilians. There could be problems."

Mercer shook his head slightly. "My men were civilians just a few weeks ago. Lots of 'em have sisters. Some of 'em are even born-again Christians."

"I am glad to hear it," Lamb said.

"Even if they weren't," Mercer went on, ignoring him, "they'd watch their step because I'm watchin' over 'em.

You will have no problems with my men."

Three days later, not long after sunset, three men on bicycles came through the canyon from the Carmel Valley. They were stopped at Checkpoint Alpha, where the road climbed out of the canyon into the upper valley. After radioing the ranch, the soldiers on duty allowed the men through.

Allison met them in the living room. Another lightning storm was breaking over the hills. The men introduced themselves: all were ranchers in the Carmel Valley. Their spokesman was a powerful old man named Olson.

"We heard about the soldiers you got here and how they cleaned out those survivalists," Olson said. "We got the same kind of problem. People holed up here 'n' there, come out at night, steal cattle and anything else they can find. My oldest boy got shot in the foot a couple weeks by somebody tryin' to swipe hay."

"Can't you do something yourself?"

"We're law-abiding people, Mr. Allison. I know everything's gone to hell, and some people are taking advantage and running wild. But that's not for us. We couldn't just go up to some fellow's house and shoot him dead. And we don't have jail or anything. Even if we did, we couldn't spare anybody to guard it, or feed prisoners, or any of that. We're having a hell of a time just looking after our families."

Jesus, thought Allison, it was like something out of *Seven Samurai.* He rubbed his beard solemnly. "Can you help support Lieutenant Mercer and his men? Food, shelter, that kind of thing?"

"I guess. Give us an idea what it'll cost—"

They dickered and argued for some time. At last all agreed on terms: Mercer's two platoons would patrol the part of the Carmel Valley occupied by the ranchers and their neighbours. Allison had been appointed Designated

Administrator of Escondido Valley by General Miles; the appointment was vague enough to permit him to operate in neighbouring areas as well, enforcing martial law and trying offenders. In exchange the ranchers would provide two-fifths of the soldiers' food and supply adequate quarters for up to three squads at a time. Food, tools and weapons would also be contributed to a central store in the ranch compound.

When the ranchers left, Olson gripped Allison's hand. "We're glad to have you folks for neighbours," he said. "You're good people."

Later that night, as lightning flashed through the skylights and hail rattled down, Allison looked in on Sarah, sleeping in what had been his dressing room. She was small and pale, her dark hair tousled on the pillow. He thought she was the most beautiful child he had ever seen.

Shauna came out of the bathroom on the far side of the bedroom. She wore her ratty bathrobe; Allison wondered irritably if she ever wore anything else these days. She was taking a long time to snap out of her current depression.

"So you got to borrow an army after all," she said, dropping the robe and sliding into bed.

"Huh?"

"Remember? The day of the waves you were going to ask Ernie Miles to lend you some soldiers. For the movie."

"My God. That seems so long ago. Maybe we ought to make *Longrangers* after all." He sat heavily on his side of the bed and began to undress.

"You're having too much fun being a real soldier."

"Fun, my aching ass. Most of the time I'm scared out of my mind. Now at least I'm only anxious. If Mercer makes us a few more friends, I might even relax a little."

"Friends." Shauna turned off the Coleman lamp. "Those aren't friends, they're vassals."

He laughed in the darkness, surprised that she knew the word and pleased at its aptness. "Better to have 'em than be 'em, kid."

She made love to him with uncommon passion, and he responded fiercely and hungrily. Later, when she lay snoring in his arms and the storm grew into a blue-flashing roar, he kept seeing Helen Burk's face at the instant of her death. Not until the storm passed, and grey dawn filled the skylights, did he fall asleep. As he did, he thought: This is what it's like to be haunted.

10

The car, a three-year-old Pontiac, arrived at the Kennards' house promptly at 2:30 in the morning. Don and Kirstie put their luggage—a single duffle bag—on the seat beside the driver, and settled down in the back seat.

"What luxury," Kirstie sighed. "Actually going somewhere without walking."

"No kidding," the driver agreed. He was a young Chicano, part of the Berkeley local council's full-time work force. "We got fourteen, fifteen cars converted to propane or natural gas. Wish we had more. I don't care what anybody says, it ain't natural to have to walk all the time, you know?"

"A lot of people are converting, aren't they?" Don asked. "We've been seeing more trucks and cars on the streets lately."

"Yeah, I guess so. Trouble is finding the equipment and then finding the propane or gas. But a lotta guys are using their heads to beat the shortages."

That was true enough, Don reflected. Berkeley was even beginning to look different as people began to experiment with different kinds of energy resources. Some had made solar panels and were heating their homes with them. But that was only a piecemeal solution, he knew. Perhaps one household in twenty had self-generated hot water and space heating; one in fifty had its own electric light, usually from a bicycle-powered generator. Berkeley as a whole was down to ninety minutes of electricity, every other day.

The streets at night were busy, almost crowded in some places. Hundreds of bicycles were out, and a few trucks. Here and there a building glowed with electric lights: hospitals, a few local-run clinics, the food-distribution centres. Otherwise candles burned everywhere. People had begun to adjust to staying up all night and sleeping most of the day.

Down near the wreckage zone, the driver turned into a side street along a park, and found his way blocked by a truck. "What now?" he growled.

A backhoe was operating in the park, its engine roaring as it dug a long, deep trench parallel to the street.

"What a waste of fuel," Don said.

"No it's not," said Kirstie. "Smell. There's quite a pong in the air."

Don nodded, wrinking his nose. A work crew of ten or fifteen men and women, wearing the orange armband of the Berkeley local, stood by the truck; several held furled stretchers. Other people, adults and children, were crowded along the sidewalk. Some were crying.

"It's a burial," Kirstie whispered. "They've got to work fast."

Someone opened the back of the truck. In the headlights of the Pontiac, the Kennards could see bodies stacked three or four deep. Members of the work crew, wearing white surgical masks and gloves, climbed up and began hauling out the corpses, swinging them onto waiting stretchers whose bearers took them to the trench and dumped them in.

One of the workers came up to the car and said to the driver: "I think you better back up and go another way. We're going to be here awhile."

"I can see that," the driver answered. "Man, that's real sad, ain't it? Really sad. More typhoid?"

"Yeah. The doctors say it's getting worse."

"Uh-huh. Listen, on our block you can take your pick, you know? Typhoid, meningitis, hepatitis, stomach bugs they ain't got names for yet."

"I believe it. Well, take it easy." The worker turned and plodded back to the truck. The stink of putrefaction thickened; swearing, the driver threw the car into reverse.

"It never quits, does it?" Don said quietly. "No energy, no clean water. No clean water, people get sick. No energy, no transportation and no medical technology, so people die."

The western edge of the wreckage zone, facing the bay, was beginning to resemble a shoreline. A crude harbour was in operation. Sailboats and a very few power craft crossed the bay to San Francisco and Marin, carrying passengers and small quantities of trade goods; payment was in goods or in local-council scrip. The Kennards had anchored *Naiad* here after their return from Monterey Bay in March; now, in early April, the little sloop was equipped for the much longer run to Vancouver.

Their crew waited on the dock: Bill Murphy and Chief, just off the ferry from San Francisco, and Einar Bjarnason. Sam Steinberg was there too; he was on the Berkeley local executive now, and had come down to see them off.

"You know," Sam remarked as they all walked down the dock, "when Don first suggested this salvage idea, the executive thought he was nuts. Now they're all terrified that maybe they were right the first time, and we won't get the oil after all."

Don laughed. "They'll get it, all right." He looked up at the night sky: stars glittered among the scattered clouds. "We've got good weather. I hope it stays that way. We won't have any weather reports between here and Vancouver."

"Don't remind me," groaned Bill Murphy. "All the way up the coast in a dinky little sloop, without a working compass or radio. The executive was right—you *are* nuts."

Naiad was moored at the end of the dock; they all went aboard, including Sam, who opened a bottle of champagne. They sat on deck in the cool April night, drinking and talking quietly. Sam said good-by and left, and then it was time to take the tide.

Far out from the coast, the sea was strewn with floating debris—logs, trees, shattered lumber, sometimes the recognizable fragments of a house or dock. It was exhausting to beat against the west and northwest winds while steering around half-submerged logs. But Don saw that his crew worked well together; they had been chosen partly to give representation to the locals supporting the trip, but all had experience in small craft and were enjoying the challenge of pitting *Naiad* against the sea.

It seemed strange to Don to sail within sight of the coast yet see so few signs of life. Twice they saw other sails and, once, a derelict Japanese freighter loomed up out of early-morning rain and drifted slowly past. The coasts of northern California, Oregon and Washington were wrapped either in clouds or in smoke; at night, the flames of vast forest fires glowed all along the eastern horizon, and sometimes half the sky pulsed red and pink above the fires.

"I wonder if there's a stick of wood still standing between Alaska and San Francisco," Don said. "I've seen bad fires, but nothing like these. They must have been burning for weeks."

"It is sad," Einar said. "In my country we have no forests since a thousand years. When I came to Berkeley, the trees were like magic to me. Often I go walking in the hills just to see the trees."

"You and my grandfather will get along," Don said with a wry smile. Then: "Einar—look. To starboard."

With a splash and a gasp, a humpbacked whale broke the surface. Then another one, and more; in less than a minute, six whales had appeared around the sloop.

"My God," said Don, "look at their backs."

A whale rose right alongside *Naiad*; its enormous back was a bleeding, oozing mass of sores and rotting flesh. From its blowhole came a strangled squeal. Then it dived, showing flukes the size of *Naiad*'s sails. Another surfaced. It circled the boat, followed by the others. All showed gaping lesions in their backs and in the upper sides of their fins and flukes. Some seemed hardly able to breathe: their blowholes were almost sealed shut by swollen flesh.

"Ultraviolet," said Einar without expression. "The water does not protect them much."

"They're asking for help," Don said. "I believe they're asking us to help them, and we can't. We can't do a thing for them."

For fifteen minutes the pod circled the boat. The whales' cries were thin and shrill. At last the leader turned away, and the others followed. Don and Einar said nothing for a long time.

A week after leaving San Francisco, *Naiad* was sailing through Juan de Fuca Strait along the coast of Washington. Don could see the scars of the tsunamis: hillsides scoured down to bedrock, beaches buried under immense piles of shattered trees. But the waves had not propagated far into Juan de Fuca Strait; the channel looked to Don much as it always had, except for the lack of ships in what was normally a busy waterway. The peaks of the Olympic

Range were dazzlingly white; so were those on Vancouver Island, on the north side of the strait. Along the horizon hung a brownish pall of smoke and haze, thick enough to sting the eyes and catch in the throat.

Naiad sailed through the San Juan and Gulf islands, and crossed the Strait of Georgia to the mouth of the Fraser River. After days of silence or static, *Naiad*'s radio came alive: three Vancouver stations were broadcasting news, weather and music, and there was a lively chatter among the fishing fleet.

"It all seems so damn normal," Bill Murphy commented.

"Not really," said Don. "The only fishing boats we can see from here are all sailboats. They've got a fuel shortage too." He looked worriedly at the skyline of Vancouver, rising to the north. "I just hope my grandfather managed to put away a little diesel fuel."

They cautiously entered the Fraser River's North Arm, a narrow waterway lined with docks, shipyards, warehouses and sawmills. Apart from docks where fishermen were unloading their catches, the waterfront was quiet and deserted. In many areas the rising sea had flooded far inshore, leaving buildings intact but isolated from the nearest dry land.

A green-and-white sign over a sawmill had been blistered by uv but was still legible: KENFOR. The mill stood on the north bank of the river, a sprawl of buildings and yards above a string of docks and boat sheds. As Don brought *Naiad* alongside the nearest empty dock, he pointed to the tug moored next to it:

"There's *Rachel*."

It was a big seagoing tug, forty metres long and ten wide, painted white with green trim. No one was aboard, or anywhere on the docks.

They left *Naiad* and walked through the mill to the front gate, seeing no one. A young bearded Sikh, wearing a turban, came out of the administration building beside the gate. He was carrying a shotgun under one arm.

"This is private property," he said. "I must ask you to leave."

"I'm Geordie Kennard's grandson. We've just arrived from California. I need to get a message to him. Would it be possible to send a courier?"

"I don't really think so," the Sikh said, shaking his head. "But you could use the phone if you know his number."

"You mean the phones work?" Bill Murphy laughed. "Wow! We've hit the big time."

Two minutes later Don was standing in the reception area of the administration building, dialling. After three rings he heard his mother's voice.

"Hello?"

"Hi, Mum. It's Don. Mind if Kirstie and I bring some friends home for dinner?"

"Oh my God! Is it really you? Where are you? How are you?"

"We're down at the mill, Kirstie and I and three friends. We just sailed in from San Francisco."

"I'll send Samuel down to pick you up. He'll be there in twenty minutes. Are you all right? No, of course you are. Listen, I've got to hang up before I start crying or something silly like that. We'll get things ready for you. Five people for dinner?"

"Yes, Mum."

"I'll see what I can do. 'By."

It was the same old Cadillac that Geordie had always sent to meet Don and Steve when they were coming home from summer camp or university. And Samuel the chauffeur was driving, wiry and trim as ever, dressed as always in a black suit, white shirt and blue bow tie. He walked from the car to the main gate, where Don and the others stood.

"Welcome home, Donald. And you, Kirstie. It's good to see you both again. You're looking well."

"Samuel, you look marvellous. You haven't changed a

bit." Don gave him an affectionate hug and introduced him to the others.

Everyone fit comfortably in the limousine, with Don and Kirstie in front and the three men stretching their legs in the rear.

"How does Geordie manage to pay a guard for the sawmill?" Don asked.

Samuel looked surprised. "With money, of course."

"You've still got a money economy?" said Kirstie.

"Of course."

"Is the federal government still in charge?" Don asked.

"Oh, no. Nor the provincial. We just have our local councils, working with the municipal governments."

"Then how do you still have money?" Bill Murphy asked from the back seat.

"Why, it was . . . there. So we still use it. I know it doesn't have any real backing, but then again they're not printing any more, so it's getting more valuable as it gets scarcer. Don't you do the same sort of things in California?"

"It's almost all barter," said Don, "and a little scrip put out by the locals. Samuel, how on earth can you still run this old gas guzzler?"

"Ah," said Samuel with a knowing smile. "It runs on natural gas now. We've still plenty of it coming down the pipeline from the north. And when gasoline got so scarce last year, I suggested to Mr. Kennard that we convert all our automobiles to natural gas. I expect most of these other cars run on it too—maybe a few on diesel, but that's hard to find now."

As the Cadillac carried them west and then north into the city, Kirstie saw Don fall still. He gazed out the window, a fist over his lips, and she realized he was nerving himself. What a strange man he was: full of physical courage, yet frightened and resentful of a frail old man. When he reminded her of the ancient grudges and unhealed wounds in the Kennard family, she was almost grateful for her own upbringing with her cousins.

Soon they were in Shaughnessy, the richest of the city's neighbourhoods, but now looking shabby and decrepit.

"A lot of people have moved out of town," Samuel said. "Gone off to their summer places in the Gulf Islands, or up into the Cariboo. Some have just moved in with friends. Cheaper than trying to keep warm in a big old house. Mr. Kennard would never do that, of course. He'd be just miserable anywhere but home."

He turned in to a driveway flanked by yellowing laurel hedges. The grounds, covering half a good-sized city block, looked autumnal. A few brown leaves clung to the maples and alders; the monkeypuzzle trees had gone rusty orange. The fruit trees—cherry, plum, apple—were dead or dying except for a few small ones sheltering under plastic. Only the hemlocks and cedars seemed healthy.

Despite himself, Don felt a pang of sadness. This place had been a prison for him, and he was glad to have escaped, but it had always been beautiful; it did not deserve this scarring. The house itself, three stories of Victorian turrets and stone chimneys, looked older than he remembered it: the white paint was blistered and peeling, and the roof was mottled with dead moss. Around the house, the rhododendrons that Don's mother had nurtured for years were masses of withered brown.

Elizabeth Kennard welcomed them at the door. She was tall, slim, her white hair piled into curls and contrasting sharply with her deep tan. She wore a pale silk blouse and a grey tweed skirt; Don thought she looked as if she were about to go off for an afternoon at the art galleries.

"You look wonderful," she said, giving him a brisk, cheerful hug. He introduced Bill, Einar and Chief. "I'm delighted to meet you all. Of course you're staying here. Samuel will show you to your rooms, and after you've had a chance to freshen up a bit, we'll have drinks and then supper.

"Donnie and Kirstie, I made the mistake of letting Geordie know you were coming, and he insists on seeing you both at once. Do you mind? Good. It won't be for long—he tires pretty quickly. Almost as quickly as I do."

"Really, how is Geordie?" asked Don.

"Much frailer, but still his old self." She lowered her voice. "Be careful what you say about Steve. We heard from the Commonwealth Antarctic Research Program just after the tidal waves. They told us a plane had been sent from New Zealand to evacuate Steve's station, but it never came back. I've just told Geordie that they were all evacuated to New Zealand and we ought to hear from Steve any day now."

"That's all you've heard? After almost two months?"

"Donnie dear, it's more than we've heard from you until today."

"Do you think Steve is dead?"

What else can I think?" She shuddered a little. "Well, you turned up at last, so perhaps he will too. Now let me catch my breath. Geordie fusses so if he thinks I'm upset."

"Go on back downstairs. We'll talk to him."

Geordie Kennard was almost as tall as his grandson, and very thin. Unkempt white hair fell thickly over his freckled forehead. At ninety-four he wore glasses, but only to conceal hearing aids; his eyes were a clear blue. Like his grandsons, he had a big nose and a slightly protruding lower lip.

He sat in the library, the largest room in his second-floor suite, in a leather armchair. On a little table beside him were his five-o'clock whisky and a long Cuban cigar. The room was comfortably dim, aromatic with tobacco smoke. It was furnished with Edwardian heaviness except for an Apple V computer beside a big roll-top desk.

"Come in and shut the goddamn door," he barked. "It's cold out in that hall. Hello. That Kirstie? You've lost weight. Samuel says you sailed up the coast. That right?"

"That's right, Grampa."

"Used to do that sometimes, when I was younger. Only we used the fastest goddamn boats we could find. Don ever tell you I was a rumrunner?" he asked Kirstie. "Those were the days when I was young and stupid. My dad finally retired just so I'd have to take over the business and quit risking my ass. Sit down! Have a drink." Puffing his cigar, he poured them each a sizable glass of neat Scotch from the bottle beside his chair.

"I hear there's a lot of forest fires down in Washington. That true?"

"Yes. All the way down the coast, until about Mendocino."

"We had such a dry winter, we had fires in January. Jesus Christ. Some of 'em are still burning, too." He took a deliberate sip. "We lost some good timber on Vancouver Island and up the coast. Not that it matters."

"Why doesn't it matter?" Kirstie asked.

"The goddamn business has gone belly-up, that's why," Geordie snarled. "No demand. Most of the lumber we had stored, these goddamn socialist unions just took over without so much as asking."

"What unions?" said Don. "Do you mean the local councils?"

"Yeah, that's what they call themselves. A bunch of reds, just like the dumb assholes I used to run out of my camps back in the old days. Well, they got what they want now. Everything gone to hell, all the industries bankrupt, and the forests burning down." He smiled. "Y'know, I just hope to hell I hang on a little bit longer. With any luck at all I'll be around for the end of the world. Wouldn't that be a shame, to drop dead just before the end of the goddamn world, and miss it?"

Don smiled. "You may think it's bad around here, Grampa, but to us Vancouver looks like paradise. We're fighting to stay alive down in California."

"Well, you're here now. Your mother is really relieved. What're you gonna do with yourselves?"

"We're not staying. We're going back to San Francisco."

"What? Why?"

"You might say we're very involved with people down there," Kirstie said. "We can't just walk away from them."

"Huh. Why'd you leave, then?"

Don took a deep breath; he had not expected to face this moment just yet. "Grampa, I want the *Rachel*."

Geordie gurgled with sardonic laughter. "You want *Rachel*, huh? What for, and what price?"

"I want to take her down to Monterey and salvage a half-million tonnes of gas and oil. I need a big, powerful ship that doesn't need a big crew, something that can haul a barge with a submersible down the coast."

"A submersible?"

"The tanker's capsized in about a hundred metres. We need to go down in a submersible, cut a hole in the tanker's hull, and rig a pump to get it to the surface. Then we haul it in barges to San Francisco."

"That's a fortune in fuel. How come somebody else isn't salvaging this great tanker of yours?"

"Most of the professional salvage operators are dead. Anyhow, the Monterey area is being run by some general who doesn't seem interested in trying to get the oil out."

"Jesus Christ on a crutch, boy—who's in charge down there? What's happened to the government?"

"The government is gangs of soldiers and black marketers. The local councils who are running things sent us here."

"The locals. Like the ones we got here, right? You're working for those assholes, and you want me to give you *Rachel*. I'd rather tie on a tin beak and peck in the shit with the chickens."

Don met his grandfather's pale blue eyes for a moment

and glanced away. His hands felt light and shaky. He took a deep breath.

"This is a deal I'm looking for, Grampa, not a present. And if you only dealt with people you liked, you'd have been pecking in the shit with the chickens a long time ago. Now, do you want to deal?"

"What's your offer? It better be a good one."

"Give me *Rachel* and six months, and I'll come back to take over the business."

Geordie laughed, almost silently. "I just got through telling you there isn't any business. We're broke, if that means anything."

"It doesn't mean a thing, Grampa. You're one of the richest bastards in British Columbia, and you know it. You've got ships, sawmills and the pulp mill. You've got more hydro power than most *cities* have these days. Broke my ass."

Geordie placidly puffed his cigar.

"What you haven't got," Don went on, "is markets. The markets will come back, and they'll go to whoever holds on to some physical plant, whoever gets transport going again. It might as well be KenFor."

"Well, I'll certainly drink to that. But you tell me where the markets are."

"California. Maybe Oregon and Washington too, after all the forest fires. The locals in California are looking after a couple of million homeless people. We've got to get people back on their feet, working, producing, growing. The oil from the *Sitka Carrier* will get us through the worst part."

"What if the government gets back to normal too? Suppose they kick your precious locals right in the ass and tell us to get lost? They weren't too keen on importing our wood before this all started."

"We'll smuggle it in if we have to. You used to run booze into the States; it'd be like old times."

"Christ, you're even dumber than you look. I can just see you tryin' to outrun the Coast Guard with a log boom tied to your ass." But he was smiling. "I just don't like the idea of playing footsie with all these goddamned radicals."

"You leave that to me and concentrate on getting rich. Do we have a deal?"

"Jesus, listen to you talk. 'Getting rich.' How come the high and mighty scientist wants to get down in the gutter with his old granddad?"

"I can't do oceanography without money, Grampa. If I'm running KenFor, and KenFor's making money, I can steal enough to do some science on the side."

"That makes sense. Okay, buster, you got a deal."

Early the next morning, Don drove one of the other family cars—a Honda Accord—over Second Narrows Bridge into North Vancouver. Burrard Inlet, the city's great harbour, was covered by a tangled mat of debris formed by the flooding of the low-lying shore. At the far end of the inlet, east of the bridge, four or five freighters rode at anchor; but no ships moved in the harbour.

Taking the first exit from the bridge, Don drove to the light-industrial zone behind the waterfront. He parked in front of an anonymous cinder-block building, got out, and tried the door. It opened.

The reception room was silent and dusty. Its walls were decorated with colour photos of submersibles and scuba divers; Don recognized himself in one photo. He went down a corridor into a large, high-ceilinged machine shop at the rear of the building. Skylights cast yellow-moted beams onto the floor and walls.

In one of the beams stood a submersible on a modified flatbed trailer. It was no longer than *Plummet,* and only a little wider, but it was taller from keel to sail. Its nose was a hemisphere of glass; floodlights and twin manipulators were recessed into the sharply tapering hull.

A man stood near the sub's pointed stern, his feet buried in tangled cables and hoses. He was adjusting a diving plane; his wrench made soft metallic noises.

"It'll never fly," Don called out. Morrie Walters lowered his wrench and turned, squinting into the shadows. In the beam of sunlight he looked almost skeletal: tall, emaciated, with stringy brown hair fringing a bald scalp.

"Don Kennard! What brings you back to the scene of the crime?"

They shook hands casually, unmindful of the three years since they had last met.

"This is your new baby?" Don asked.

"Yeah. She's called *Squid*. She was supposed to be operating in the Beaufort Sea, before everything went to hell. Hey, did you know I'm bankrupt? Not that it matters. Let me show you what she's like inside."

Inside were two bucket seats, side by side, and banks of instruments arrayed on the inside of the hull. Behind the seats were lockers, batteries and electronic equipment, covering the circular rear bulkhead. Morrie ran through her specifications while pointing things out with a flashlight.

"She's beautiful," Don said. He settled himself in the pilot's seat and crossed his legs. "And plenty of room. You've done yourself proud."

"I know. If the sea level gets much higher, she'll float right out of here. Think I'll take her to Hawaii."

"Bring her to California. I've got work for her."

Don told him about the *Sitka Carrier* and *Rachel*. Morrie, sitting beside him, listened thoughtfully and stared through the bubble at the roll-up metal door in the rear wall of the building. He rubbed his sunburned scalp.

"When do we go?"

"Next week, if we work fast enough."

"I'll have to talk it over with Jenny. She and the kids couldn't come. For how long?"

"Depends. Probably all summer, unless we're really lucky."

"How are you going to pay me? I'm not taking U.S. dollars."

"How about a bargeload of gasoline and diesel?"

"Oho. Not bad."

"You can tow it back with *Rachel* and use her until Kirstie and I come back for good this winter."

"For good? Hey, wonderful. But I thought you never wanted to live here again."

"Well—Geordie's dying, Morrie. He's looking pretty frail. When he was still in his eighties, it wasn't so hard to hate him, and my dad hadn't been dead for long. After a while you can forgive a lot. And forget the rest. My mum's not looking all that great, either. I can't just leave her here, with poor old Samuel to look after her. Anyway, I made the deal with Geordie. For coming back, I get *Rachel*."

Morrie nodded. "Good. Hey, it's gonna work out. And we're gonna have a blast with this baby. She is so state-of-the-art, even *I* don't know everything she can do."

The sun, climbing higher, blazed through the skylight and down onto the glass hemisphere. It sparkled and glittered. Don looked up at the glare of the sky.

The preparations took five days. With Bill, Einar and Chief, Don took *Rachel* out of the Fraser River and into Burrard Inlet. Once they had moored in North Vancouver, it took half a night to move *Squid* to her new home on the barge. Setting up a maintenance shop and fuel supply on the barge took four days.

On the night of *Rachel*'s departure, the crew had supper in Shaughnessy and then squeezed Geordie and Elizabeth into the limousine for the last trip to North Vancouver.

"Everybody sleeps all day," Geordie said, "and then they

run around all night. Lucky bastards. I don't sleep more'n two-three hours, day and night. Nothing to do but play solitaire and think about my sins."

"That ought to be enough to occupy you and two helpers," Elizabeth chuckled.

"It's more fun than listening to you and Samuel tell me all the things I'm not allowed to do any more." He subsided into testy silence, glaring out the window. Elizabeth looked at Don, rolling her eyes.

When they reached the dock, Geordie and Elizabeth stayed in the car. Don and Kirstie sat with them to say good-by.

"It's like sending you off to Harvard," his mother said.

"Only more expensive," Geordie growled. "Well, get going. The sooner you get down there, the sooner you can come back and peck in the shit with me and the chickens."

Geordie's supplies of diesel fuel had been large; *Rachel*'s tanks were full, and *Squid*'s barge carried a sizable reserve. Don and the rest of the crew swung between exhilaration at having so much energy at their disposal, and anxiety about wasting it.

The tug ran south through the Strait of Georgia, dodging deadheads and other floating hazards, and then turned northwest into Juan de Fuca Strait. The sky was cloudless but smoky; long, steep swells rolled up from the south. Off the mouth of the Columbia River, the weather turned stormy, and the swells became wind-torn waves. Einar, doing a periodic check for radio broadcasts, picked up a news bulletin from Portland:

"*. . . accordingly, President Wood has agreed to suspend his responsibilities until normal conditions are restored and has urged all Americans to support the new Emergency Administration formed by the Joint Chiefs of Staff. The Joint Chiefs are now empowered to proclaim and enforce whatever regulations are deemed appropriate. Their first Emergency Regulation reads as* follows:

" *'The United States of America is hereby placed under martial law. All military reservists are ordered to report for active duty within twenty-four hours. Commanding officers of military installations are to extend their responsibilities to administration of civilians residing near such installations. Municipal, regional and state governments shall place themselves and their resources at the disposal of appropriate commanding officers or their designates. Failure to comply shall be considered a breach of the Uniform Code of Military Justice, and offenders shall be tried by court-martial.'* "

The broadcast faded out in static. Don and Kirstie, standing just behind Einar, looked at each other.

"It can't work," said Kirstie. "The military in California are in worse shape than we are. How are they supposed to step in and run things?"

"If a few officers take over the locals—"

"They couldn't!"

"They could with enough armed men behind them."

"I know what happened to the National Guard the night of the waves," Kirstie retorted. "They got slaughtered."

Don shook his head. "It wouldn't happen again. The army would come in ready for anything." He looked unhappy.

South of Point Reyes, almost at the Golden Gate, *Rachel* hove to. The sea had calmed, and a dense fog hung in the windless air. With the radar dead and the radio direction finder unreliable, Bill decided to wait for the fog to lift.

The radio still worked, but so poorly that Einar was sure another solar flare must have hit. He picked up frantic messages from Bay Area locals and ham operators, and occasional broadcasts in code. The details were vague, but it was clear that military units were trying to take over in San Francisco and the East Bay, against strong resistance from the locals.

After a day and a night in the fog, Einar picked up a conversation between a ham operator working for the Berkeley local and another one in San Francisco. Army units from Sacramento were occupying Richmond and El Cerrito and attempting to break through into Berkeley. The push had been stalled, but missiles had begun falling all over the East Bay, killing scores of people and disrupting the defence of Berkeley.

"*The missiles seem to be coming from the west. Has the army in San Francisco got that kind of hardware? Over.*"

"*Not that we know of. But we heard a cruiser was off the Golden Gate a couple of days ago. God knows where it came from. It's all socked in out there now, but maybe they're the ones. Over.*"

"*Christ, I didn't think they had things like cruisers any more. Listen, tell your people we're hanging on, but it's rough.*"

Kirstie turned away, not wanting to hear any more, and paced furiously across the wheelhouse. "Those bastards—those bloody navy bastards. Bill, we've got to get in there as quickly as possible."

Bill Murphy snorted. "What for? So we can get shot up?"

"So we can help! Those are our people. Don, shouldn't we go in?"

He had walked to the wheelhouse door and stood looking out at the fog.

"Listen," he said.

Kirstie, Bill, Morrie and Einar followed him outside. The air was damp and grey. Off to starboard, something hissed and faded away.

"It's the cruiser," said Don. "It can't be more than two or three kilometres away. I'll bet their radar is as dead as ours; they're just firing blind." His face was grim. "Morrie, I need to put *Squid* in the water. You don't have to come with me."

"What are you going to do?" asked Morrie.

Don shrugged and shook his head. Kirstie thought he

looked scared and determined.
"I'm going to try to sink them."

11

As soon as reports of the mutiny at Ford Ord reached him, Mercer set up a defensive perimeter on the crest of the ridge between Carmel and Monterey. Then he sent word to Allison. An hour later, Allison was at Mercer's headquarters in the principal's office of Carmel High School.

"Man, I can't believe this," Mercer said through a cloud of cigarette smoke. "We got the word yesterday about the president being arrested and the Joint Chiefs taking over. I figure, big deal, we been on our own for months here. But, man, the troops went apeshit. They figure their hitches are over 'cause their commander-in-chief is locked up. I hear General Miles was pretty drunk when the men started liberating trucks and heading for home—he ordered the MPs to open fire on some dudes driving off the post, and they told him to forget it. So he shot at 'em himself, and the MPs wasted him."

"Christ," Allison whispered. On the wall behind Mercer's head, photographs of the president and the state governor beamed down.

"Well, it's been getting worse ever since. The troops started fragging officers, trashing everything they could reach, getting bombed and stoned, and taking off. They started comin' out of Ord around dawn. Half of 'em still shitfaced. Couple of 'em drove jeeps and started shootin' up Alvarado Street just for a smile. When they get tired of that, some of 'em gonna head here."

"Can we handle them?"

"Sure we can handle 'em. They're mostly kids, you know? No organization. The smart ones are already long gone. Going home." Mercer sipped hot coffee. His sunglasses were propped on the bill of his olive-green baseball cap.

"If any of them come this way, will your guys fight their buddies?"

"Course we will. Man, we own this place, this is our home now. We'll wax 'em, they ask for it."

Allison nodded. Mercer's army was over three hundred now—mostly army kids, with some civilians and a handful of retreads. The force was in charge of the whole Carmel Valley and down the coast to the northern fringe of Big Sur. Monterey, until now, had been policed directly from Ord. Allison didn't like thinking about the sudden insecurity on his doorstep.

"Next question. Can we take over Monterey ourselves?"

"Ho-ho." Mercer grinned. "Maybe. Sneak in, pick up a few dudes and find out what's going on down there. Then we could go in tonight, when they're getting drunked up again. Lock 'em up overnight and work on 'em tomorrow."

"What does that mean?"

"Uh, that means shoot and recruit. There'll be a few real assholes, you know, rapists and like that. We get them identified really quick, shoot 'em, and then tell the others they can re-enlist in the Carmel Valley Army."

Allison shook his head. "I wouldn't trust the bastards."

"Hey, come on! What do you want, girl scouts? Or you want to kill every swinging dick we find in town?"

"All right, all right. How many men will you need?"

"All of 'em. Pull in the guys up the valley and down by Big Sur."

"Now, goddamn it, Odell, you know that's impossible. Frank Burk's still out there, and if he even guesses we're all in Monterey he'll kill everybody on Escondido Creek. Uh-uh, that's out."

"You have really got a thing about Burk, you know that? A thing. Sure, he's out there. But we don't know where. Ain't even seen a trace of him lately. Maybe he even left the Zone to find his people."

"My ass. The son-of-a-bitch is up in those hills, waiting for a chance."

"And a couple hundred sons-of-bitches are in Monterey, man. Now think: if you throw all your men into town tonight, this time tomorrow you got double the men we have now, and Burk is through. You send in just a few squads, they get shot up and you're worse off than before."

"I want two squads stationed at the ranch. Minimum."

"Okay. But you stay at the ranch too."

"What the hell for?"

"You're my insurance, man. You think everybody in the valley likes me? Uh-uh. They like you, the big movie celebrity with the private army. You get shot, man, and we're just another bunch of dangerous blacks, far as these folks care. They'll hide their food and start pickin' us off."

Allison drew in a breath and slowly let it out. "All right. I'll stay at the ranch." He didn't know whether to feel relieved or insulted: Mercer had said, in effect, that Allison was only a figurehead. But Mercer had also admitted that—for all his firepower and tactical cleverness—he felt alone and vulnerable in a white community. Then perhaps being a figurehead wasn't so bad after all.

Allison's group of friends had, not surprisingly, become the Leadership Committee: each had special areas of responsibility. That afternoon the Committee met in the ranch house living room. Rain pounded on the windows, and logs burned behind the glass doors of the fireplace. The curtains, as always, were drawn.

Allison outlined the meeting's agenda and settled back to hear reports. They were much the same as last week's: Hipolito Vasquez was keeping the cars and generator in shape, but worried about fuel supplies. Ted Loeffler was running all over Carmel Valley, co-ordinating civilian support for Mercer's troops, and worried about fuel supplies. Bert D'Annunzio kept running patrols into the hills, searching for Frank Burk; he could use more people and vehicles. The women were spending less time in the greenhouse—food was not a real problem, since every household in the Carmel Valley contributed to the ranch's support —and wished they could get out more.

"I hear you," Allison said. "I think we may have a solution to the gas problem, and that might solve most of the other problems."

"How?" asked Bert.

"The *Sitka Carrier*. If we can get some of that gas and oil out, we'll be okay."

He saw at once, by their guarded expressions, that the idea was too big for them. They were caught up in the immediate problems, too caught up to see the long-range solution. Okay, let it soak in for a while.

"What about this mutiny?" Ted asked, changing the subject. "Have you heard anything more, kemo sabe?"

"Mercer's moving into Monterey tonight, with every man he's got except for two squads here."

The news startled everyone, as he'd known it would. Allison sketched out the reasoning behind the move and its expected benefits.

"We'll have more administrative problems," he said, "but more resources to solve them. And if we're in control of Monterey harbour, we can get access to the *Sitka Carrier*."

"We don't have any ships, for God's sake," Bert objected. "There isn't even a rowboat between here and Oregon."

"Bullshit," Allison grunted. "There's half a dozen freighters down in Morro Bay, and I've heard of more up around San Francisco. We can get hold of a ship."

"And how do we get the oil out?" Bert persisted.

"I'm not sure of the details yet. We'll find some engineers."

"If you think so, Bob Tony," Ted Loeffler said. "I'll start head-hunting whenever you give me the word."

"Are we agreed?" asked Allison, glancing from face to face. "Okay, Ted. Start looking tomorrow." He looked at his watch. "Mercer should've had those squads here by now. Move to adjourn? Okay. Bert, you want to do a quick sweep around the place?"

Bert nodded and left. The others dispersed: to the kitchen, the generator shed, the bunkhouse. Allison went upstairs to the bedroom. Shauna sat in a bentwood rocker, staring out at the rain through a gap in the curtains.

"Hi," he said, pulling off his shirt. She nodded. He stripped off the rest of his clothes and went into the bathroom. Setting the wind-up oven timer for three minutes, he showered and was out again before the timer could ring. Hot water was a scarce luxury. If only they had more fuel, more gas and diesel—

"Rain getting you down?" he asked quietly as he came back into the bedroom.

"No. I just needed some peace and quiet."

"Get it while you can, kid. We have a new war tonight."

"I don't want to hear about it."

He yanked fresh clothes out of a dresser. "Jesus Christ. Guys are going to die tonight to help keep us alive, and you don't want to hear about it. What *would* you like to hear?"

"Don't shout, Bob."

"I'll shout if I want to. Look, kid, I know where you're coming from. It's been heavy, sure. But, God, it could be so much worse. We've got Sarah, we've got our friends, a whole goddamn army, plenty of food. Up in San Francisco they're starving to death. Kid, you can't just fold up and quit. We're getting through this. It's going to get better, really better. Believe me."

"Have you ever lied to me before?" she asked with a wan smile.

"Not in days." He dropped his clothes on the floor and drew her out of the rocker; she let him carry her to the bed.

"I always forget how strong you are."

"Not that strong. You're just getting skinny."

It was true: as he slid her jeans off and undid her blouse, he was struck by her thinness. Her figure hadn't gone, but she seemed frailer. How long had it been since he'd paid any attention to her? Two weeks? A month? The work of running a private army was too much—he would have to cut back, spend more time with her. And Sarah. Allison knew he'd been neglecting her too.

"Pay attention," Shauna hissed. "You're a million miles away."

He took the rebuke in good spirit and put more thought into his caresses.

"What's this?" His hand paused on the nape of her neck; he pulled back her thick hair. "You've got a mole. How long has that been there?"

"Ow! That hurt. I don't know. But it's really tender."

"Sorry. Listen, kid, we ought to get it looked at. I'll dig up a doctor somewhere."

"Forget it. It'll go away."

"Kid, something like that could be trouble."

"Trouble? What are you saying? What kind of trouble? Does it show? Does it make me ugly?"

"Hey, hey, easy," he murmured, running his hand down her side. "If it's an infection, it could be a nuisance, that's all. No big deal, kid."

He worked harder to bring her to arousal and then to climax, wondering all the time how Mercer was doing.

The squads which Mercer had promised never showed up. Allison and Bert took shifts on sentry duty, patrolling the compound in the rain. Nothing happened. Before dawn, a private on a civilian motorcycle came up the road to report that Monterey had been secured. Three of Mercer's men had been wounded; eighteen mutineers had been killed, and another twenty would be shot before noon.

Allison, Bert and Ted discussed the news over coffee in the kitchen.

"I feel like a mass murderer," Ted murmured.

"Bullshit." Bert shook his head. "Violence is a legitimate right of any government. Hell, it's a government monopoly. And we're the government."

"Thirty-eight guys."

"Ted—" Allison put a hand on his shoulder. "Some of those guys could've come up here and blown you and Suzi and Ken—away. Hey, get your priorities straight. We're protecting our own, any way we can."

"Yeah. Yeah . . . I just feel shitty about it."

"We all feel shitty about it. I mean, who wants to kill people? But we've got a duty to our families, and Lamb's crazy people, and the Carmel Valley people."

"And now the Monterey people," said Bert.

"Right on," Allison agreed.

"Does it ever stop?" asked Ted. "Today Monterey,

tomorrow the world."

"Sure it stops," snapped Allison. "It stops when we're reasonably secure. Now that Monterey's under control, we don't have any major threats from the outside. We'll take over Ord, just to save whatever we can, but that's it. So can that shit about tomorrow the world."

"Hey, kemo sabe, I'm your faithful companion, remember? You don't need to bark at me."

"Okay. Let's forget it, right?" Allison felt angered by Ted's conciliatory tone and blinking eyelids. What a time for him to go soft. "I'm going into Monterey to see what's happening. Probably be back around sunup."

The Range Rover's tires hissed on the wet road. Allison looked at the gas gauge and silently swore to himself: he was burning gas and exposing himself to an attack by Frank Burk, just to get away from Ted. True, the guy was an organizational genius; they would have been lost without him. But he was coming apart at the seams. It was depressing and alarming; despite all that he and Ted had been through together in the last six or seven years, Allison realized that Ted would have to be exploited or dropped.

The drive through Carmel and into Monterey took a long time. Muddy water rose above clogged culverts and swept across the road in many places; here and there the asphalt was gone completely. Another year, and horses would be more useful than trucks even if the gas held out.

—Gas. He kept thinking about the *Sitka Carrier*, just a few miles away with enough gas and diesel fuel to keep them going for years. Somehow it had to be salvaged, whatever the cost—

The stink of oil-soaked beaches was heavy in Monterey and mixed with the smell of smoke. The debris left by the waves always smoldered a bit, but now fires were burning all over the undamaged parts of town. The streets were empty in the rain. In the civic centre, a squad of soldiers in ponchos flagged him down. In the blue light of dawn they looked cold and sleepy.

"Morning, Mr. Allison," said the buck sergeant in charge. "The lieutenant's operating outa the library." He pointed down the street to a glass-and-brick building on the corner, near the edge of the wreckage area.

Allison parked and went inside. Three or four Coleman lanterns made pools of light on the main floor. At a desk beneath one lantern sat Mercer, drinking coffee and eating a sandwich. He waved a dispassionate greeting as Allison came in. Across the floor, a dozen soldiers were smoking dope and playing cards.

"Want a sandwich?"

"No. It's all gone okay?"

"It was a fucking picnic. People here were so glad to see us, they wet their pants. Told us where the guys were, how many, all that."

"You're a genius. A genius. How much do we control?"

"Up into Seaside, I guess."

"The Leadership Committee wants to take over Ord."

"That makes sense. Sure. Take a day or two."

"Then we stop."

"I don't know about that. Might still be an idea to take over the whole Martial Law Zone."

"The whole MLZ. Wow. Can we handle that?"

"Man, we can handle anything if we got enough gas."

"All *right*. And maybe I can get you the gas." He sketched out his salvage plan. Mercer ate.

"Might work," he said at last. "Need some professionals. What do we do if it doesn't work out?"

"Damned if I know. I keep hearing that San Francisco's got no gas, the San Joaquin Valley's got no gas. If we can't salvage the tanker, we'll have to start cooking alcohol."

Mercer smiled. "Man, come on. I'm talkin' transportation for hundreds of trucks, not some funky way to get you up and down the creek."

"Then let's get at the *Sitka Carrier*."

"Okay. Come on," Mercer said, standing up.

"What?"

"Time for the big recruiting speech."

They went back outside. Across the street was a broad, sloping lawn below the fire station. Soldiers, bareheaded and unarmed, were filling the lawn; behind them came Mercer's men, rifles levelled. Allison estimated over five hundred mutineers must be in the group. They looked tired and scared; most were kids, trainees. But a few were older men, senior NCOs and a few officers.

Mercer and Allison crossed the street and walked up the driveway to the fire station's main entrance. It was brighter now, under a low overcast that streamed by from the west. Civilians, scores of them, were gathering in front of the library and on the nearby city hall lawn.

"Long as you're here," said Mercer, "you might as well be the emcee." He nodded towards a microphone standing by the fire-station entrance.

"For what?"

"We're executing twenty dudes caught raping or robbing civilians, or firing on our men. They're like a warning that we mean business and we're righteous. Anybody co-operates, they'll be okay. They don't, they get shot."

"Jesus, Odell, you really get me into some of the—"

"Do it. We got a million more things to do today besides this."

The battery-powered speakers crackled and squealed while Allison introduced himself. He began diffidently, but gained confidence and spoke with growing fervour about the hardships everyone had faced, about the need for soldiers and civilians to stand together. After a few minutes, people began to applaud. At the end, the applause was long and loud.

It swelled even more as the twenty men were marched

out. Their hands were tied behind them; gags were stuffed in their mouths. Many were bruised and blood-streaked. Each was escorted by two soldiers, who gripped him by the elbows. One, a young man with a captain's bars on the collar of his fatigue shirt, tried to break free; a blow to the head from a pistol butt quieted him.

Five young soldiers carrying M-16s came around the corner, marching in step. They wore glossy chromed helmets and bright-blue neck scarves; mirrored sunglasses masked their eyes. The crowd quieted almost in a breath, except for the squallings of babies.

At a sergeant's command the five soldiers lined up at parade rest, facing a patch of grass just a few feet from the microphone where Allison stood.

The first five prisoners were thrown onto their bellies on the wet, dead grass. The firing squad raised their rifles. Allison looked up, at the crowds on the lawns and the street and in the windows of the buildings. This was the civic centre of a small California city. Until a few months ago, no one here could have imagined such a scene. He wondered if the others saw it with the same dreamlike lucidity and sharpness.

"Fire!" snapped the sergeant. Allison's ears rang, and he remembered the woman he'd shot. The prisoners bounced and twitched under the impact of the bullets. Their escorts dragged away the bodies to make room for the next five.   Allison made himself watch, and when one of the prisoners looked up and met his gaze, Allison did not look away. So what if the son-of-a-bitch was a living, thinking human being; that was why he'd been a problem. An instant later the prisoner's face was concealed in the red-soaked grass.

The civilians cheered as the last bodies were hauled away. Allison relaxed. This was what the great leaders of the past had known, this power of life and death. No other power compared with it.

Allison did not get back to Escondido Creek for many days. The Monterey area was crawling with deserters. Women were raped and murdered, men shot dead before their children, houses burned, food stocks destroyed.

Mercer force-marched his men at night, across the muddy fields where artichokes had once grown. In pre-dawn rain they emerged out of darkness, slipping silently into towns while the deserters slept. Not many shots were fired except in the executions.

Allison went with them, sharing the wet and tiredness. When a town or village was secured, he went in and pre-sided over the executions. Then he met with the local people and appointed a government; by nightfall he was off again.

He had been so long at the ranch that the world beyond Monterey looked foreign. Roads were breaking up; farm-lands had turned into weedy bogs. Whole neighbour-hoods in Watsonville and Salinas had burned down. Mold spread across sodden carpeting in empty offices. Dogs had learned to hunt at night, in packs of fifteen and twenty; Allison often heard them bay in the dark, but they never challenged the soldiers. Rats were everywhere.

So were people. It seemed as if every building in the MLZ, intact or not, was jammed with people. Some were refugees from the coast, others from the towns and cities to the north—Santa Cruz, Los Gatos, San Jose—where food was scarce and gangs fought each other in the streets.

First out of curiosity, then out of necessity, Allison inter-rogated many of the refugees. The local councils in the Bay Area, he learned, had survived the attempted military takeover, but were desperately short of food and fuel. They were planning to salvage the *Sitka Carrier*.

When he heard that, Allison's skin prickled. He gave orders that anyone recently arrived from the Bay Area was to be brought straight to him; the three or four people he then saw were able to give enough details to confirm the rumour.

Allison sent word to Ted to recruit a salvage team as quickly as possible. He did not intend to be ripped off.

It was a cold, misty day in early June when he drove back home. To the east the sun was baking the valleys beyond Salinas; air rose shivering with heat and the fog over the ocean swept in to replace it.

Allison sat in the rear of a Cadillac limousine. His chauffeur was black, as was his bodyguard. Ahead was a truck full of soldiers; behind was another. Two motorcyclists led the way. A waste of gas, Allison had thought. Mercer had disagreed.

"You are the main man now. A lot of people might like to take a shot at you. Then we're all back in the shit." Allison had reluctantly agreed.

He and Mercer made a good team: Mercer worried about internal betrayal, Allison about external threats. First it was Frank Burk, next the mutineers in Monterey, then the Bay Area locals. For now, no outside threat was really serious. The Carmel Valley Army was almost seven thousand strong; it controlled the whole coast from just south of Santa Cruz down to Big Sur, and inland to Highway 101 north of Watsonville. He had the support of the people; in Salinas, they'd even donated hidden food supplies without being asked. With Fort Ord's armaments at his disposal, he could even consider taking over all of central California.

—Except that he had no gas. And the *Sitka Carrier* sat out there, slowly bleeding diesel.

The motorcade reached the ranch just before sundown. Most of the escort went back down the road to the now-permanent camp known as Fort Apache, half a mile away. Allison went into the kitchen and found Lupe giving Sarah some breakfast: tortillas smeared with butter. No one else was around. Lupe explained that the señora was still asleep, as were most of the others; Señor Bert was out patrolling the edges of the Brotherhood's property. Allison nodded and let Lupe serve him a big meal of eggs, fried potatoes and ham. It no longer felt odd to eat breakfast at sundown, or supper at dawn.

"How ya doin', squirt?"

"I'm fine," Sarah beamed. "Did you bring me anything?"

"No, doggone it. I'm sorry, I forgot. Next time for sure."

"Did you see Mommy?"

"No. We only went places around here. Salinas, Castroville. Your mom's down in L.A."

"How come she never phones?"

"Phones don't work any more, love. When things get better, we'll call her."

"Shauna says they'll never get better," Sarah pouted.

"Oh, she's just saying that. Things are better already. We've got lots of food, electricity and all these nice soldiers to look after us."

"They scare me. Kenny says they kill people."

Allison made a mental note to speak to Ted about his kid. Then again, Kenny was just relaying his father's half-baked ideas. Better to have it all out. If Ted didn't smarten up, he'd have to be dropped from the Leadership Committee. Or they could set up an Executive Group—sounded good—and leave him off it.

"Kenny's just trying to scare you, silly. If we didn't have the soldiers, all kinds of bad people would come and take everything away from us. Like Frank Burk."

He saw fear, real fear in her eyes, and regretted his words. Burk was a bogyman for everyone these days: the lurker in the shadows, the avenger. The bastard's corpse was probably rotting somewhere in the woods, but until it was found they would all jump at the thought of him.

"Daddy, can we go somewhere else? Can we go home?"

"Sarah, love, we *are* home."

"I mean the old home. Before the 'partment."

—The house in Topanga Canyon, in the long-ago days of two years ago.

"No, love, but listen: how about watching a movie on the TV? *Popeye? Superman?*"

"Only if you watch it with me."

"Sure. I'd like that."

They went into the den, where a big Hitachi projection screen dominated the room. Allison got out a videodisc and put it on; then he took a beer and a can of Pepsi out of the fridge behind the bar and settled down to watch *Superman*. They snuggled together, giggling; soon Sarah was lost in the movie, slurping her Pepsi. Allison put aside his beer after one sip. It was definitely past its shelf life.

When Krypton exploded, Sarah started screaming. Her body went rigid in Allison's arms. Lupe hurried in, clucking in Spanish, and whisked her away. Sarah's screaming went on for a long time.

Allison turned off the sound and watched the blinking, fuzzy images. Despite its foul taste, he drank the rest of his beer. As he put down the empty can, he saw that his hand was shaking.

—Oh, Sarah—it's all for you, for you.

12

It took less than an hour to prepare *Squid* and lower it off the rear of the barge. Morrie, more experienced with the sub, sat in the left-hand pilot's seat. Don kept an eye on the gauges, set along the rim of the glass bubble.

"Jesus," Morrie complained, "I put in this great viewport, and you give me solid mud." They were barely submerged, and the water was an almost opaque caramel colour. *Squid*'s little electric motor hummed softly.

"You also put in a beautiful sonar system," said Don, "and you must have shielded it perfectly. Look—there's the cruiser."

Morrie was silent for a moment. Then he said, "You sure you want to do this, Don? I mean, you didn't even really ask the rest of us or anything."

"They didn't stop me. They know that if that cruiser keeps shooting, we're finished."

"That's the United States Navy we're going up against."

"No, it's a bunch of homicidal maniacs in a big ship."

"You look kind of homicidal yourself."

Don switched on the outside microphone. A dull thump

came from the speaker. Another. The cruiser was launching missiles every two to three minutes.

"They seem to be manoeuvring in an oval pattern," Morrie said. "Another few minutes and they'll be back."

"Cut across and we'll wait for them."

"What about *their* sonar?"

"Chances are it's on the blink. Even if it's working, we'll just look like floating junk."

The water cleared a little; horizontal visibility was almost ten metres. Three or four metres above, the surface was an oily shimmer. The outside microphone picked up a salvo every two minutes, and the steadily increasing growl of the cruiser's engines.

"Okay," said Don. "Start moving us forward." He switched off the speaker; the sound of the cruiser was coming straight through the hull. The sonar's liquid-crystal readout showed 100 metres, 80, 60, 40—

"There she blows," Morrie shouted.

"Get right under their stern."

The cruiser's dark bulk blocked out much of the shimmering glow from the surface. *Squid* sank deeper. Don and Morrie saw the blur of the huge twin propellers, then felt their turbulence. The sub dipped and yawed, edging forward of the propellers until the cruiser's hull was a solid black mass overhead.

Don threw a switch. Compressed air hissed into a plastic float on *Squid*'s hull. The sub rocked heavily while he counted seconds, then pressed a button.

The button glowed white under his fingertip, confirming that the float had been released. He looked up through the bubble, and saw the float, a vivid Day-Glo orange, rising towards the propellers. It rose unnaturally slowly, pulling a heavier cable than it had been designed for.

The cable drum, mounted just forward of the sail, shrieked. *Squid* shuddered. The roar of the cruiser's propellers changed pitch; seconds later a muffled thump came through the sub's hull. The propellers fell silent.

Morrie looked at Don.

"Well," he said, "we got her roped and hog-tied. Now all we gotta do is brand her."

Using his manipulator, Don drilled a hole partway through the cruiser's hull, about ten metres forward of the tangled propellers. Rotating the tool module at the end of the manipulator, he brought an air-driven riveter into position. Morrie, using his manipulator, took an aluminum disc from the basket below the observation bubble. The disc had a flat rim, but bulged out in the middle on one side. While Morrie held the disc against the hull, Don drove a rivet through the rim. *Squid* glided fifteen metres forward, and the two men repeated the process. Ten minutes after the cable had snarled the propellers, three powerful explosive charges were attached to the cruiser's hull.

Morrie steered the sub back towards *Rachel* and the surface. It was brighter now; when they reached the surface the fog had thinned enough to allow a glare of sunshine.

Einar and Chief winched *Squid* aboard the barge and helped the two men out. Morrie checked his watch.

A moment later three concussions, close enough to feel almost like a single one, struck them. A siren began to whoop in the distance.

"D'you think we really did it?" Don asked Morrie as the men clambered off the barge and onto *Rachel*'s stern.

"We did it," said Morrie. "Those aluminum jobs are built to be quick, not tough." He shuddered suddenly and jammed his hands in his pockets. "I just hope we didn't hurt too many people," he added hoarsely.

Chief started the tug's engines, and Bill Murphy steered cautiously through the fog. Don and Kirstie acted as lookouts in the bows. Through the open windows of the wheelhouse came sporadic thumps and the endless whooping of the cruiser's siren.

For the next hour or more, as they moved through the fog, they could hear the sounds of steady destruction: sirens, explosions, the rush and bang of flames. Then *Rachel* was out of earshot, moving slowly through fog that thinned and thickened.

"It sounds bad in Berkeley," Einar told Don as the tug entered the Golden Gate. "The soldiers are pushing east from the freeway, and the militia are retreating to the campus. They think they are fighting maybe five hundred soldiers, with a lot of firepower."

"What about San Francisco?" Don asked.

"The Presidio has surrendered. Many soldiers have gone over to the locals."

Don turned to Bill. "Can you take us to Hunter's Point?"

"Sure, but why?"

"To get some help for Berkeley." Don paced across the wheelhouse, his arms folded and his hands in fists.

During much of the afternoon, the soldiers had taken cover from the sun; from office buildings around Shattuck and University, they fired at the militia's defensive positions between Shattuck and the campus. Twice, the militia had tried to rush the attackers' forward positions; both times the assaults were turned back, leaving dozens of dead and wounded in the square and nearby streets.

Late in the afternoon, with the sun in the militia's eyes, the soldiers left their positions and assembled for a full-scale attack on the campus. It started with mortars and recoilless rifles, shattering the militia's forward positions and disrupting their communications across the campus. Fires broke out; black smoke rose above the tower of the campanile.

The soldiers, meanwhile, formed into three groups: while the main body stayed on University, west of the square, two other groups formed wings that moved north and south on Shattuck. The wings would draw off some of the defenders, while the main body thrust onto the campus.

Within a few minutes, the sputtering gunfire from north and south showed that the wings were in position and engaging the militia. The main body, over three hundred men, poured from doorways and alleys onto the sidewalks and sprinted east across the square towards the campus.

Almost at once, rifles and machine guns opened up behind them. The surprised soldiers slowed and turned; with the sun almost on the horizon, they could not see their attackers. In seconds, fifty or sixty soldiers were dead; the rest ducked into doorways, or ran along Shattuck towards the wings. Enfilading fire from farther down Shattuck cut them to pieces. Retreating towards University, they ran or crawled for cover under heavy fire. No coherent defence developed, only clusters of frightened men shooting blindly into the yellow glare of the sinking sun. Many tried to escape through buildings into nearby streets and alleys; some succeeded, but more were cut down.

The attack on the campus collapsed into short-lived firefights and panicky surrenders. Running up University came two hundred militia, while another fifty came up Shattuck from the south; most of them were blacks from Hunter's Point. They disarmed the surviving soldiers and herded them into a parking lot. A few minutes later the remnants of the wing groups were marched in to join them.

Mitchell Eldon, commanding the Hunter's Point militia, found the senior surviving officer in a corner of the parking lot. He was a bearded black man wearing captain's bars on his filthy fatigues.

"I don't exactly know what to do with you, brother," Mitchell said softly. "You cost us at least a couple hundred dead and hundreds more wounded."

"I was carrying out my orders," the captain said.

"Well, I expect you will carry out the local council's orders for the next little while. We can't massacre you, and we ain't gonna turn you loose, and we sure as hell ain't gonna give you free room and board. So I guess you and your boys will be doing some community improvement for a while. For starters, you can pick a detail of ten men to collect the bodies."

"Like hell I will."

Mitchell reached up and took off the captain's sunglasses. "How'd you like to run around tomorrow without your shades on, brother? How long do you think your eyes would last?"

The captain turned and stabbed a finger at the ten nearest men. Mitchell handed him back his sunglasses.

The crew of the *Rachel* stayed in Berkeley harbour after offloading the militia. Towing the barge and three sailboats, the tug had brought almost three hundred local militia from Hunter's Point. Many were ex-soldiers, and some of the older ones were veterans of Vietnam. They were armed with M-16 rifles, M-50 machine guns, grenade launchers and bazookas; their ammunition, taken from the Presidio, was almost limitless.

The crew sat in the wheelhouse, talking very little, listening to the buzz and crackle of the radio. The local had devised a crude code, but under pressure of combat the militia leaders were reporting their predicaments in clear. After listening for a while, Einar got up.

"I am too worried. I must go to see Sam."

"You're not likely to find him," said Kirstie. "He'll probably be with the local executive, wherever they are. The wrong side of the soldiers, anyway."

"I will go at least to his house. It is not so far. If he is not there, I come right back."

As Einar stepped onto the dock, the popping of distant gunfire sounded clearly.

"What happens if we lose?" Morrie asked Don.

"God, I don't know. Run like hell back to Vancouver, I guess. Or to some surviving local. But I'd be damned angry, after we've got this far."

"Personally, after what I've seen of California so far, I'll be damn glad to be home again. This is a scary place."

"Not as scary as it'll be if the army wins," Kirstie said.

The radio let them follow the soldiers' assault on the campus and their sudden defeat by the Hunter's Point militia. Don grabbed Kirstie, hugging her and yelling; Chief and Bill howled at each other, and Morrie slumped relievedly into a chair. In the trailer at the foot of the dock, people started cheering. The twilight turned to darkness, and men and women and children seemed to materialize out of the wreckage zone, laughing and shouting.

The Kennards and the rest of the crew joined in the celebrations, drinking neat gin with the harbourmaster and her family. The sky over Berkeley glowed from scattered fires; across the bay, more fires burned in San Francisco.

Einar appeared out of the darkness, his face grim in the candlelight of the harbourmaster's office.

"What is it?" Don asked.

"I found Sam. He was shot dead on University Avenue."

Kirstie snatched up an empty gin bottle and flung it through a window. The sound of shattering glass was loud.

With the civic centre burned to the ground, the local executive moved its offices to the high-rise student residences south of the campus; that at least made it easier for Don and Kirstie to commute to the endless meetings that followed the battle of Shattuck Square. Morrie, concerned with *Squid* rather than the politics of launching the salvage operation, shared Sam's old house with Einar and walked down to the harbour every night.

No one knew for sure whether the Joint Chiefs' coup had succeeded elsewhere; it had certainly failed in central and northern California. But the Bay Area locals were faced with worse problems than ever: most of the city had no electricity at all any more, and those portions that did got no more than thirty minutes a day. The crowded hospitals were turning away the typhoid and typhus cases, and something like cholera was beginning to appear. Antibiotics were unavailable. Yet somehow a kind of calm hung over the region.

Equipping *Rachel* for salvage and recruiting a team took longer than Don had expected. Week after week passed while he lobbied the local for one job or another to be done; often he ended up doing the job himself. Even when workers, raw materials and tools were all available, work went slowly: people were too hungry, and often too sick, to work quickly and efficiently.

After a long night of work on *Squid*, Don bicycled home, dead tired. It was just past five on a beautiful July morning, and the sun was not yet high enough to be a hazard to unprotected eyes; Don took his sunglasses off and enjoyed the natural colours of the city. Green was rare these days, and all the more precious. Even a patch of weeds gave pleasure through its rank vitality.

Kirstie was already home, after a night of committee meetings, and as tired as he was; they ate a silent meal of rice and onions, and prepared to go to bed.

A car horn honked outside, loudly and insistently. Surprised, Don went to the living-room window and looked out. A Ford van was parked in front of the house, the first car on Alvarado Street in weeks. The honking stopped, and out of the van stepped Dennis Chang and his wife Mei Ming.

"Gene power!" Dennis chuckled as they sat down in the kitchen. Mei Ming set up a two-burner camp stove and proceeded to boil water for tea. "We've come all the way from Palo Alto on home-brew methane, the same stuff we've got in the camp stove."

"It's weird to be driving," Mei Ming said. "Sort of like the old days, except there's no traffic and the roads are getting awful. And Dennis has forgotten how to drive."

"Does this mean you're ahead of schedule?" Don asked.

"Just the reverse. I need more help and more time. We thought a live demonstration would encourage the locals to find some more people for us."

"What's the problem?" Kirstie asked.

"Viability," Dennis snapped. "After a few dozen divisions, the cultures start to die off. I know what's causing it, I think. It's just going to take a few more months to confirm the cause and design a way around it."

"How long?" asked Don.

"It's almost August now . . . call it November. By Christmas we'll have methane to burn. So to speak."

"Damn." Don shook his head. "We've been delayed by all sorts of problems, mainly transport. And God knows how much longer it'll take to get us underway."

Dennis nodded. "Tell us about it. We're short of all kinds of things in Palo Alto—food, drugs, chemicals and fuel."

"It's worse than that," Mei Ming said. "People are starving. Kids are getting sick and dying. People are killing themselves because they just can't handle it."

"Have you got any gangs?" asked Don.

"No, thank God," Dennis answered. "We didn't even have to deal with the feds the way you people did. Palo Alto's pretty quiet. But Mei Ming's right—people are committing suicide because they can't cope. Whenever it gets me down, I tell myself it could be worse. We could be in San Diego with radiation sickness, or getting butchered in Monterey."

"What's happening in Monterey?" Don asked, surprised.

"Didn't you hear? Apparently the army went crazy down there, after the great coup. Deserters were running around all over the place, shooting people, raping, the works. Now they've got some soldiers and civilians running things, but it doesn't seem to be a whole lot better. They have mass executions all the time. The lucky ones get kicked out."

"That's daft," Kirstie said. "We need every person we can get—even those bloody soldiers who tried to take us over, we've got them working. We've too much to do."

Dennis shook his head, smiling cynically. "The Monterey mob are just looking after themselves. They don't need a whole lot—hey, what's that?"

The wind chime outside the back door was tinkling, without a breeze. The joists beneath the floorboards began to squeak. Then the whole house was vibrating, shuddering. The big kitchen window shattered in a cascade of glass fragments.

"It's an earthquake," Don said. "Quick—out the back door."

They bolted out into the back yard and ran round the side of the house into the street. The ground jerked violently; Dennis staggered against the side of the van. A cypress swayed and fell across the driveway with a thump. A low, almost subsonic rumble filled the air; shouting, people began to pour into the street.

The retaining wall at the bottom of the Kennards' front yard toppled across the sidewalk, every stone in place, and was partly buried by a miniature avalanche of earth and sod. A moment later, the house crashed in upon itself. Other houses on the street were falling as well, some quickly and some slowly.

Another shock hit, brief and hard. A long stretch of Alvarado Road cracked and slid about two metres downhill. The surviving houses on the downhill side buckled and disintegrated. Dust rose into the morning sunshine.

Then it was very still. The only sounds were the hysterical barking of a few dogs and the rattle of loose pebbles. The people in the street stood silently, staring at the ruins of their homes.

"That was the worst one I've ever felt," Don said softly. "My God, the ground still feels as if it's shaking. Is everybody all right?"

"Yeah," said Dennis, "but it doesn't look like we're gonna be able to drive away from here anytime soon. Not with the road like that."

It seemed very funny, and they all giggled. Then Don said, "Let's see who needs help. We'll be a long time waiting for the local to get here."

To Kirstie it was like the day of the waves, a sudden shift from routine to a world of dust and blood and people screaming. They worked much of the day, trying to find and rescue neighbours trapped in the wreckage of their homes. Fires started in many of the houses and spread into stands of eucalyptus; smoke was thick in the air.

Late in the afternoon, Einar Bjarnason came up the road. He looked tired and gaunt.

"The executive sent me to find you," he told Kirstie. "They want us to take *Rachel* to Monterey Bay as soon as possible."

Kirstie laughed bitterly. "At this rate, that'll be a year or two."

"I think they mean tonight or tomorrow. They need fuel right away to cope with all this."

"Well, in that case we may have to go without Don. He lost his sunglasses, and he's been doing rescue work outside all day without them. Now he's snow blind."

13

Allison woke up suddenly around seven in the morning—the dead of night on Escondido Valley time. The bed was shaking. He snapped at Shauna to be still, but she didn't answer, and the shaking got worse. Downstairs, something shattered on the kitchen floor.

"Oh shit," Allison muttered. He rolled out of bed and strode to the doorway into Sarah's room. The curtains were parted a little; he could see her sleeping, curled up with her knees under her and her thumb in her mouth. The windowpanes rattled, and Allison hesitated. The doorway was a safer place to be, if the quake got worse, but he didn't want to rouse her needlessly. Almost any surprise seemed to set her off into hysterics these days.

"Bob?" That was Shauna, awake at last.

"Daddy?"

He walked casually into Sarah's room and picked her up, just as a windowpane cracked.

"What's happening?" She clung to him, warm in her flannel nightie.

"Just a little earthquake. See—it's going away already."

He carried her into the other bedroom, where Shauna lay curled in bed. Allison turned on a battery lantern rather than open the curtains. In the white electric light, Shauna looked drawn and pale despite her tan.

"All over, see? You guys slept through the best part of it."

"I wasn't asleep," said Shauna. "It was a big one." As she sat up, he was struck by how much thinner she'd become. Her collarbones, framed in the neckline of her night-gown, jutted; the bones of her face stood out sharply.

"Let's go get some breakfast," Allison said as he carried Sarah downstairs. "Hope the kitchen's not too messed up." Why wasn't Shauna eating more? They had plenty of food, most of it canned but still perfectly good. Something must be bugging her; when she was ready to talk, he'd be ready to deal with it.

The kitchen was a mess: pots and pans still swung on their hooks above smashed bowls and plates that had cascaded from the cupboards. The big refrigerator was all right, but the little one had toppled. In the dawn twilight, filtered though the curtains, it all looked depressing.

Bert came in from the D'Annunzios' quarters in the old bunkhouse, wearing jeans and carrying a .45.

"Jesus, if it ain't the sheriff," Allison bellowed clownishly, trying to relax Sarah. "Put down your shootin' arn—we give up."

"Getting to be second nature," Bert said, putting his pistol on a countertop. "Man, some shake. The twins are screaming their heads off."

Allison matter-of-factly got milk—powdered but palatable—out of the big fridge, and cut a slice of corn bread. Smeared with margarine and cherry jam, it was Sarah's favourite breakfast. She settled down to it, oblivious of the mess, and Allison began to cheer up a little. At least she wasn't freaking. He lit the Coleman stove and made instant coffee as others began coming in: Hipolito and

Lupe, Ted and Suzi Loeffler, Diana Marston, and Sergeant Hoops—a sergeant major now, just as Odell Mercer was now a colonel. When the babble got too loud, Allison banged a spoon on the coffee pot.

"Okay! We got some cleanup and maintenance. Bert, check the fences and booby traps. Burk might try to take advantage of the uproar."

Ted Loeffler rolled his eyes and sighed.

"Something the matter?" Allison asked quietly.

"No, kemo sabe. I just wish you'd get over Frank Burk."

"You think I might be getting paranoid? Got any doubts about my judgment?"

"No, no. You just come on like the Sheriff of Nottingham waiting for Errol Flynn."

"Ted—we're not in the movie business any more, okay?"

Allison assigned jobs, asked questions, demanded answers. He authorized two hours' generator time and two gallons of gas for Hoops's jeep, so he could run down to Carmel to see how things were. The radio was out of action; judging by the static, Allison guessed that another solar flare had hit overnight.

When the impromptu meeting broke up, Ted caught Allison's eye: "Can you give me a minute, Bob Tony?"

Ted sat down and leaned forward, elbows on his knees and hands folded almost prayerfully before his face.

"Okay, for openers I'm sorry about the wisecracks. In the old days, I thought you were maybe off base, a joke or two and you'd see what the problem was. Not now, and I realize it's the wrong way to deal with what we're facing. If I wasn't so frazzled and uptight I'd just say, 'Hey, do whatever's right,' and—instead, gee, I'm ready to—"

Allison waited in silence while Ted composed himself.

"I—I guess I feel like we're operating under false pretenses."

"False pretenses," Allison nodded. "Want to expand on

that?"

"Bob Tony, we've gotten to be a sovereign fucking state. You noticed that? We tax people, we feed people, we shoot a hell of a lot of 'em. I don't know if that's what Suzi and Ken and I signed on for."

"Ted, none of us did. It was just one damn thing after another."

"Hey, I know it. But I don't know if we're really coping."

Allison raised his eyebrows. He waved a hand at the room, at the women's bustle and clatter as they cleaned up the kitchen. "We're a running organization. No small thanks to you."

"Oh, sure, Bob Tony. But what's it doing to us?"

Keeping us alive and well, Allison wanted to shout. Instead he said, "Tell me."

"Not only can't I sleep, I can't get it up. Never before. I'll spare you the details. And it's not like I'm confessing, okay? I'm just starting with me and Suzi. Who is sleeping fine, on Demerols. And Ken has nightmares and goes two days at a time without talking to anybody.

"Then there's Bert. See the way he loses his temper? Man, remember how he blew away that kid in the Trans Am, the night we left L.A.? That was just for openers. Bob Tony, he's killed five people so far. That I know of. For diddlyshit things. Holding back on a case of powdered milk, for God's sake, so he shoots the family's oldest boy."

"Does Mercer have the details on that one?"

"Mercer's got the details on everything."

"I know where you're coming from. Okay, how about me?"

Ted looked at him. "Want it straight, or funny?"

"Straight."

"Bob Tony, you haven't been out of this house in over three weeks. You won't let us even open the curtains. You've lost what, fifteen pounds? The more you try to run things, the less you look like you're doing it."

"Anything else?"

"Shauna's sicker than hell, and nobody's done a thing about it, because she doesn't talk about it and neither do you."

"Everybody's got skin troubles, Ted. And the runs, and flu, and we got typhus and typhoid in Salinas and Watsonville. All the doctors are working their butts off."

"Jesus, Bob Tony, call one in for a day and have him just take a look at her, would you? She's lost twenty-five, thirty pounds. She coughs all the time, she hardly ever talks, and she's doing some kind of drugs."

"Shauna is a big girl; if she's really feeling bad she'll tell me. And she's not taking drugs."

"Was I ever wrong in the old days? You used to say I saved you a fortune just by keeping the dopers out of the company. Anyway, Sarah is *not* a big girl, and she's really fucked up."

Allison leaned back on the couch and crossed his arms and legs. "I don't want a lecture about Sarah. She's had a hell of a time, sure. But at least she's safe and secure."

"You know she shits her pants? She walks around holding onto Lupe's skirts, with her thumb in her mouth. She—"

"I *said* she's had a hell of a time. She'll be fine. Don't say anything else about her."

Ted rubbed his face. "Sure, Bob Tony. Hey, if I said anything out of line, I'm sorry."

"That's okay. Listen, I *need* you to be up front with me. Now I'll be up front too. I'm taking you off the Leadership Committee. Like a holiday."

"What—"

"You can stay on here at the ranch. You and Suzi and Ken can do the jobs you're good at, but without the responsibility of being on the Committee. We're making some heavy decisions, and it gets to us all, one way or another. So take a break. Give us advice, but let us take the heat. Be a devil's advocate."

"Sure." Ted stared at the wall. "Any objection if we check out?"

"Check out? Leave?"

"Back to L.A. I don't want to overstay our welcome, and I think I left a tap running."

Allison stood up. "Please yourself. I just can't give you any gas."

Couriers began arriving at the ranch around noon; Mercer, in Monterey, relayed news as soon as it came in. The MLZ seemed to have escaped the worst of the quake, though it had been bad enough: scores of dead in Salinas and Watsonville, fires in Seaside and broken water mains everywhere. CB radio reports, through bursts of flare static, gave a far worse picture of cities in the north. The dead in Santa Cruz alone were estimated at well over three thousand. A fragmentary message from Paso Robles, to the south, seemed to indicate that the whole town had collapsed.

Allison sat in the living room, curtains drawn and lanterns burning, while the messages arrived. Bert was in now and then, offering advice or asking questions. At three in the afternoon, Mercer himself arrived.

"We are in some trouble," he said when the room had been closed off. "Half the people in Monterey and Pacific Grove are out in the streets. Lots of houses just came down, bang. Lots more will come down next time somebody sneezes. Most of the MLZ has no water. Ord's okay. Some of the old barracks are kinda creaky, but the concrete ones are good."

"Can we move people into them?" Allison asked.

Mercer put his muddy boots up on a Barcelona chair and sighed. "Sure, Bob. But once we got 'em there we gotta take care of them. Food. Clothes. Bedding. Some way to heat those buildings. They all got electric heat, you know. Even if we had enough generators to heat and light all those buildings, we'd use up all our gas in about two days."

"Gas. It always ends up with gas. What about that salvage team? They come up with anything yet?"

"Not much. They say they might be able to do somethin' if the tanker was right side up. But it turned turtle."

"Shit. I want the leader of that team up here right away, tomorrow. He can show me how he's going to salvage the boat, or he's fired."

"I'll have him here. But listen: we better face the fact that we just might not get all that good stuff. Then what?"

"Have to go liberate some," said Allison, rubbing his beard.

"You talkin' more expansion?"

"No, just some quick raids."

"Better plan on liberatin' some food too. We're running short already, and winter's comin'."

"Okay, okay. But we can't expand any more."

"Raids are no good. You clean out some place, and their locals will come down here and beat us to death. Come *on*, man."

"Hey. We had an earthquake today. Let's worry later about conquering the world."

Mercer stared wearily at him. "When the food runs out, you and me don't have any later."

That was the trouble with opportunists, Allison reflected: they lost heart when they couldn't see an opportunity. Somehow he would have to make sure that Mercer never saw a new opportunity arising somewhere else, or the black son-of-a-bitch would sell them all out without blinking.

"We got this far, Odell. We'll have more later than most people . . . Off the subject, can you get a doctor up here, the next day or two?"

"Somebody got the sniffles? You think my doctors don't work enough?"

"By tomorrow afternoon, Odell. You can have him back tomorrow night. Now, let's get back to relocating all these people. How about putting them in those barracks and not worrying about heat and light?"

"Bob—I just said they'd need food, clothes, doctors. And we'd still need gas and oil."

"Okay, okay—let 'em sit where they are. Or come up with a better idea."

"See what I can do." Mercer stood up and put on his olive-drab baseball cap with the eagle on it. "Like you said, we got this far."

At ten that evening, Allison took a tray upstairs. Shauna had taken a sleeping pill around noon, and hadn't even stirred when Sarah had been put to bed at two-thirty. The child was still asleep; Shauna was just waking.

"Hi," he said softly. "I brought you breakfast in bed."

"Oh." She sat up drowsily. "Put it on the night table. Gotta go pee." When she returned, she took only the coffee; the bacon and scrambled eggs slowly cooled.

"How are you feeling?" he asked, sitting on the edge of the bed.

"Tired. My head always aches."

"I've been neglecting you. Too much going on."

"Was the earthquake bad?"

"No. Listen, how's that sore on your neck?"

"Still there. So what?"

"Can I see it?"

"What the hell for?" She was angry. "You come up here just to stare at my sore?"

"Hey." He took her hand. In the harsh light of the Coleman lantern, she looked gaunt and haggard. "I worry about you. You're a tough cookie, you never complain, and you let things go on too long. I should've had somebody look at it a long time ago. C'mon."

Grudgingly, she lifted her hair from her shoulder. Allison leaned forward and delicately pulled the band-aid from her neck.

"Ouch."

"Sorry." It was bigger: a dark patch the size of his thumbnail, like a big, flat mole. It made a distinct lump under her left ear, extending towards the nape of her neck well beyond the dark patch. A lesion, near the centre of the dark patch, oozed a yellowish fluid.

"Looks like God's own boil," Allison said. "Take the doctor about two seconds to clean it out."

"I don't need a doctor. I just need some peace and quiet. Peace and quiet. No doctor."

"Okay, okay. If you don't want to let him see you, that's fine."

The couriers kept arriving with more news: casualty figures, damage reports, rumours from outside the MLZ. Allison felt relieved to hear that the Bay Area had suffered the worst of the quake. Maybe it would slow them down a little. The locals were bound to move south on him eventually; it was as logically inevitable as his own move north against them.

Around dawn, Allison took a nap. At nine, the leader of the salvage team arrived. He was a nervous blond man who had somehow managed to avoid sunburn. He went through the three cups of coffee with plenty of sugar and evaporated milk, while describing in detail the problems his team was facing. Allison listened patiently.

"What would you need to do the job?" Allison asked.

"A submersible. One that could drill through that hull and attach a valve to it. Then I could just pump the stuff ashore, or onto a barge."

"Where do I find a submersible?" The blond man looked at the floor. Allison glared at him. "Okay, thanks.

You're off the job."

When the man had left, Allison sat thinking for a long time. Rain slashed against the glass behind the drawn curtains. A submersible. Would the Naval Postgraduate School know where one was? Some ex-employee of some defunct offshore-oil company?

The household was full of comings and goings, footsteps outside the closed-off living room and murmured voices in the kitchen. Someone tapped at the door: Lupe, announcing the doctor from Monterey. Allison went out to welcome him, and sent him upstairs with Lupe to see Shauna. Still thinking about salvage, Allison went back into the living room. He decided to talk to Ted. The guy was a pain in the ass, but he would know how to go about finding a submersible.

"Hipolito! Quiero hablar con Ted. Immediatamente."

"Si, señor."

But Hipolito was back in a minute, saying no one answered in the Loefflers' quarters, and their door was locked.

—Oh Jesus, has he killed himself? And Suzi and Ken?

His Spanish deserted him. "Break down the goddamn door. Quick!" He nearly followed Hipolito outside, into the rainswept courtyard; thoughts of Frank Burk stopped him at the door. Hipolito loped back a few minutes later, holding a piece of paper.

Allison took the note. *Bob Tony, you owe me a big one. I've called it in. Love, T.*

"What the hell is this? —Hipolito, al garaje. Quizás Ted ha robado un automóvil."

When Hipolito returned, by now soaking wet, his face was grim. The Range Rover was gone. So were four jerrycans of gas and two spare tires. Allison sent for Bert.

"The son-of-a-bitch won't get far," Bert told him. "Everybody in the Zone knows that truck."

"They know him, too. The troops'll just wave him

through. Once he's out of the Zone, somebody's likely to wipe out the whole family for those jerrycans."

"Out of the Zone?" Bert repeated. "Why?"

"I fired him yesterday. Then he asked to go back to L.A. I told him sure, but not on my gas."

"Jesus." Bert shook his head. "You're right. Someone's gonna knock him off. The dumb shit. Well, maybe we can still stop him. I'll get couriers out."

As he strode out of the room, the doctor entered. He was a tired young man with a wiry beard and dark rings under his eyes.

"Can I talk to you, Mr. Allison?"

"Sure, for a minute. We've got a small emergency."

"You've got a big emergency too, I'm afraid." The doctor closed the door. Allison's senses sharpened suddenly; he could smell the other man's sweat and fatigue.

"Your wife is a very sick woman. I don't think we can do much for her, except for the pain."

"What are you talking about?" His own voice seemed to come from very far away.

"Your wife has malignant melanoma. It's a kind of skin cancer, very rare, very serious. It's well advanced and must be all over her body by now."

"Malignant—"

"I've seen a lot more of it in the last year than most physicians see in a lifetime. Maybe it's the ultraviolet. But I'm afraid I can't offer you much hope, Mr. Allison. I'm sorry.

"You didn't tell her."

"No."

"First smart thing I've heard you say. I don't know where Colonel Mercer dug you up, but you can shove your diagnosis up your ass. Get out of here."

The doctor's eyes widened. "She's going to need methadone, not just those analgesics she's been using. I left enough to keep her comfortable—"

"Get out!"

"—for two weeks. By then there'll be no arguing about it. I'll be back in four or five days to check on her. Is there anyone else I should look at while I'm here?"

"Get out and don't come back."

The doctor shrugged into a dirty windbreaker and put on a black Stetson. "See you soon, Mr. Allison."

Lupe came out of the kitchen. "Mister Allison, have you seen Sarah? It's time for her snack."

"I thought she was with you. She's not upstairs. Go look in the basement."

A few minutes later everyone in the house was searching for her. Lupe checked through the other buildings; nothing. Allison went back upstairs and searched. Sarah's room was its usual mess; she wasn't in the closet, or the bathroom, or under the bed.

When he returned to the kitchen, Bert was there, listening to Lupe's shrill account of the search.

"Kids can be really creative hiders," Bert said. "She'll pop out in a minute, laughing her head off."

"Don't give me that shit. I want the whole compound gone over, inside and out. Don't quit until you find her."

"Okay. Hey, why don't I get one of the twins? They might guess where she's gone."

"Good idea." Allison waited impatiently until Bert came back with Ryan. The three-year-old was sleepy; the twins usually woke only after sundown.

"Ryan," said his father. "Sarah is hiding. Do you know where she's hiding?"

Ryan shook his head fuzzily, then collapsed on his father's shoulder. "Think, Ryan. Does Sarah have a secret place, a hiding place?"

"Unga Teh."

"What? Come on, Ryan."

"Unca Ted. Said they goin' shoppin'."

Bert glanced at Allison. "When, Ryan?"

"Bedtime."

"Five this morning," Bert said. "He's had seven hours."

"That son-of-a-bitch. I'll kill him. Where the fuck does he think he can take her? Back to L.A.?"

—Yes. It had to be. Allison pulled Ted's note out of a pocket. *Bob Tony, you owe me a big one. I've called it in.* You owe me—Ted had said that as they drove away from the apartment building in Santa Monica with Sarah on his lap.

"He's taking her back to Astrid. Jesus Christ, Bert, he's insane. It's three hundred miles. Somebody's going to pick them off for sure, as soon as they're out of the Zone."

"We'll see about that," Bert muttered. "We put together a flying column, fifty or a hundred men, we'll catch up. She'll be back here by morning."

"Do it."

Around six that evening, a motorcycle engine bellowed and fell silent outside. The courier was in the house a few seconds later. He was a stocky Chicano, with zinc oxide smeared all over his lips and ears.

"Mr. Allison. Sergeant Chavez reporting. Colonel Mercer got an urgent message for you."

Allison felt his legs trembling. Arms folded, he said: "Is it about Sarah?"

Chavez looked puzzled. "I dunno, sir." He drew a brown envelope from an inside pocket of his fatigue jacket, and handed it over.

Allison tore the envelope open. He read the message twice before it made sense:

A tug with two barges anchored in the bay this afternoon. Right over the tanker. They say they're from San Francisco and going to salvage the Sitka. No reply when I ordered them off. Mercer.

"Chavez! Go get thirty men for escort duty in fifteen minutes. We're going into Monterey."

14

They had to carry Don on board *Rachel*; Bernie, the medical student, examined him while the tug's engines warmed up.

"I think you're gonna be lucky. You have a low threshold, okay, so it didn't take much exposure or a very long latency period. But you're also recovering fast. Another two days and you'll be all right."

"Two days of this? Christ." The insides of his eye sockets felt full of grit; tears oozed continuously between his swollen lids. It took enormous effort not to rub at his eyes. The tiny cabin was dark, but even the light of Bernie's pencil flash was painful.

"Listen, you've done well to go this long without getting photophthalmia. I see lots of people on their fourth, fifth episode. Most of them are right on the edge of permanent blindness, okay, and they still can't get it through their heads that they shouldn't go outside anymore without protecting their eyes."

"Bernie, I'm supposed to be diving tomorrow. Can I do it with my eyes in this condition?"

"Keep your shades on, okay? Have a good trip."

As *Rachel* ran through the Golden Gate and south down the coast, Don lay in a restless doze. Kirstie looked in on him from time to time, before finally climbing into the upper bunk and falling asleep.

He woke at dawn, feeling a little better, and left the cabin without disturbing Kirstie. Morrie was in the galley, drinking instant coffee. They had a breakfast of cornmeal muffins, and talked quietly about the earthquake.

Its epicentre had been right on the Hayward Fault, running east and west through Berkeley and up into the hills, but it had been felt over a wide area. The Hetch Hetchy Aqueduct had been severed, so almost the entire San Francisco peninsula was without water. Hundreds of fires had broken out; the emergency medical centres were crowded with burn victims. Landslides had erased whole neighbourhoods, and aftershocks had brought down many buildings weakened by the first quake. Tens of thousands of people had moved into parks and other open spaces, preferring to risk blisters and snow blindness rather than burial.

The local councils, scarcely recovered from their battles with the feds, were almost paralyzed. Without fuel to run generators and vehicles, they were reduced to what could be done by dazed, disorganized, hungry people. It was not enough.

Another storm had swept in during the night, and *Rachel* battered through it all the next morning. But the skies cleared behind it; when *Rachel* anchored in Monterey Bay over the tanker, it was on a beautiful summer afternoon.

The oil barge was anchored a short distance from the tug, while *Squid*'s barge was brought alongside *Rachel*. A crew of mechanics transferred to the barge to prepare the sub; Don went with them, wearing dark sunglasses.

"Let's take her down tonight, if you're up to it," said

Morrie as they were eating dinner in the barge's tiny wardroom. "I want to get a look at how the ship's lying."

"Sure," said Don. He wiped up the last of his rabbit stew with a scrap of bread. Rabbit had become a popular food lately, a cheap source of animal protein; it was the bread that was the luxury.

The radio squawked. Leaning back in his chair, Don picked up the microphone. "Kennard."

"*Don, it's Bill.*" The captain's voice was almost unrecognizable in the static. "*We just got a message from Monterey. The natives don't sound very friendly.*"

"Ah. What's the message?"

"*It's from a guy called Colonel Mercer. Calls himself the commanding officer of the Provisional Defence Forces of the Martial Law Zone. He says we're on their territory and we better go home.*"

"What did you tell him?"

"*I said I'd pass the word to the man in charge, but I don't think I got through. He kept saying, 'I repeat, you are to depart at once. Do you acknowledge?'*"

"Uh-huh. Well, keep trying. Tell him we're sorry to trouble him, but we're a duly constituted salvage operation engaged in peaceful work. We won't cause him any problems."

"*What if he doesn't buy it?*"

"Well, I don't know. But we're not going home."

"*That's the spirit.*"

"By the way, we're going down for a trial run in about an hour."

When *Squid* was swung up and out on its crane, the seas were still choppy but predictable, and the operator dipped the submersible into the water without trouble. Morrie let them drop quickly.

"It's a lot clearer than I expected," he said as he switched on the floodlights. Orienting himself quickly, Morrie put *Squid* on a southeasterly course and a steep descent. Sonar pinged briskly, and the screen showed the profile of the bottom. Don had trouble reading the instruments through his dark glasses, but when he took them off the reflected glare of the floodlights made him wince.

"There's the hull," he said after a few minutes, pointing to a bulge on the otherwise flat profile on the sonar screen. "We should be right on top of it. Yeah, there she is."

A thin coating of algae clothed the hull, new growth since Don and Kirstie had first seen the tanker. Colonies of marine life—seaweed, starfish, barnacles—had taken hold here and there. The hull stretched away into the gloom; *Squid* glided above it, from near the stern to the vast, blunt bows. The water thickened rapidly until visibility was no more than two metres in a brown-black murk.

"There's the main rupture," Don said. "It's not putting out as much oil as it was in the spring."

They surveyed the whole expanse of the hull and found no new leaks. But Morrie spotted patches relatively free of algae, where the metal shone brightly in the sub's floodlights. Don called *Rachel*; Bill Murphy answered.

"We're amidships, and just found an area that looks like someone's been testing the hull."

"*Copy. Can you judge how recently?*"

"The scratches are clean and bright. It must have been since Kirstie and I were here."

"Maybe our Colonel Mercer," Morrie suggested.

"*Could be,*" said Bill. "*Maybe that's why he doesn't want us around. Do you feel like claim jumpers?*"

"No," answered Don, "but I don't like the idea of having to fight somebody for the privilege of pumping gas. We're continuing with the survey."

Several places along the hull showed similar marks, though none were deep enough to penetrate the steel. They found no new ruptures.

"We're in luck," said Don as *Squid* rose towards the surface. "Tomorrow morning we'll secure the valve mounting, and bring the umbilical down. Day after tomorrow we'll be in business." Condensation dripped on his head and shoulders. "Unless those people in Monterey make trouble."

Allison stood on the roof of the Monterey City Hall and looked northeast through binoculars. The sun was long since down, and the bay was black. The ship's running lights were tiny but bright.

"Think they can do it?" he asked Mercer.

"I dunno. They got that tug and a couple of barges. They don't look like a holiday cruise."

"Griswold says they'd need a submersible—one of those minisubs."

"Maybe they got one." Mercer squatted down against the parapet, out of the wind. "The hell with 'em. We'll go get our gas somewhere else."

"No," said Allison. "They're not getting a goddamn drop of our oil. None. None."

"Hey, okay—I hear you. No need to yell. But what's the difference? They get our oil, we get somebody else's."

"No. The bastards get that oil, they'll be back for our food—"

"What food?"

"Our food, our weapons. Jesus, there're millions of people in the Bay Area. Give 'em gas and they'll be down here in trucks, like locusts. Uh-uh. I'm stopping 'em right now, while I've got 'em by the balls."

"Oh, we got 'em by the balls, huh? I didn't notice."

"You get some artillery in place. That ship isn't more than four miles offshore from Moss Landing. We'll sink the bastards."

"Aw, shit." But Mercer stood up. "I'll try it, but—"

"Just do it, Odell. Do it. By tomorrow morning."

"Hey, Bob—something the matter?"

"Nothing you need to worry about. Just get those god-damn guns set up, okay?"

"Yeah, yeah." He walked away, a shadow in the dark-ness. Allison didn't notice; he had already turned to study the ship's lights again.

Just before sunrise, Don and Morrie boarded *Squid* again. An hour later, after various items had been loaded aboard and tested, the submersible sank into the sea. The eastern sky had been a pink-and-white smear of clouds; within seconds, *Squid* was sinking through blackness.

While Morrie piloted the submersible, Don ran through a long check list. He found he could read without too much strain, though his eyes still felt scratchy. The descent was uneventful.

When the tanker's hull emerged out of the darkness, Morrie steered *Squid* east, towards the bows. The water was browner and murkier than yesterday; the current must have shifted west a little.

"This'll do," said Don. He gripped a manipulator knob. The arm went out, poised over the hull, and began to whine. Don inspected the disc-shaped multiple tool at its end, rotating it until a drill bit locked into position.

The other manipulator, controlled by Morrie, drew a heavy plate from its carrier on Squid's belly. It was well over a metre square, with a sixty-centimetre hole in its centre and smaller holes near its corners. The plate slid onto the hull with a muffled thump; *Squid* wallowed upward until Don corrected its buoyancy. Then his hand went back to the manipulator knob. The tool arm went out, poised over one of the plate's corner holes, and descended. The drill bit slid through the hole and touched the steel of the hull; *Squid* began to vibrate as the drill dug in. Morrie shifted the sub's balance to keep it level.

The drilling took a long time. Sometimes the water

turned dark brown, opaque with oil droplets, and Don waited until he could see the drill bit again.

"Through," he said at last, and withdrew the drill. A jet of pale gasoline shot up. As the gas spread, Don rotated the tool head to lock in a bolt driver and lowered it into the corner hole. Squeezing a trigger produced a loud clang; the submersible shuddered, and the gas flow stopped. One corner of the plate was secured.

Three more times Don drilled through the hull; when the plate was fully secured, he began to cut around the central circle. The diamond saw was effective but slow, and gasoline swirled out of the lengthening cut. The noise and vibration went on and on. When the radio crackled, Don gratefully stopped cutting.

It was Bill Murphy. "*We got another message, Don. It's from some guy named Allison. Says he's Colonel Mercer's boss. He wants to talk with you.*"

"Can you patch him through?"

"*Will do.*" A moment later, a strange voice sounded scratchily in the speaker.

"*Hello? This is Robert Anthony Allison. Am I talking to the head of the salvage operation?*"

"Yes. Donald Kennard."

"*I understand you're in a sub, down on the tanker.*"

"Yes."

"*Well, my friend, you have just one hour to get back up to the surface and start moving out of the bay. One hour from now.*"

"Can't do it."

"*My friend, you will do it. In one hour, six howitzers will start firing on you. They will keep firing until they sink your ship.*"

"That's insane," Don snapped. "You'd set the slick on fire. It'd burn till the tanker was empty."

"*You're full of shit,*" Allison shouted. "*That's diesel oil and it won't burn. Even if it did, only one tank is leaking. My people tell me the other tanks are still intact.*"

"Mr. Allison. We've already cut into another tank. A lot

of gasoline is escaping right now. Some of it's already on the surface. It will burn and it'll ignite the diesel. That'll make the rest of the cargo unsalvageable for months, if ever."

"*Great. I'd rather have that than see you bastards walk away with it. You've got fifty-six minutes.*"

"I need more time than that," Don said. "I'm coming in to talk to you."

The answer was a long time coming. "*What's to talk about?*"

"Sharing the tanker."

Again, silence. Then: "*Have you got the authority to negotiate?*"

"This is my project, Mr. Allison."

"*Okay. Come into Monterey harbour. How long will it take you?*"

"Maybe two hours, three hours tops."

"*All right. You'll be met.*"

The transmission ended, and Bill Murphy came on. "*This is a hell of a note, Don. That guy sounds crazy. You sure you'll be okay?*"

"No, but don't tell Kirstie that. Look, we've come this far. We're not going to turn around and go home empty-handed because of some bullshit threat. If they're willing to see me, they're willing to bargain."

"*I hope you're doing the right thing.*"

"So do I. Anyway, we'll finish this and get back up as soon as we can."

"You're not going in there," Kirstie said. "It's insane."

Don shook his head. "They were ready to start shooting. Just getting them to talk is an achievement."

"Those buggers will just lock you up and hold you for ransom. Or shoot you just to prove they mean business. Don, you can't go."

"I know it's dangerous, but it's the best chance we've

got." He paused. "And I'm not going to let those people chase us off. It's as simple as that."

"You bloody, bloody egomaniac. You're as bad as Geordie."

"You know, I wish to God *he* could come with us. He'd end up with *their* oil as well as the tanker."

She kissed him. "Why don't you bog off, then, if you're so eager?"

The Monterey waterfront reminded Don of Hunter's Point on the day after the waves: a jumble of rocks, timber and debris, piled into a dike up to three metres high. Cannery Row was in ruins: oil floated in thick brownish-black clots on the water and coated the dike as well. The stink was foul.

About where the old wharf had been, two black soldiers stood on the top of the dike. One of them waved; Don waved back and steered his Zodiac towards them. They clambered down the face of the dike, slipping on the greasy logs and boulders, and moored the Zodiac. Don stepped out and followed the soldiers over the rubble, through the wreckage zone, and up into the streets of Monterey.

"Something the matter?" one of them asked.

Don was wiping his face with a handkerchief. "I'm getting over snow blindness. Makes my eyes water."

"Man, that's bad shit. I had some of that once. Like gettin' chili sauce in your eyes."

They said nothing more. Blinking and squinting behind his sunglasses, Don looked around at the remains of Monterey. The earthquake had left many new buildings collapsed, while some of the older adobes had come through almost undamaged. He saw no civilians, only a handful of soldiers patrolling the deserted streets. The stink of oil mixed here with the sharp, fresh smell of burned wood.

The city hall had lost its plate-glass windows, and a sentry stood in the doorway. He stepped aside; Don and his escort walked over broken glass and through the empty doorframe. Soldiers sat in the lobby, playing poker for cigarettes. They glanced incuriously at Don. His escort guided him up a flight of stairs to an office facing south across a dead lawn.

Two men sat before the windows of the office, dark outlines against the glare.

"Have a seat," said one of them. Don blinked and squinted while his eyes adjusted. The man who had spoken was a bearded white man. He wore a wrinkled white cotton shirt, beige chinos and desert boots. He was self-consciously slumped back into his chair, as if trying to show himself relaxed and uninterested. His hands curled around the ends of his chair's armrests, and his face was immobile. His eyes were narrowed to unreadable slits.

The black man in the other chair wore crisply pressed fatigues with gold eagles on the collar. His fingers were steepled in front of his lips; his deep-set eyes studied Don, inquisitive and calculating. This is the strong one, Don thought. The other guy is ready to snap.

"You're Donald Kennard? I'm Robert Anthony Allison. This is Colonel Mercer. Let's cut the horse-trading bullshit and get down to it. What's your bottom-line offer?"

Don was not surprised by Allison's abruptness. "Ten per cent of all the oil and gas we take out of the tanker. You can collect your first instalment day after tomorrow."

Mercer looked surprised and a little impressed. Allison only frowned and shook his head.

"We need enough fuel to sustain a hundred thousand people for as long as possible."

"Okay, you've got a hundred thousand people? We've got three million. The *Sitka*'s got about four hundred thousand tonnes of fuel left in her tanks. Our share will carry us for four or five months. Ten per cent ought to carry you easily for a year, maybe two."

"Mr. Kennard, I said for as long as possible. Our share will be fifty per cent. That gives us five years, maybe longer, by your calculations."

"Look, you won't need that much fuel. In four to six months we're switching over to methane, produced by bacteria. By this time next year we plan to be exporting energy all over California." Don saw Mercer's eyes widen. "We've got genetic engineers working on it. We need the *Sitka*'s fuel to buy time to develop the methane."

"For Christ's sake, how fucking dumb do you think I am? How the hell do I know you're gonna have methane or alcohol or vanilla ice cream? I know this: that tanker's got fuel, and I want all I can get. All right, you people have the equipment and the know-how. But we've got guns that can turn you into scrap iron on the bottom of the bay. Fifty per cent of the tanker's cargo goes to us, off the top. You can have whatever's left."

Don thought for a moment. "If I agree to those terms, thousands of people in San Francisco will die. I'll go to fifteen per cent, delivered concurrently with our own shipments. Nothing more."

"Then you have no deal, my friend." Allison stood up. "You'll be escorted back to your boat. I expect your ship to be out of the bay before sunset. If it's not, we'll sink it."

"Uh, just a minute," Mercer said. "Mr. Kennard, would you mind stepping outside for a minute? I need to talk something over with Mr. Allison."

"Sure."

The dim corridor was a relief after the glare in the office. Don took off his glasses and wiped his eyes; they hurt again. He was distantly aware of taking quick, impatient steps down the moldy, half-rotten carpeting. How had such jerks ended up running the lives of a hundred thousand people? Neither one would qualify for a neighbourhood committee in the Bay Area, but here they had all the weapons of a major army post, and the manpower to use it.

Mercer at least seemed interested in Don's offer. He must realize that it was fifteen per cent or nothing. If Mercer could only be made to see that he'd get nowhere with Allison—

"Mr. Kennard? Like to come back in, please?" Mercer called.

Don paced into the office and sat down. Allison was slumped even deeper in his armchair, his chin on his chest.

"Colonel Mercer's suggested an alternative, Mr. Kennard. For the sake of fairness I'm willing to consider it, and at least see your reaction to it. A sixty-forty split, in your favour, divided as you bring the oil up. That seems pretty reasonable to me."

Don listened to Allison and wished he could see the man's face more clearly. The voice was thick, monotone.

"It sounds like a step in the right direction," Don answered slowly. "But the proportions are still wrong. We need the fuel to buy time to develop the methane. That'll benefit all of us. What do you think you'll use after all the tanker's fuel is gone?" He kept his eyes on Allison but was aware of Mercer's gaze, steady and unblinking. "I gave you a no-bullshit offer, fifteen per cent, and that's as high as I can go. Now, that's sixty thousand tonnes of real fuel. All this fifty-fifty, sixty-forty crap is fifty per cent of *nothing*, forty per cent of *nothing*. Without us, there's no way you can salvage that fuel. Can you understand that, Mr. Allison?"

Allison's face contorted; suddenly he grabbed Don's shirt and yanked him to his feet.

"Schmuck! Think you can fuck me around? Nobody talks to me like that, nobody!" His breath was sour in Don's face; his eyes were wide now.

"Sixty thousand tonnes, Mr. Allison." He kept his voice level. It was Mercer he was speaking to.

Allison slapped Don across the face, knocking his glasses off. Don winced, more at the stab of light than the slap, and fought against the urge to strike back. Half-blind and unarmed, he would win nothing in a fight. But Mercer would have to read him correctly, as he must already have read Allison.

"Sixty thousand—"

Allison shoved him backward, and he toppled over with his chair. Before he could move, Allison kicked him in the belly, then in the head.

"Asshole," Allison said. Then he looked at Mercer: "Haul him out of here and shoot his fucking brains out."

"Hey, hold on. Let's just put him back in his boat, all right? We kill him, we don't know what we're getting into, you know? We got enough trouble."

Allison tucked in his shirt with trembling hands. "Nobody treats me like that, Odell. Nobody. Now, get this cocksucker downstairs and see that he's shot. Do you understand me?" he added shrilly.

"Yeah, yeah, awright." Shrugging, Mercer went to the door and bellowed for guards. Three soldiers hustled up from the lobby. Mercer helped them carry Don downstairs.

"Park this dude in the basement for a while," Mercer muttered to his men as they lurched downstairs. "In the broom closet, with the door locked."

As they crossed the lobby, a soldier ran in past the sentry.

"I got an urgent personal message for Mr. Allison, Colonel. Is he here?"

"Upstairs," Mercer answered. "Room two-oh-seven." He saw that Don was securely locked away, then went slowly back up the stairs. He got to the lobby just in time to see Allison running through the door, across the lawn to where his red Mercedes 450 sl was parked. By the time Mercer got outside, the car was gone. He went back inside and found the messenger.

"Awright, what was *that* all about?"

"Uh, Mrs. Allison is dead, sir. Looks like she took an overdose of somethin'. That Mexican housekeeper found her."

"Oh shit, and that crazy fucker's gone off by himself. Okay, gimme a detail of six men out front, right now!" Mercer roared at the cardplayers across the lobby. "And get that goddamn truck out here, the deuce and a half!"

Allison drove fast, windows rolled up against the stink of Monterey. A glass bottle exploded across the hood; he scarcely noticed, except to pat his chest for his shoulder holster. It wasn't there—he'd forgotten to put it on when they'd left the ranch. No wonder, with everything happening at once. The earthquake, Ted, Sarah, the doctor, then these turkeys in the bay, and now Shauna—

It was a lie, that was for sure. She was sick as hell all right, and she might have overdosed, but she wasn't dead. He'd pull her out of it. God damn all these fucking people with their demands, dragging him away from his family.

He felt frightened and angry and exposed. Everything was falling apart, everyone was fading away. He was acting foolishly and impulsively, running around alone and unarmed like this. Get into a normal pattern, start thinking rationally again. By God, when they brought Ted back the bastard was going to *suffer* before he died. Sarah . . . please let her be all right, please Bert, find her safe and get her home.

Allison hurried on over the hill to Carmel. He saw little bands of refugees, trudging north towards whatever shelter they could find in Monterey or Fort Ord. They looked like tramps: dirty, skinny, some of them bleeding, carrying or dragging a few ratty possessions. What the hell had made him think these people were worth doing anything for? Why hadn't he stayed in Escondido Valley, instead of trying to save this inhabited ruin? He swung hard left onto Carmel Valley Road, remembering the lurch the car had made when the wave ran across the highway on that stormy afternoon long ago.

Long ago: Shauna's silver Jag coming the other way, with Shauna living the last few seconds of an ordinary life. She would have been luckier if the waves had caught her in Carmel, if she had suffered only a moment's surprise instead of this. And if he'd left Sarah with Astrid, and if the Loefflers had stayed in L.A. with Bert and poor dead Dave Marston. Then he and Shauna could have stayed on at the ranch with Hipolito and Lupe, minding their own business. Letting the survivalists rip off the Brotherhood, letting everything go to hell at its own chosen speed, not trying to save things and people not worth saving.

No. He could sorrow over some things and be angry over others, but he regretted nothing. He'd done his best, and without him things would have been worse.

The long-dead fields were streaked with the black slime of decayed vegetation. How long had it been since he'd seen a cow or horse grazing, even in those stupid goggles? Stumps and scattered slash were all that remained of the oaks and eucalyptus, fruit trees and pines and cypresses that had adorned the valley.

The entrance to Escondido Valley was still wooded, by Allison's order, though most of the trees were dead or dying. Allison slowed and turned. Something banged the right front tire, and the car swerved and stalled. From the tilt of the fender, he realized he had blown the tire. Swearing, he put on his Stetson and got out.

The tire was ripped to bits. He got the jack and tool kit from the trunk and went to squat beside the wheel. As he did, he saw a small hole in the fender: a bullet hole.

Allison's hands began to shake. He reached for the tire iron, his eyes still on the hole. The only sounds were wind in the leafless branches on the hillside, and water splashing down the creek bed on the other side of the road.

They must be up on the south side of the entrance to the valley: a lot of trees up there, dead brush, plenty of cover and a good view of anyone coming up from the west. He was lucky they hadn't hit him. If he could get around the car, roll over the shoulder of the road, and get down into the creek bed, he could cross the creek and find cover in the woods on the opposite hillside. Then work his way up to the first checkpoint and safety.

He flipped off the hubcap and stood up, walked to the rear of the car with the tire iron still in his hand, a weary motorist doing a chore. With the trunk lid concealing him, he threw himself over the edge of the road.

Stones rattled around him; he went over and over, both hands clenched on the tire iron. The world spun around him and he splashed into a shallow pool. Up, stride, splash, *umph*.

He was lying on his back in the pool, wondering if he'd already gotten up or had just imagined it. The tire iron was gone. Never mind. Up, get across the creek. Up. Up.

He realized that he couldn't get up. His hands moved; he could lift his head. His back felt cold and wet, but not his legs. His legs felt nothing. When he looked down at them, he saw red clouds and tendrils in the water.

"I can't be *shot*," he said.

Two men loomed above him, dark outlines against the bright haze of the summer sky.

"Mr. Allison," said the taller of the two. "I'm Frank Burk. Remember me?"

Allison was sure he'd heard the name before, but couldn't place it. "Help me up. I think I'm hurt." The men seemed to be receding; perhaps they couldn't even hear him. "Give me a hand. Please."

"Allison, don't you know who I am? Frank Burk."

"Yeah . . . yeah. I think we've met. Maybe in Monterey? I've got a ranch up near there. Please, help me up."

"Oh fuck," said Burk.

Allison heard another bang, very close. Something hurt in his chest.

Help me up, he tried to say. I have to bring Sarah home.

The men were gone. The sky was gone. The water was gone. Then the pain was gone.

Don came to in chilly darkness, lying on a cold cement floor. His stomach hurt, and when he lifted his head he gasped with pain. It was very quiet.

He got to his feet and groped around in the darkness. In one corner of the tiny room was a big sink, with faucets that worked; he cupped his hands and drank a little water. Feeling his way across mop handles and buckets and shelves full of dusty boxes, he found nothing that might get him through the locked door, or that might be used as a weapon. When they came for him, his one chance would lie in surprise—a sudden assault, maybe seizing a weapon from whoever opened the door, and then somehow getting out of the building and down to the Zodiac.

Kirstie had been right again, as she usually was. These guys were insane, and he'd been dumb enough to think they could be bargained with. He missed her. He missed his mother and brother, too, and Geordie. He remembered the old guy saying he hoped to live long enough to see the end of the world. Well, he had a better chance of that now than his grandson did. Don had a confused, dreamlike memory of Allison ordering Mercer to shoot him. For some reason the moment had been postponed, but surely it would come soon.

After what seemed like a long time, he heard footsteps coming down a flight of stairs and then down a hallway towards him: a single man, walking briskly. The man rapped twice on the door.

"Mr. Kennard? It's Colonel Mercer. I'm lettin' you out

now. Please don't try anything, okay? Everything's cool."

Keys jingled, and the door swung open. Without his sunglasses, the dimness of the basement was bright enough to make him squint. He snorted with amusement at his fantasies of a bold escape. With his eyes, he'd have run into the nearest wall.

"Eyes still hurt, huh? Here's your shades. You want to come upstairs, have something to eat?"

"Yes. Thanks."

They went upstairs, back to the same office, past a deserted lobby. It was mid-afternoon. Mercer drew the curtains across the cracked glass in the windows.

"I'm really sorry about all that, stickin' you down in the closet. Allison was all hot to shoot you, so I thought I better just get you out of his sight for a little while."

"Thanks. I take it Allison's calmed down."

"Wow." Mercer laughed silently for a moment and then shook his head. "He's dead, Mr. Kennard. He got ambushed by a couple of crazy dudes he'd been scared of for months. His wife had just killed herself with metha-done. Found out she was dying of cancer, you know? He got the message and took off without a bodyguard, and we followed him. Got there just in time to take care of the crazies, but it was too late for Allison."

Don shook his head, but said nothing. Mercer opened a brown paper bag and produced supper: cans of pork and beans, and metallic-tasting beer. Mercer rattled away while they ate, apologizing for the food, complaining about the shortages and morale problems he contended with.

"Old Allison, he was supposed to be the big leader, you know, the problem-solver. But he kind of turned into the problem, I guess. Just got pushed a little too hard."

"So you're in charge now?"

"Kind of looks that way. Allison's got a friend named D'Annunzio, who's mostly good for shooting people who can't shoot back. But he's off chasing around after Allison's kid, somewhere south of here. Any luck at all, he won't make it back. If he does, we'll put him in a cage. Uh, could we maybe talk about that deal?"

"For the gas and oil?" Don smiled. "Sure. What's your no-bullshit bottom line?"

"Fifteen per cent, if you give us early delivery on some of that methane you guys are cooking up."

"Sounds good."

"Listen, I need something else."

"What?"

"I need a white dude to run things here. I try to do it myself, somebody's gonna shoot me in the back."

"Is that how you and Allison did it?" Don finished his beer and started another. "Why bother? Just elect a local council and let 'em take over."

"Um ... well, trouble is, people got used to the army running everything, and then us."

"You're saying you guys aren't ready for democracy yet?"

Mercer laughed. "Let me tell you about the black man's burden. All these natives here, all they want to do is sing and dance and fool around and maybe settle a couple of old scores with Ole Massa here."

"We'll work something out. Maybe get you a transfer to the Bay Area."

"I'll pack my bag."

A couple of hours later, Don rode back out into the bay in the Zodiac. The western sky was a mass of rising storm clouds, black and orange and red. The Zodiac bounced over a light chop, through stray shafts of golden light from the setting sun. Off to the east, the tawny hills gleamed below the darkening sky. He was upwind of the slick, and the air was fresh and cold.

Fifty thousand years, Einar Bjarnason had predicted,

until the sun's heat rose again to normal. Fimbulwinter was on its way: in the antarctic night, the ice was reaching far to the north. Perhaps it had already killed his brother, as it had killed so many others. Soon, perhaps in months, snow would lie deep and bright across Canada and the mountains of America; it would not melt in next year's summer, or the summer after. And each winter would add to it, pack it down into glacial ice whose weight would draw it down from the north, from the mountains, spreading, thickening, feeding on itself—

The Zodiac seemed to dip and accelerate. *Rachel* and the barges, less than a kilometre to the north, tilted towards the east.

To the west, the sea was bunching up, rising steeply and swiftly until the horizon disappeared. Flecks of white glinted near the crest of the wave. In seconds he was looking up at it; then the Zodiac tilted up and rose with terrible speed and silence.

—He was at its crest, and then dropping again. *Rachel* and the barges had ridden it out as well. To the east, the wave now blotted out the coast in a long line of spray that caught the sun and gleamed with rainbows. A boom rose from the wave, echoed from the shore, and went on for a long time.

Rachel loomed up before him, and he saw Kirstie standing by the rail, casting a line to him. He caught it and made the Zodiac fast. Her hair in the sunset was like fire. Then he was on deck, holding her, rejoicing in her closeness. *Rachel* came around and headed out to sea, looking for deeper water to ride out the rest of the tsunamis in.

"I thought for sure you were dead," Kirstie said with her arms around him.

"Not yet," Don said. "Not for a good long while. Let's go find Morrie. We're going to have a hell of a time tomorrow, getting everything operating again."

ABOUT THE AUTHOR

CRAWFORD KILIAN was born in New York City in 1941 and grew up in Los Angeles and Mexico City. After stints at Columbia University, in the U.S. Army, and at Lawrence Radiation Laboratory in Berkeley, California, he moved to Vancouver, British Columbia. Since 1968, Kilian has taught English at Capilano College in North Vancouver and is Co-ordinator of the college's Communications Department. He lives in North Vancouver with his wife, Alice, and two daughters, Anna and Margaret.

His previous novel, *Icequake,* was a major international success, selling over 300,000 copies worldwide in less than a year. He has also published two children's books, *Wonders, Inc.* and *The Last Vikings;* a widely praised history, *Go Do Some Great Thing: The Black Pioneers of British Columbia;* and two science fiction novels, *Empire of Time* (*Publishers Weekly* called it "An absolute knockout...") and *Eyas.*

SEAL BOOKS

Offers you a list of outstanding fiction, non-fiction and classics of Canadian literature in paperback by Canadian authors, available at all good bookstores throughout Canada.

THE CANADIAN ESTABLISHMENT	Peter C. Newman
THE IVORY SWING	Janette Turner Hospital
A JEST OF GOD	Margaret Laurence
LADY ORACLE	Margaret Atwood
THE SNOW WALKER	Farley Mowat
ST. URBAIN'S HORSEMAN	Mordecai Richler
MALICE IN BLUNDERLAND	Allan Fotheringham
THE STONE ANGEL	Margaret Laurence
THE BACK DOCTOR	Hamilton Hall
JAKE AND THE KID	W. O. Mitchell
ZEMINDAR	Valerie Fitzgerald
DADDY'S GIRL	Charlotte Vale Allen
BODILY HARM	Margaret Atwood
PREPARING FOR SABBATH	Nessa Rapoport
SUNDAY'S CHILD	Edward Phillips
THE DIVINERS	Margaret Laurence
HIGH CRIMES	William Deverell
THE ESTABLISHMENT MAN	Peter C. Newman
THE HAUNTED LAND	Val Cleary
ROSEGARDEN	Kurt Palka
THE CANADIANS (six volumes)	Robert E. Wall
COMEBACK	Dan Hill
MURDER ON LOCATION	Howard Engel
NEVER CRY WOLF	Farley Mowat
LIFE BEFORE MAN	Margaret Atwood
WHO HAS SEEN THE WIND	W. O. Mitchell
GOING THROUGH THE MOTIONS	Katherine Govier
THE ACQUISITORS	Peter C. Newman
MEET ME IN TIME	Charlotte Vale Allen
THE SERPENT'S COIL	Farley Mowat
BODILY HARM	Margaret Atwood
PERPETUAL MOTION	Graeme Gibson
JOSHUA THEN AND NOW	Mordecai Richler

The Mark of Canadian Bestsellers